THE TRUCK AND TRAILER WERE GETTING CLOSER AND CLOSER...

Then, suddenly, the little car spun. I was thrown to the right, and only my seat belt kept me behind the wheel. My shoulder belt clutched my neck. Then the whirl ended, and I was sitting still.

I wasn't hurt.

Mozart was pounding against the car, and I could see the truck not ten feet away from me.

I had to get out of there. Strapped into the car I was a sitting duck, and if the guy in the truck cared enough about me to wreck my car, he might have other plans in mind for me as well.

★

Also available from Worldwide Mystery by
EVE K. SANDSTROM

DEATH DOWN HOME
THE DEVIL DOWN HOME

Eve K. SANDSTROM

The DOWN HOME Heifer Heist

WORLDWIDE.

TORONTO • NEW YORK • LONDON
AMSTERDAM • PARIS • SYDNEY • HAMBURG
STOCKHOLM • ATHENS • TOKYO • MILAN
MADRID • WARSAW • BUDAPEST • AUCKLAND

For Dave and in memory of Kaypro II

THE DOWN HOME HEIFER HEIST

A Worldwide Mystery/October 1994

This edition is reprinted by arrangement with Charles Scribner's Sons, an imprint of Macmillan Publishing Company.

ISBN 0-373-26153-5

ACKNOWLEDGMENTS

A writer is continually amazed at the willingness of acquaintances, friends, and complete strangers to help with research. Truck salesmen, for example, don't balk at suggesting the best rig for a modern-day rustler to drive, and cattlemen willingly describe the best technique for breaking ice in a stock pond or for convincing a mother cow she should adopt a strange calf. Dozens of people helped with the background for this book, many of them without knowing they were doing it.

Of special assistance were Inspector Jim Avance, of the Oklahoma State Bureau of Investigation, who made sure the law enforcement techniques accurately reflect those of a small county in southwest Oklahoma, and Tom Horschler, a rancher and educator who shared his expertise in raising and showing cattle and in organizing stock shows. If I made a mistake, they'll tell me about it.

ONE

THE DRY SNOW BLEW through the headlights and sifted over the heap of fluorescent orange at the edge of the road.

My husband Sam—Sheriff Sam Titus of Catlin County, Oklahoma—was kneeling beside the rounded shape the night dispatcher had told us was a body. As I watched, Sam flipped a raincoat over the orange heap and stood up, ducking his head to keep his hat brim between the snow and his glasses. Two orange legs and a pair of dark shoes poked out from the raincoat.

Sam stuffed his hands into the pockets of his heavy parka. The radio call had been right. Joe Pilkington was dead. Nothing could be done to help him.

Billy, Sam's little nephew, leaned against my knee. He was gawking out the windshield of the Titus Ranch pickup. Sam had left the truck idling because we needed the heater, and I could feel Billy tremble slightly with the motor's vibration.

He moved restlessly. "Why is that man lying down in the snow?"

I searched my mind for something to distract him. This was not a good place for a six-year-old. A pickup had shielded us from the scene, but it had been moved, and I knew Sam didn't realize the body was now in full view of his nephew.

"Isn't the man cold, Aunt Nicky?"

"I think he's been hurt, Billy." I tried to keep my own voice calm. "Uncle Sam will make sure he's taken care of. Did you bring a book? I'll turn on the light, and you can read to me while we wait for Uncle Sam to do his job."

I reached over and turned on the dome light. Instantly our reflections appeared on the windshield, largely blocking our view of the wire fence, the metal gate, and the dry grass poking through a crust of snow in the pasture beyond. But the reflection didn't completely hide the figure heaped in the ditch; two other pickups had been pulled into place with their headlights on those bright legs. Joe Pilkington had dressed for death in a hunter's insulated coveralls of glowing orange.

His colorful garb was a symptom of his ranch's position on the economic edge. Most ranchers wore insulated coveralls of khaki or brown to work in the fields. Orange was reserved for hunting. Joe probably had been forced to make his hunting rig do double duty because he couldn't afford two sets of coveralls.

I heard a siren behind us, and Billy twisted in the seat and looked out the back window. Flashing lights were coming fast, shifting from side to side on the uneven gravel road. The lights held Billy's attention until a Catlin County Sheriff's Department car had pulled past and parked between us and the huddled body. Sonny Blacksaddle, Sam's chief deputy, waved at me as he got out of the car. He reached inside the collar of his heavy jacket and pulled out the long braids he wore as a tribute to his Kiowa ancestors, then zipped the jacket up as he walked toward Sam and the other two men who were standing in the road near Pilkington's body.

"Turn out the light, Aunt Nicky," Billy said. "I can't see."

I couldn't see either, and I was as curious as Billy. Since the body was now hidden by Sonny's patrol car, I switched the cab lights off and watched.

Johnny Garcia was talking to Sam. Johnny had found the body on his way to his job at the Titus ranch, where he worked for Sam and Sam's dad. He was quite upset over the discovery, to judge from his gestures. He swung his arms, knocking his red hunter's cap askew and almost hitting the second man in the nose.

The man dodged back, and the hood he wore fell onto his shoulders. His back was toward me, but his ash-blond ponytail told me it was Daniel—Daniel who? I never could remember Daniel's last name, but he worked on the Mullins ranch, a mile or two up the road. And he was a singer. He'd entertained for the county employees' Christmas party. I knew a lot about him, and he lived right near by. Why couldn't I remember his name?

Daniel turned and I could see his deeply tanned face. His dark tan contrasted with his fair hair and made his looks unusual, dramatic, maybe even sexy.

Johnny had probably used Daniel's phone to report Pilkington's death, I thought. The raincoat over the body looked like Johnny's. He kept a long cowboy-style coat in his truck.

Sam was nodding solemnly, his western hat jammed firmly over his earmuffs, and Sonny knelt, apparently making his own inspection of Pilkington. A steer stuck its head over the wire fence behind Sam and chewed calmly, indifferent to the ridge of sleety snow frozen along its back. Across the pasture, a hay shed and a line of large cylinders of hay were taking shape in the predawn light.

Law enforcement was going on routinely, once again taking precedence over our personal lives.

Sam had planned to take this particular day off, or at least to take it off from the sheriff's department.

Days off had been few since Sam had returned to his family's ranch two and a half years earlier and our lives had abruptly changed directions. Sam and I had been newlyweds, and he'd been planning on at least fifteen more years in the Military Police branch of the U.S. Army. Then his father was the victim of a murderous attack, an attack that left big Sam Titus permanently disabled. Next, Sam's brother, Bill, was killed. This left no one in charge of the

3,000-acre Titus Ranch, and Sam—who had sworn he'd never go back to rural life—was the only Titus available to step in. Soon afterward the Catlin County sheriff resigned, and Sam was offered the appointment.

Now, with one election and more than two years in office behind him, Sam was a county official for forty hours a week. But he seemed to be a rancher for forty-one, and his dad was pressuring him to give up law enforcement completely and become a full partner in the Titus Ranch. Sam's divided professional loyalties caused his dad to make sarcastic remarks about "Rexall ranchers," Big Sam's variation on the ultimate cattleman's insult, "drugstore cowboy."

Big Sam thought ranching was enough career for anybody. He didn't make any effort to understand why Sam would prefer a different line of work. Although he told the world he had officially retired, and he declared Sam boss of the ranch, Big Sam felt free to overrule Sam's decisions. This was a situation that wasn't always easy for Sam to handle.

Johnny Garcia, as the Titus Ranch's only full-time employee, took care of a lot of the routine work, but Sam had a pair of tan insulated coveralls like the orange ones Joe Pilkington had died in. Before dawn every winter morning he put them on and went out with Johnny "to feed."

Beef cattle are not kept in barns. They live in pastures, and every morning and every evening cattlemen must make sure they have feed and water. In winter this means breaking ice in ponds and stock tanks. When the grass is covered with snow and ice or has become too sparse to satisfy the cattle's hunger, it means hefting hundred-pound sacks of cattle cubes and spreading the feed in troughs and over the ground. It means checking those cattle for signs of illness and keeping an eye on cows who might decide to give birth in a snowbank. It means chapped cheeks and hands split from the cold. It means the chance of getting a pickup stuck in a back pasture and having to walk several miles through a blizzard to get the tractor to pull it out.

I'd gone along to drive the truck a few mornings, and seeing how hard Sam and Johnny worked and in what miserable conditions—well, it sure made me appreciate a hamburger.

And this had been a rotten winter. The first two winters I'd spent in Oklahoma had been fairly warm. A heavy, wet snow in January, or maybe a bad ice storm in February, but most of the weather had been mild and pleasant. Big Sam had said things such as "This warm weather makes me jumpy as a toadfrog on hot gravel. Somethin' ba-a-ad's gonna happen." Nothing much had.

But this winter was bringing the averages back down to normal. We'd begun with a pre-Christmas ice storm, and now, with Groundhog Day just past, we'd had six straight weeks of ice, snow, sleet, freezing rain, frozen pipes, cars sliding off the roads, and bad falls. An elderly Catlin County woman had slipped and broken a hip while trying to sweep snow off her back porch. She wasn't found for two hours, and now she was hospitalized for hypothermia.

Just yesterday the temperature had climbed higher than freezing for a few hours, but a new front—what Big Sam called "another durn norther"—had blown in around midnight. It had brought only a light snow, but the temperature was down around zero again.

Johnny pulled down the silly-looking fur-lined flaps on his red winter cap, the ones that usually stuck up over his ears. Sam grabbed for his own hat as a gust of wind clutched at it, and I decided I didn't want to estimate the current windchill factor.

Sam and I were on our way to pick up Sam's dad to go to a livestock show in Lawton. We were taking Billy along, partially because both Sam and Big Sam tried to spend time with the boy, but also because Billy had become the owner of a heifer calf, Dogie. Billy was to show Dogie for the first

time later that month, at another show, one set for our local fairgrounds. So he needed to see how a livestock show
worked.

Sam had been looking forward to getting away from
county business. I'd been afraid the new cold front would
cancel the trip, but the roads were expected to be clear, so we
had picked up Billy on schedule, at six-thirty.

Then the two-way radio in the truck gave us the word
about Joe Pilkington. Sam immediately shifted from
rancher into lawman and headed for the spot where Johnny
Garcia had discovered the huddled body.

I didn't know much about Pilkington. He seemed to be a
typical southwest Oklahoma rancher; in other words, he had
a full-time job in town.

A machine shop? Was that where Pilkington worked?
Somehow that seemed right. His wife worked, too, in a
Wichita Falls beauty shop. I knew her only by sight. But she
was quite a sight, thanks to a head of hair she kept a deliberately phony peach color.

Pilkington had apparently gone out to feed his herd and
had been hit by a car when he got out to open the gate to his
pasture. Johnny had found Pilkington's old blue Chevy
pickup still running. The driver's door had been gaping, the
truck's lights had been trained on the gate to the pasture,
and the tape deck had been playing a Willie Nelson song.
Joe Pilkington had been lying about twenty feet away, his
body in the ditch parallel to the road.

I kept watching as Sam and Sonny opened the gate and
went into the pasture. I could see their flashlights prowling
around, then they came out and Sam walked directly up to
my window. I rolled it down, and the dreadful cold came
rushing in. Big Sam would have said there was nothing between us and the North Pole but a "bob-war" fence, and
somebody had left the gate open.

"Is it bad?" I asked.

"Bad enough. You'd better take Billy on over to the folks' house and then go on to the show. I'll be stuck here for a while."

"Do you think you'll be able to come later?"

Sam shrugged. "I don't know. It looks like a hit and run. It could be the guy that hit him just went on off to find a phone, and that he'll be back. Then we'll work it like an accident. But it looks kind of funny to me."

"Funny?"

"Yeah. There's been a pickup and a trailer out in that pasture, and it looks like somebody tried to mess up the tracks. Maybe I've got a tarp in the tool chest. I'll try to save what I can."

"Do you need me to take pictures?" I'm a photographer by trade, and I help Sam preserve evidence when he needs me.

"Nope. Frankly, this little dab of snow messed the tracks up. They're not much use. If I find any worth saving, I'll make casts of them. Sonny can handle any photos with the point-and-shoot."

Sam opened the metal tool chest that fits across the pickup's bed right behind the cab, and pulled out a heavy plastic sheet. It crackled stiffly in the cold.

"See y'all later," he said.

I rolled the window back up, watching as Sam walked into the pasture and began spreading the tarp over the ground.

A pickup and a trailer out in Joe Pilkington's pasture. What did that mean?

Shades of the Old West. Sam might have to get a posse together.

It was cattle thieves. Maybe the ones who had been giving southwest Oklahoma ranchers problems for six months.

Rustlers, twentieth-century style.

TWO

NATURALLY, Big Sam and I had to have an argument before we could go on to the steer and heifer show.

My father-in-law felt obliged to object to Sam's change in plans, and I had to object to his objection, but we didn't take too long to get our yelling done.

The house where Big Sam and Marty Titus live was put up by Big Sam's father in the 1920s, and Sam says it was barely adequate shelter while he was growing up, during the years his father was using all available resources to build the Titus Ranch to its present prosperity. But three years earlier Big Sam had felt economically secure enough to give Marty the go-ahead for a major remodeling and redecorating effort. Marty, an artist who knows good design and has an acute sensitivity to color, had turned the house into an understated showplace. It's comfortable, beautiful, practical, and completely unpretentious—the kind of place either Big Sam's fellow ranchers or Marty's artistic crowd can hang out.

Big Sam was sitting at the round table drinking coffee when Billy and I came in the kitchen. Billy threw his jacket on the antique church pew by the back door, handy for sitting down to put on boots, then accepted a quick hug from his grandfather before he headed into the living room, calling for his grandmother.

Since Big Sam never goes outdoors without his wide-brimmed hat, he has the traditional cattleman's complexion, and it happens to match Marty's kitchen's color scheme. He has terra-cotta cheeks the color of the walls and a pale forehead the color of the natural oak cabinets. Now he looked at me, and his cheeks deepened from terra-cotta to red brick.

"Godfrey Daniels!" he hollered. "Where's Young Sam now?"

Sam was on the verge of turning thirty, but he was still "Young Sam" to his dad and to about half of Catlin County.

"Just calm down," I said. "Joe Pilkington's been killed and—"

"I know that!" Big Sam whammed his palm on the kitchen table. "Johnny already called to tell us. And I know that the Catlin County Sheriff's Department doesn't take care of traffic accidents. So where is Sam?"

"He had to look—"

"He had to look two places at once, that's his problem! That boy's got to make up his mind. Either he's a rancher, or he's a lawman! I'm gettin' sick and tired of him foolin' around playin' Dick Tracy!"

"Wait a minute! He's an elected official!" I yelled back. "He's got to do his duty. He just can't walk off—"

"Elected official, my foot! And why? There wasn't a bit of use of him runnin' for that office—"

"No use? You want him to waste all that training? All his background—"

"That's all well and good, Nicky, but this ranch needs his full attention."

"Why? It's got the full attention of two grown men already. Sam doesn't need to give up—"

Big Sam whacked the tabletop again. "What Sam needs is to watch out or he'll wind up—" He paused, and when he spoke again he put a sneer into his words that showed he regarded them as the most damning epithet he could utter.

"—he'll wind up a Rexall rancher!"

That's when I got tickled. Big Sam always affects me that way. In the two and a half years since I became part of the

Titus family, I've learned to love the guy, peppery temper and all.

So now I gasped, pretending to be shocked. I clasped my hand to my chest and rolled my eyes. "Not that!" I cried. "Not the awful"—I dropped my voice to a whisper—"the dreaded—Rexall rancher!"

Then I went around the table and kissed his cheek.

Big Sam's anger passes, he admits, "fast as salts through a widder woman." I don't understand the medical theory behind that saying, but I wasn't surprised when he grinned and patted my hand. The storm was over.

"I'm an obnoxious old son of a biscuit," he said. "Useless as buttons on a boar hog. But I worry about him. He's doin' too much."

"I know, Big Sam, but he has to work it out himself."

Big Sam reached for his coffee. "I just hope he works it out by May."

Yes, May was going to mean major changes for the Titus Ranch. But there was no point in worrying about it at that moment.

"You ready to go?" I asked. "I saw Marty's car out there warming up for us."

IT WAS CLOSE TO NOON when Sam turned up backstage at the Heart of the Great Plains Classic Steer and Heifer Show.

I was in the middle of the crowded main barn, surrounded by rows of steers and heifers. They were tied to fences made of pipe or white pickets, each placid animal brushed and groomed until it seemed to be wearing mink or sable. Kids and parents and grandparents, all in insulated overalls or waterproof suits, carried pitchforks and shovels or worked on the cattle with currycombs and giant blowdryers.

Folks who weren't busy lolled on the upholstered lids of coffin-like show boxes—storage bins five feet long, three feet wide, and three feet tall that are lugged from ranch to show and home again in stock trailers or pickups. Others dangled their heads into the bottoms of the boxes, almost turning upside down to dig out cattle hair spray or electric razors big enough to give half-ton steers a trim. The only beauty aid missing was bleach; it's illegal to dye the contestants.

Trimming chutes, which are portable metal racks used to hold cattle immobile during grooming, stood shoulder to shoulder at the end of the barn and were scattered among the tethered animals.

Mechanical noise bounced off the metal roof and walls—noise from powerful floor fans on stands higher than my head, from cattle hair-dryers that looked like vacuum-cleaner tanks with long vacuum-cleaner hoses, from the giant electric clippers, and from the gasoline generators that powered all that equipment. Human noise came from those dozens of kids, parents, and grandparents as they shouted over the buzz of machinery or muttered below its whir.

The scene appeared confused, but I had found I was usually the only person there who didn't know exactly what he was doing.

But that day I did know what I was doing. I was taking pictures.

Over the past two years I'd changed from a purely artistic photographer into a slightly commercial one. I'd discovered magazines would actually pay money for photographs of southwestern scenery.

I had linked this to my artistic work, of course. My photographs of the giant prairie skies had won me a spot in a major show to be held in Houston in April. I was one of only a dozen southwestern photographers invited. My pleasure in reaching this new professional plateau had paled a bit when Sam said he wouldn't be able to get away to come with me. So I was planning to tackle Houston on my own. It seemed I was tackling a lot of things on my own these days.

But on that day, among the contestants in the Heart of the Great Plains Classic Steer and Heifer Show, I was indulging an experimental interest in human interest photography.

My current subject was a tall, lanky kid whose closely trimmed and molded haircut almost matched the closely trimmed and molded clip job on his Black Angus steer. He was using the giant electric blocking clippers to trim a ridge of hair at the end of the steer's spine into a right angle, an angle designed to make the animal's back look absolutely level. The steer's legs had already been trimmed into ebony columns. I knew the kid's goal was to make the Angus's body look like a box set on fence posts.

Then I saw Sam come in the outside door, the one closest to the main arena. He stopped and looked around, his collar turned up against the windchill factor that had followed him in. He took his glasses off. They'd probably fogged up, though it was pretty cool inside the barn, too. Even with the blank look he gets without his glasses, he looked good to me. Six feet plus, sandy hair, strong features—pretty terrific.

I held my strobe unit over my head and flashed it, just in case he was looking for his wife. Sam immediately put the glasses back on and walked in my direction, smiling slightly. The sight made my hormones do a little flip.

Sam is private about his feelings. His slight smile, I'd learned, could be translated as "Darling! Am I ever glad to see you!" I was awfully lucky to have him, even if he couldn't go to Houston for an art show.

He patted me on the shoulder, his public version of a big, wet kiss, and I squeezed his hand, because I know how to show a little restraint in public, too.

"Glad you were able to make it," I said. "What did you find out about Joe Pilkington?"

"Still up in the air. OHP took over."

The Oklahoma Highway Patrol would be in charge of investigating a traffic accident, even one on a county road. Did that mean Sam had dropped his suspicions about the evidence that a truck and trailer had been in the pasture?

"What about the tracks you found?"

Sam touched my shoulder again. "Tell you later." Then his gaze shifted to a spot behind me. When he spoke, his voice was a little louder.

"Hi, Buck."

Buck Houston.

I turned and put on as nice a smile as I owned. All of us Tituses needed to get along with Buck. Just in case he turned out to be the solution to our problems.

Buck walked toward us, all six feet, four inches of macho. I liked Buck a lot. So why did he make me so nervous? Buck's face was on the handsome side, but too rugged for the "pretty-boy" tag Sam's dad hung on men he thought too good-looking. With his standard black western hat, tan insulated overalls, boots, and padded poplin jacket, Buck looked like a working cattleman.

There was nothing wrong with his education—master's degree in farming and ranch management. His background was respectable—conservative ranching family; worked his way through college. He had old-fashioned, courtly manners of the "Yes, ma'am, don't worry your pretty little head about it" type rare in a man in his early thirties.

Buck was also openly ambitious. He worked at two jobs, he'd told Sam, to save money toward buying his own place some day. He wanted to get into breeding registered cattle on his own. Big Sam respected Buck. "He's got the know-how and the want-to," he'd told me. Then he'd added his highest accolade: "He's a hard worker."

So why did I get such a knot in my stomach when Buck approached? I'd known him a year, but he'd only begun to make me nervous two weeks earlier, when I'd learned he'd asked Sam's sister-in-law for a date.

Brenda was twenty-six, a few months younger than I am, and she had been a widow more than two years. Out loud, we all said she ought to start dating, and Buck was certainly a suitable person. If he and Brenda really hit it off, he might become part of the family, Billy and Lee Anna's stepfather. And even if Brenda remarried, she and her children would remain part owners of the Titus Ranch.

Buck might want to have a voice in running the ranch. He certainly had more education for the job than Sam did. He might even know more about it than Big Sam did. He might be a valuable addition to the team, but Buck represented a possible change in the Titus family's status quo, and change is always a little disturbing.

My lips felt stiff, but I tried. "Hi, Buck. You frozen?"

"Pert' nigh, Nicky. This weather's 'bout to get me." Buck smiled, and his smile was only a little too broad. It probably looked more natural than mine. He turned toward Sam, and his expression changed to a concerned frown. He dropped his voice, as if he didn't want me to hear. "What's this about Joe Pilkington? Is it true he's dead?"

"'Fraid so, Buck. How'd you hear about it?"

"Mike got it from one of the 4-H kids. Listen, I need to finish up that heifer's tail. Come over and talk to me while I do it."

Buck gestured over his shoulder, and I saw his special charge, Mike Mullins, two rows over. The boy stood beside a grooming chute, combing the Hereford heifer in it. Mike's black hair stuck out from under a yellow, billed cap. Mike was twelve, I knew, and he was beginning to get long legs, but the heifer was still as tall as he was.

Buck was herdsman for Mike's father, Dr. Franklin Mullins. Dr. Mullins had bought a ranch in Catlin County two years earlier, dubbing it the Circle M. He spent weekends in a snazzy house he'd built there, but he stayed in Oklahoma City during the week. Mike lived at the ranch all the time, under the supervision of a housekeeper and, I supposed, of Buck. He went to school in Holton, the county seat.

Daniel, the one whose last name I couldn't remember and who had been at the scene of Pilkington's death, worked for Buck on Mullins's Circle M Ranch. Daniel was standing beside Mike, dumping wood shavings out of a giant plastic bag and spreading them in a wide stall area.

Sam and I followed Buck across to Mike's station. I could see the wooden sign that read "Circle M—Registered Herefords" wired to the fence. The heifer was one of five Herefords lined up in an area marked off with blue flags. Four director's chairs and an expensive-looking walnut show box had been set up at one end, forming a sort of living room. Daniel waved as we approached. His ash-blond hair and well-disciplined ponytail gave him a rakish look.

Buck patted Mike on the shoulder, and the boy gazed at him almost adoringly.

"That looks good, Mike," Buck said. "Now you work on Harry down there, and I'll do Proud Mary's tail."

Mike nodded and stuck his currybomb into his hip pocket—the approved spot for Future Farmers and 4-H members to store such items. He picked up a brush, went down to the steer at the end, and began to stroke his side. In spite of the chilly temperature in the barn, a powerful electric fan was trained on the animal. Cool air helps the cattle's coats look lush, cattlemen say, and keeps their appetites sharp. I knew the fan's noise would keep Mike from hearing our conversation.

Buck pulled up a camp stool and sat down on it, directly behind the heifer in the grooming rack. The hair at the end of her tail was tangled and standing out in all directions. Buck pulled out a comb, an ordinary people comb this time, and began to tease the white tuft of hair at the end of the animal's tail, exactly the way a beautician would add bulk to a human customer's hair.

"Mike's dad got all excited when he heard about Pilkington," Buck said.

Sam nodded. "Yeah. It happened pretty close to his place. Just over two miles from your house."

Buck ran a big-time show cattle operation for Dr. Mullins. He lived on the Mullins place in a new brick house, much better than the mobile home Dr. Mullins provided for Daniel. I felt a bit smug because Johnny's mobile home was better than Daniel's.

As a second job, Buck was area field representative for the Sooner State Cattle Growers' Association. This meant he worked closely with Big Sam, who was area board member for the Sooner State Association. Each put a lot of miles on his respective pickup, touring an eighth of the state to listen to cattle ranchers' concerns. Buck and Big Sam would be working the crowd at today's show, I knew. Big Sam concentrated on listening and looking for new members, and Buck handed out advice on embryo transfers and the latest test results on the new vaccines.

Buck picked up an aerosol can labeled "Tail Adhesive" and sprayed Proud Mary's tail before he spoke again. "What happened to Joe?"

"Hit and run, we think. He went out to feed his cattle. Looks like a car hit him when he got out to open the gate. I don't suppose you heard anything this morning?"

"I wasn't home. I brought the cattle over here last night. Stayed at the Holiday Inn."

That surprised me. The Lawton show was in the next county, no more than thirty miles from the Circle M. I would have expected Buck to stay at home and drive over. But since Dr. Mullins apparently provided him with an unlimited expense account—well, it was none of my business.

Sam blinked. "The vehicle probably went up your way. Too bad you weren't there. You might have heard something."

Buck shrugged, but he continued to mold the tail. "Of course, Dr. Mullins says he heard something." His voice was noncommittal, but he punched the word "he" just hard enough to inspire disbelief. "He didn't mention it until after we heard about Pilkington."

It would be like Dr. Mullins to claim he'd heard something, I thought. Marty and Big Sam considered the doctor a neighbor, which meant he got polite treatment from all of us and Big Sam didn't sneer openly at his "Rexall rancher" status. But as far as I was concerned, Dr. Mullins would fit right in at a livestock show—in the jackass division.

I didn't say this out loud; after all, the man was Buck's boss. I was immediately glad that I'd kept silent, because Dr. Mullins's son popped up at Buck's elbow.

Mike's chin didn't have quite so much baby fat as it had had a year before. He was a nice-looking kid, but he tended to have a sullen expression—except when he looked at Buck.

Buck smiled and rested an arm on Mike's shoulder. "Yeah, Mike. What do you need?"

"I think there's a little rough spot on Harry's side, Buck. Did we use up the conditioner?"

"There should be a new can in the box. And see if there's a plastic sack in there for Proud Mary's tail."

Mike nodded. The boy walked over to the walnut show box. Its top was upholstered in what looked like leather. Mike opened the box. A roll of paper towels and a rack holding several show sticks, the long rods used to control cattle during judging, were mounted inside the lid. The Circle M gear was top of the line, the fanciest rig in the barn. Most folks settled for metal or fiberglass boxes with vinyl upholstery.

Buck molded the stiff hair at the end of the heifer's tail into a big ball, then tied a few strands up with twist ties from bread sacks and sprayed it again. He looked up at Sam.

"I hope you don't think this business with Pilkington had anything to do with the cattle thefts," he said.

"There's no particular reason to think there's a connection," Sam said mildly. "Did you think there would be?"

"Of course not! It's some bee Dr. Mullins has in his bonnet. I think he's laying for you." His voice's lack of inflection made it contemptuous. Mullins wasn't the only southwest Oklahoma cattleman who was talking about cattle theft that year—ever since a regular crime wave had broken out the previous summer. More than two dozen ranches had been hit and between three and four hundred head of cattle stolen over an eight-county area. The Titus Ranch had lost twenty head, which was a bit embarrassing for Sam. And Catlin County was the geographical center of the thefts. Did this have any significance? No one knew. But it made Sam uneasy.

Mike came back, and Buck was silent as the kid handed him a plastic sack. Buck tucked the heifer's tail into it and tied it on with more twist ties. He looked up at Sam and lifted his eyebrows significantly. "If I can help you, let me know."

Sam nodded. "Thanks," he said. "Mike, that's a nice-lookin' steer you're working on."

Mike grinned, then ducked his head. He went back to his steer. I thought Buck was going to say something more, but right then Daniel came over. He flipped a twist tie around the open end of the giant bag of wood shavings and tossed it into a corner beside the show box.

"I'll head on back, Buck." He grinned broadly. "I'll take care of the truck as soon as I get there."

Buck glanced at Daniel, nodding. Then he turned back to us, but he didn't speak to Sam either. After an awkward pause, we said our good-byes and walked away.

"What did Buck mean about Dr. Mullins?" I asked as soon as we were out of earshot.

"Probably trying to warn me that he's thinking of making trouble with the Sooner State Association over these cattle thefts."

"What could they do?"

"Hire their own investigator."

I thought about that. "How would that affect you?"

"If they hire the right person, the Catlin County Sheriff's Department could benefit. If they hire the wrong person—" Sam shrugged. "Well, we're not getting anywhere very fast, and neither are any of the other sheriff's departments involved. We wouldn't be able to refuse any legitimate help, especially since the OSBI's resources for investigations of cattle thefts are limited." The Oklahoma State Bureau of Investigation provides technical assistance to small law enforcement agencies, such as the Catlin County Sheriff's Department with its three deputies, two jailers, and one clerical worker.

Sam patted my arm again and grinned. "But at the moment Big Sam and Billy are getting hungry. You ready to help me rustle up some lunch?"

I rewrapped myself in my heavy ski jacket and cap—the red ones I'd been told looked good with my curly black hair. Then I slung my camera gear over my shoulder, and we headed outdoors and over to the main arena. As we crossed the drive, a sapphire-blue pickup passed us, and I saw the Sooner State Cattle Growers' Association logo on the door. Daniel was driving Buck's truck. He gave us a casual wave.

At the concession stand under the bleachers of the main arena we loaded up with chili dogs, Frito pies, nachos, and plain chili in paper bowls, then joined Sam's dad and Billy in the front row of the bleachers.

Big Sam, who finds stairs pretty difficult, had hauled himself up three steps from the arena level and planted himself in an aisle seat. The metal seating and concrete flooring were cold and hard, but Big Sam had a complete view of the judging and the traffic in and out of the dirt-lined arena. His spot was okay.

Except that Dr. Franklin Mullins was in the seat right behind him.

Mullins was a wiry little man; even the two-inch heels on his boots didn't make him more than five-six or so. In fact, I wondered if the height he gained from the boots wasn't offset visually by the extra-wide brim on his hat. The hat also hid his one attractive feature, a gorgeous head of thick, expertly styled gray hair.

The doctor's face glowed triumphantly when he saw Sam. "There you are!"

"Hi, Doctor. You lookin' for me?" Sam's voice was calm.

"I want to know what's going on with these rustlers," Mullins said. The remark was typical of Mullins's playing-cowboy attitude toward ranching, I thought. Hardly any modern-day cattlemen and no modern-day lawmen used the term "rustler."

"So do I," Sam said mildly. "Here, Billy. Here's the chili dog you ordered." He handed his dad the flimsy cardboard box the concession stand had provided for our food, and I stood by with the cardboard rack of soft drinks. Even Dr. Mullins didn't dare interrupt until Billy was settled with his potentially messy lunch in his lap and his Coke firmly between his knees.

I sat next to Billy, and Sam settled into place down the row, leaving the folding seat between us pulled down to use as an uneven table for our own drinks. When I turned to pick up my paper cup, I bumped into the brim of Dr. Mullins's hat. He'd stuck his head between us.

"What happened to Pilkington?" he asked. "Was it the rustlers?"

I knew Sam wouldn't tell him the answer to that one; he never discusses cases with anybody outside the department. So I wasn't surprised when he answered Dr. Mullins with a question of his own. "What makes you think it might be the cow thieves?"

Mullins gave himself a self-important shake. "Well, it seems that has been the main crime we've had around here."

"It's certainly been a problem, but we do have other crimes. The Oklahoma Highway Patrol is investigating Mr. Pilkington's death as a hit-and-run accident." Sam took a bite from his chili dog.

"Then it wasn't anything to do with the cattle thefts." Mullins sounded disappointed.

Sam swallowed his bite, then repeated his first question. "What made you think it might be mixed up with the thefts of cattle?"

"Well, I heard something."

"Oh? Who'd you hear it from?"

"Oh, no! Nothing like that. I don't mean gossip!"

Sam picked up his Dr. Pepper and took a drink. "Then what was it?"

"Well, you know our house is just a few miles on down Split Creek Road from the Pilkington place."

Sam nodded. "A half-mile to Daniel's trailer, almost exactly one mile to the house where Buck lives, then nearly a half-mile on to your place."

Mullins sat back, and when I glanced over my shoulder at him I saw that he looked surprised. "I never measured it," he said, "but I imagine that's approximately right."

Sam took another bite, chewed, and swallowed before he answered. "My chief deputy and I ran it off on his odometer this morning. It's a mile and a tenth to Buck's and another four-tenths on to your drive."

Mullins's eyes widened. "Oh?"

Sam nodded. "Yep. The Highway Patrol planned to check with the neighbors, but you had already left before anybody could get by your house."

"Then you're not handling the death?"

"OHP handles traffic accidents, but we cooperate." Sam turned in his seat and looked directly back at Dr. Mullins. "Just what did you hear, Doctor?"

Mullins leaned forward slightly and gave himself another self-important shake. I was reminded of Big Sam's description of him. "That banty rooster can strut sitting down."

Mullins cleared his throat. "Well. I guess it may seem odd, but I'm sure of what I heard."

He looked at Sam, and Sam looked back. Sam didn't speak, but he kept looking at Mullins expectantly, his eyes wide behind his glasses.

Mullins dropped his eyes. "I heard Mozart," he said.

Sam blinked, and I imagine I did, too.

Mozart? I pictured the frozen pasture, barbed-wire fencing, and cold cattle that had been at the scene of Pilkington's death. That memory mixed with Mozart made me turn to face the arena and quickly plunk a chili-covered corn chip in my mouth. I didn't want to laugh, when Sam was taking Mullins's report so seriously. But the idea of Mozart wafting over the cow pastures and hay sheds through the blowing snow was—well, incongruous.

"I said it sounded odd." Mullins's voice was defensive. "It sounded odd at the time. That's why I noticed it."

"I assume it was coming from somebody's tape deck," Sam said.

"Oh, yes. Some truck was passing down at the end of the drive, and I could hear Mozart very clearly. It got louder and louder, then faded away as the truck went on past."

"Did you get a look at the truck?"

"Not really. It was just a set of headlights and tail-lights."

"Big truck or pickup?"

I looked back at Mullins then, and I saw that he was frowning. "Well, from the lights I'd guess it was a big pickup pulling a trailer. That's why I associated it with the thieves."

"But you didn't see it? How about the other people there at the house? Mike or the housekeeper? Did they see it?"

"No. I was letting the dog out. Nobody else was downstairs yet. I'm the only early riser. All those years of seven A.M. surgery, I guess."

Sam nodded. "Well, I appreciate your telling me about it, Dr. Mullins. I'll pass this on to the Highway Patrol, and they'll be by for a statement."

Mullins "strutted" in his seat again. "Then it may be important?"

"It's too early to tell," Sam answered. "It might just have been somebody who always listens to a classical station and who got out early to move cattle. But very few ranch trucks would be down that road unless they came from the area. We'll have to find out."

"Then you don't think it's linked to the rustling?"

"As I said, it's the OHP's investigation. But Joe's cattle were still in his pasture."

Mullins nodded glumly. "I'd sure like to see you catch those guys." He got up and walked away.

A small rancher in our area, such as Joe Pilkington, might have only twenty or thirty head of cattle, and a big operation, like the Titus Ranch, a few hundred. The thieves were taking a deep cut out of the area's cattle production.

Law enforcement agencies were stumped, I knew from Sam's comments.

Lawmen often locate stolen cattle by finding out where they're being sold, then finding out who sold them. But none of these cattle had turned up at sale barns.

At least ten Catlin County ranchers had been hit. In each case either the cattle were in pastures remote from a dwelling or else the ranch family had been away from home. Often the cattle had not been properly branded or otherwise identified, sometimes because they had just been purchased.

Cattle that could be sold for beef were prime targets for the cattle thieves. They let breeding stock alone. In each case a truck the lab guys thought was a one-ton pickup pulling a twenty-five-foot gooseneck trailer had been driven into a pasture at night. The cattle had been enticed aboard with feed, and the load had been driven away before dawn.

The trailer had Kelly tires, and the truck a set of bald Bridgestones. If the law ever found the truck, they felt pretty certain they'd be able to identify it by the tires.

But finding it wasn't going to be an easy job. This type of rig is the most common type of working outfit used on ranches. There were hundreds in the eight counties that were involved.

It was such an efficient operation and covered such a wide area that Sam believed the cattle thieves were scouting carefully to identify cattle ripe for stealing. But so far nobody had been discovered touring southwest Oklahoma in a cattle truck without a good excuse for being there. Sam and the other sheriffs involved were trying to match up visits by people who had reasons to drive around the area—servicemen who deliver butane fuel to rural homes, for example—but no pattern had been found.

For the past three months, the Oklahoma State Bureau of Investigation had coordinated the attempt to catch the thieves. They had casts of the truck's tire tracks. They knew the kind of shoes and boots the thieves wore, and they knew there were two of them. They didn't have enough manpower to completely take over the investigation, of course. Sam and the other sheriffs involved were still the front-line detectives.

But nobody had ever identified the truck and trailer. And nobody had ever seen the cattle thieves.

Except, perhaps, Joe Pilkington.

I'd been staring at the arena, eating nachos and thinking about cattle thieves, so I was surprised when Sam stood up. He was wadding up the paper that had held his chili dog and stuffing it into the sack from his potato chips.

"I'm going to go get a candy bar," he said. "Be right back."

Then he walked away, without offering to get one for anybody else. Which was sort of odd.

By this time Billy was through eating, and he'd joined another little boy for a game of tag at the top of the bleachers. In a few minutes he came back to announce, "I'm going to the men's room."

This was a point of pride for a six-year-old, of course. Until recently Billy had called it the "boy's room," the way they did at kindergarten. Billy dreaded shopping alone with his mother because she did not want him visiting men's rooms in shopping malls by himself. I knew she wouldn't want him roaming around loose among the thousand or so people at the Heart of the Great Plains Classic Steer and Heifer Show.

So I jumped to my feet. "Come on, Billy. I'll walk down with you."

Billy's lower lip protruded instantly. "I'll go by myself."

"Sure. But I need to walk down that way. I want your Uncle Sam to get me a Baby Ruth." And maybe Sam would feel inspired to visit the arena men's room. Unclehood was proving quite an experience to Sam.

Billy wasn't sure about my plan, but he allowed me to accompany him. He was even first to see Sam.

"There he is!" Billy took off, dodging through the acres of insulated overalls as he ran toward Sam, who was standing at the end of the long concrete-walled area under the bleachers. Billy nearly knocked over a heavyset man in a purple cap, then he banged into Sam, grabbing him around the waist.

Sam turned and placed a calming hand on Billy's shoulder. For the first time I saw that he was talking into a pay phone.

Who was he calling? I wondered about it as I followed Billy's path among the padded overalls, jeans, sweatshirts, heavy jackets, and "gimme" caps of the exhibitors and their parents and grandparents. I tried to apologize to the man Billy had nearly knocked down, but he'd disappeared.

Sam raised his eyebrows to greet me, but he kept talking into the phone.

"Yeah, that would tie in real neatly with the broken glass," he said. "And with the missing gun."

THREE

MISSING GUN?

Broken glass?

"I'll go on out there in a while," Sam was telling the phone. "So long."

He didn't have the receiver back in the cradle before I spoke up. "What's going on?"

"Well." He drawled the word out, and he grinned before he said anything more. "It's pretty hard to have a private conversation in the middle of this crowd."

Billy bounced from foot to foot. "Uncle Sam! I'm going to the men's room! By myself!"

Five minutes later Sam had managed this visit in a way that salvaged a six-year-old's pride and his relatives' caution, and Sam and I were leaning against a concrete block wall, waiting for Billy to emerge.

I kept my voice low. "So what's with the phone call?"

"Just checking in with Sonny. For one thing, the OHP and the Catlin County Sheriff's Department have agreed to a public position that Pilkington's death was a traffic accident. So I'm not involved." He raised his eyebrows slightly.

"I'll remember. But what's this about a missing gun?"

"We don't know for sure. Pilkington's pickup had a gun rack, and he had shotgun shells in the glove compartment. But the rack was empty."

"Somebody took his gun?"

"Maybe. Or maybe he didn't have it with him. His wife says she's too upset to decide if it's missing or not. So at four o'clock I'm supposed to go out to the machine shop where he worked. The owner's going to call in the guys Joe worked with. They may know if he had the gun last night.''

"Oh. But what about the broken glass?''

"We found some in the pasture. It was safety glass—windshield glass.''

"But that could mean—''

Billy reappeared and grabbed Sam around the waist.

"Ooof!'' Sam said. "You're gonna knock me flat, Billy.'' Then he nodded at me. "Yeah. It has a lot of possibilities. But you can see why we need to keep them absolutely quiet.''

Billy and Sam got into the candy-bar line, and I went back to my seat, pulling my ski jacket around me and letting this new information settle.

If Joe Pilkington had had a gun with him when he discovered a pickup pulling a stock trailer in his own pasture, where the rig had no business, he probably would have immediately yanked that gun out of its rack.

If there was windshield glass out in the pasture, he might have actually fired and hit the truck. That might mean somebody was driving around southwest Oklahoma in very cold weather with a hole in his windshield, or maybe with no glass in his window at all.

And maybe with a few shotgun pellets under his hide.

I could see why Sam the Lawman was excited. It gave the law enforcement agencies something to look for. They would check all the hospitals and doctors to see if any gunshot wounds had been treated. They could check all the auto-glass repair places.

Or they could do that if the word didn't get out that they were looking for broken auto glass. Then the truck would disappear, or be driven clear to Denver for repairs.

But if Joe Pilkington hadn't had his shotgun along that morning, the glass might mean nothing.

Sam was right. There was nothing to do until he could talk to Joe Pilkington's coworkers at four o'clock.

Maybe he'd let me go with him.

Billy came running up the steps of the bleachers, yelling. "Mommy's here! And she brought Johnny!"

Big Sam shushed him, since a livestock show is not a rodeo, and spectators are expected to be reasonably quiet.

Brenda and Johnny Garcia came in with Sam. Brenda sat down on the row behind Big Sam. Brenda still looks like a china doll, all blond hair and blue eyes, but I've learned that her mild manner can hide strong resolve. One thing Southern Oklahoma State University seems to be teaching her is self-confidence.

As Sam and Johnny took front-row seats, I stood up to join Brenda. This gave me a good look at a solid phalanx of good-looking Titus Ranch men. Johnny's Latin handsomeness contrasted with Sam's sandy-haired all-American look, Big Sam's solid and imposing maleness, and Billy's misleadingly cherubic blond curls and clear blue eyes. They were almost the only bare-headed men in the building. Sam never wears a hat if he can avoid it, and Big Sam holds to the old-fashioned idea that a gentleman removes his hat—even his western hat—indoors. Johnny, I'd noticed, respected this opinion and habitually left his trademark red hunter's cap in his truck. He had tucked his other trademark, his aviator sunglasses, into his shirt pocket.

Big Sam looked at Johnny and nodded. "Wait'll you see how this judge picks 'em," he said. "I believe she knows her stuff."

I knew Big Sam was happy that Johnny had come by. When it comes to cattle, Big Sam would rather talk to Johnny than to anybody else, except maybe Buck Houston. He had a high opinion of Buck's professional expertise.

Johnny Garcia is not just an ordinary ranch hand, though he seems to regard himself as one. He comes from a Holton family and not a rich one. That doesn't seem to matter a lot in Holton, where it's considered bad form to act "high-toned." Wealthy Catlin County families may travel abroad, but they don't talk about it a lot when they get home, and they are careful to wear jeans and J.C. Penney Company shirts and to drive ordinary cars. Somehow the flamboyant Texas rancher style missed this section of the Southwest. Maybe that's because there are so few rich families that the handful in existence seem ashamed to show off their wealth among their less affluent neighbors.

But even by Holton standards, Johnny's family was poor. His father was dead, and his mother, who spoke English with a heavy accent, worked as a cook in the Holton High School cafeteria. There were six kids in the family, and as far as I'd heard, they'd all turned out pretty well. A brother was a sergeant in the army, I knew, and a sister worked at the tire plant in Lawton. Johnny was the first one to go to college.

He'd met Big Sam when he was a sophomore at Holton High School. Big Sam was a director of the First State Bank of Holton, and the bank had a loan program for Future Farmers of America students. The kids could borrow money to buy a sheep, pig, or calf to raise and show as part of their class work. At the end of the school year the animal was sold, and—with luck—the bank got its money back and the kid made a little on the deal.

As a director, Big Sam had kept a particular eye on this program, of course, because he was a big supporter of FFA. So when the ag teacher told him this Garcia kid had a real feel for cattle, and Johnny's calf won at a regional show, Big Sam wound up offering Johnny a summer job at the Titus Ranch. He'd earned the "hard worker" rating from Big Sam, and he'd been around since, with a couple of breaks when he'd worked summers with a harvest crew.

Johnny was twenty-six—he'd graduated from Holton High two years behind Sam's brother Bill and in the same class with Brenda. He'd taken a few hours each semester at Southern Oklahoma State University, and he was now a senior, majoring in agronomy.

He'd been a godsend after Big Sam was left handicapped. Not only did Johnny know how to do things around the ranch the way Big Sam wanted them, but he seemed to have a genuine fondness for Sam's dad. He'd cheerfully helped Marty push Big Sam's wheelchair over rough ground, for example, back before Big Sam learned to cope with a cane. Once or twice Big Sam had fallen, and Johnny was able to help Marty get him up without hurting his pride.

Perhaps because the emotional links of physical fatherhood were missing, Big Sam got along with Johnny better than he did with Sam.

So we all dreaded May.

May was the month Johnny would graduate from SOSU. He had good grades, a pleasant personality, and good looks. Add this to his experience at the Titus Ranch, and he was bound to land a job at a salary Big Sam wouldn't be able to match. We all wished him well, but I could see why Big Sam was urging Sam to give up law enforcement after Johnny left. He was going to be impossible to replace.

Unless Buck Houston wanted the job.

But for now Johnny was still the mainstay of the ranch, and among his other duties he was teaching Billy how to take care of his heifer calf and preparing the boy—and the calf—for his first show.

"Look at that little heifer, Johnny!" Billy spoke through a mouthful of Hershey bar. "Dogie's lots prettier than she is."

Johnny spoke into Billy's ear, but I caught the words. "Now, talk quiet, Billy. You don't want to make that girl feel bad because her heifer's not as pretty as Dogie. Remember? You want to be a good sport."

Billy nodded seriously.

"But that girl's doing a good job," Johnny went on. "Watch how she holds her show stick right down by her side."

Billy looked up at Johnny. "I learned to be careful about that!" An early misuse of the show stick by Billy had left Dogie very nervous about these gadgets. If the heifer felt at all threatened by the stick, she jumped. She had yanked Billy off his feet more than once.

"I'll never hold the show stick over my head again. Ever!" Billy's eyes were wide.

Johnny laughed. "I think Dogie taught you that lesson pretty well. But this is a nice-looking bunch of heifers."

We all got quiet then and watched the arena. Half a dozen boys and girls were showing their heifers. The smallest one, a little blond girl with a blue ribbon in her hair, was shorter than her animal. The tallest, a brunette of sixteen or seventeen with hair teased into the latest glamour style, had a lush figure and wore jeans so tight I was surprised she could bend over to tap her heifer's feet into position.

We all huddled down in our jackets. The show facility had some kind of heating, of course, but the building was constructed of cement blocks and metal, and it was drafty because it was big. It could hold basketball tournaments with ease, after the concrete arena floor was covered with hardwood instead of the foot of dirt layered over it today. Cattle were being brought in some invisible door when it was time for them to compete. The wind whistled in along with them, and I was convinced that door was on a direct route from Siberia.

The six Hereford heifers being judged were quite a bit bigger than Billy's Dogie, who was only eight months old. The judge, a blond woman in khaki pants, a heavy blue jacket, and cowboy boots, walked up and down behind them, pacing in front of the show officials sitting at a long table in the center of the ring. The young cattle were posing like so many beauty queens.

The comparison seemed apt. Like beauty queens, these were young females who were not yet mothers. Also like beauty queens, they had been on special diet and exercise regimens for months. And for today's show they had been washed, dried, curled, clipped, sprayed, combed, brushed, and otherwise adorned until they were at the peak of their personal prettiness.

Even after two years in cattle country, I can hardly tell one cow from another, or even a year-old heifer from a cow. I can tell either from a steer, of course, since I do know the facts of life. I can tell a bull from any of them.

A heifer, to a cattleman, is a cow that's never had a calf. This is not necessarily a virgin, because there's such a thing as a "bred heifer," a heifer who's pregnant with her first calf. A bovine female is a heifer until she actually gives birth. Then she becomes a cow, known to a rancher as a "mother cow," or a "mama cow" or just as a "mama."

For a cow-calf operation like the Titus Ranch, "mamas" are the most important asset of the ranch. Big Sam loved his "good mothers," the foundation of his herd, with a passion that rivaled the intensity of his feelings for Marty.

A "good mama," he had explained to a new daughter-in-law, is a cow that can be relied on to raise a big, fat calf every year. This means she is a healthy cow with plenty of milk—at best an "easy keeper," a cow that doesn't require a large amount of feed to stay healthy and produce milk. A "good mama" is also extra protective of her calf and keeps it from danger—or what she believes is danger. Since her definition may include ranchers, as well as coyotes and rattlesnakes, it means a "good mama" may be hard to handle. I'd seen Sam jump into a pickup mighty fast when faced with 1,800 pounds of mama cow who didn't want her calf vaccinated.

For Sam, Big Sam—and Johnny—Billy's heifer calf was a way to teach the boy how to handle and care for cattle. They had little interest in major show operations like the one Buck Houston ran for Dr. Mullins.

Maybe that was the reason we all stayed quiet when Buck joined us, sitting down beside Brenda on the second row.

Even Brenda's greeting was quiet. Johnny and Billy were concentrating on the show ring and didn't look around.

Then Johnny leaned forward and spoke to Billy again. "See that girl on the right, Billy? Watch how she's got her heifer's feet positioned. That's real good."

Buck cleared his throat. "It is pretty good," he said. "If she had the rear feet about three inches forward it'd be perfect. But three inches probably won't hurt her with this judge."

Instantly Johnny's head whipped around. His expression grew hard. "Hi, Mr. Houston. I didn't know you were here."

"Just this minute sat down, Johnny."

Johnny shrugged. "I'd better get going," he said. "I just dropped Brenda by. See y'all later."

Billy looked up, his face distressed. "Can I practice when I get home, Johnny?"

"You may be too late tonight, Billy. We'll work tomorrow."

"But, Johnny, I don't understand—"

Johnny frowned. "It's okay, Billy. Your granddad can explain everything here to you. Or Mr. Houston can. He's the real expert."

Buck waved. "Adios, amigo."

Johnny gave the rest of us a casual wave.

Brenda spoke softly. "Good-bye, Johnny. Thanks for driving me over."

"No prob," Johnny said. He disappeared down the steps.

"Does Johnny drive you to class all the time?" Buck asked. Brenda was a full-time student at SOSU.

"No. I suppose it would be smart for me to carpool with someone, but I usually like to have the car in case I want to do errands. And Johnny goes straight back to get to work. He drove me today because I was nervous about the roads."

She went on to assure Big Sam that the roads were still safe, but I was wondering about the whole little scene. Was

I imagining the slight sneer when Buck said "adios" to Johnny? And a similar sneer from Johnny when he called Buck "a real expert"? Why had Buck's remarks seemed to make Johnny angry? Or was it his mere presence that had riled our good-natured Johnny?

Then Buck leaned forward and spoke in Sam's ear. "Can I talk to you a minute? It's about this Joe Pilkington thing. There's one more thing I ought to tell you."

Sam looked around at him. "Sure." Then he raised his eyebrows at me. Was this the explanation of the awkward pause at the end of our earlier conversation?

I decided to be tactful and leaned over to talk to Brenda. Buck stepped over the back of the row in front of him and sat down beside Sam. He moved in close, almost rubbing Sam's head with his hat brim, and his voice began to rumble.

"I probably shouldn't pass this on," he started. Then he dropped the sound level, and I couldn't hear.

Brenda put on a bright expression and began to tell me some story about her economics professor, who was something of a wit. I was too curious about what Buck wanted to tell Sam to pay much attention. But I couldn't catch another word until Buck leaned back. He was still speaking softly, but I clearly caught the words.

"I'd be willing to swear it was his truck," he said.

I could see only a corner of Sam's mouth, but it looked as if it had been hacked from granite.

"I'll check it out."

"I just thought somebody in authority should know."

Sam nodded. "Yeah. I'll make sure the right people find out."

He stood up and turned to face me. "I've got to get out of here. You want to come along?"

I jumped to my feet, then looked at Brenda.

She smiled. "Go ahead, Nicky. Just leave the keys to Marty's car."

I gave her the keys, then began to sidle toward the aisle. The judge had awarded the blue ribbon for this group of heifers. Now, according to stock show protocol, she had to justify her choices, so she picked up a microphone from the official's table in the center of the ring.

"This heifer in first place is functionally sound and retains more femininity," she said. The second-place winner, she decreed, "should take a little longer stride off her back wheels," while the third "needs a little more femininity in her front quarters."

Buck snorted. "Just like a woman," he muttered.

Big Sam nodded sagely. "Well, I would have switched first and second places," he said. "But I follow her thinking."

It was gibberish to me. I don't yet understand the standard for "femininity" in cattle. What do they want, a lace collar and a little cleavage? I packed up my photo bag and followed Sam down the steps into the area under the bleachers.

"Where are we going?" I said.

"Out to the machine shop to talk to Pilkington's boss."

Sam took the camera bag. He'd already pulled on his heavy leather work gloves. "They're saying that the high today was fourteen degrees. But I like you in that jacket." He leered just slightly. "It reminds me of Garmisch."

I dug in my pockets for my heavy gloves. Ah, Garmisch, in the Bavarian Alps. Where I'd shared some romantic moments with a handsome army captain who had a marvelous southwestern drawl. Thanks to this dreadful winter I was wearing clothes that I hadn't had on since Sam and I skied at Garmisch before we got married.

"It's colder here than Garmisch ever considered being," I said. "What happened to the Sun Belt?"

"The jet stream chased it into south Texas. And I've never been in a machine shop that wasn't pretty drafty, so you'd better zip every zipper."

I linked my arm with Sam's, and he took my hand. We hadn't gone to many places together lately. It was fun just to feel him squeeze my mitten.

We went out to the Titus Ranch pickup, ducking our heads against the bitter wind. Luckily, the pickup's heater worked fast. My voice box thawed out rapidly, too.

"Do you want me to do anything at the machine shop? Or just stay out of your way?"

"Well, I may tape some. And I need to list the things in Joe Pilkington's locker. You can help. You're still a paid-up member of the Sheriff's Reserve, right?"

He turned west, toward the end of Lawton I knew held one of the city's industrial parks. Neither of us said anything for a few minutes, but then I couldn't stand it any longer.

"Well? Whose truck did Buck see where? And why wasn't it supposed to be there?"

Sam's chin got real granitelike again. He didn't speak.

I tried again. "Are you going to tell me what Buck said?"

Sam looked over at me before he answered.

"Nope," he said.

FOUR

I DIDN'T ARGUE. It's undignified. Besides, if Sam doesn't want to tell me something, he has a reason.

So I stayed quiet. But in a minute Sam reached over and patted my ski mitten with his leather work glove. "Buck's news was pure-dee gossip, and I'm not sure I believe it."

My resolve of silence ended. That remark demanded an answer. I resented the implication that I gossiped. I turned to face Sam.

Sam held his hand up as if I were oncoming traffic. "I know! I know! You're real good about not broadcasting on the Holton News Network. But I feel that I owe it to the other guy to ask for his version. There may be some explanation."

He squeezed my hand again. But he looked worried.

The Slater Metalwork Shop was in a fairly large cement-block building, one of several machine shops in a west Lawton industrial park. A mammoth tire plant, a major employer for the whole area, sprawled across the prairie to its west. The front had blown the cloud cover on down into Texas, and now the sky was clear and icy blue. The Wichita Mountains stood out against the horizon, hunkered down in the pale, cold late afternoon sunlight. Trees had been planted in the industrial park, but they were still small and, in February, bare. They looked as if they were shrinking back from the bitter wind, just as I was. I pulled my red stocking cap down all around my face before I could force myself to get out of the truck.

Sam had said machine shops were always cold and drafty, but the office we entered was like an oven. A giant space heater radiated heat, and a thick haze hung in the air.

A tall, thin woman with dyed black hair was standing beside the only desk in the room, talking on the phone. She glared at us as we came in, then took a deep drag on a cigarette.

She exhaled, almost disappearing into the cloud of smoke that poured out, then she spoke into the phone. "Git your fanny down here, Bubba. We're short for the evening shift besides. The world's going to keep on turnin', no matter who dies."

She slammed the receiver down and looked at us.

"Afternoon, ma'am." Sam can sound real Okie when he tries. He pulled off his glasses, which had fogged up, of course. "I'm lookin' for B.J. Slater."

"Well, you've found her," the woman said. She took another deep drag from her cigarette and lifted artificially arched eyebrows as she puffed out another cloud of smoke. "I take it you're the Catlin County law."

"Yep. Just helpin' out the Oklahoma Highway Patrol with the investigation into Joe Pilkington's death."

B.J. Slater shifted her eyes in my direction and arched the eyebrows even higher. Sam introduced me and explained that I took care of the tape recorder he used for interviews.

Smoke snorted out B.J. Slater's nostrils. "I didn't know this was all that formal."

"Well, I hate to ask people to drive down to Holton to give their statements." Sam slid his glasses back on. "That probably won't be necessary. The main thing we need to do is pin down when Joe left. What kind of a worker was he, anyway?" He nodded at me, and I switched on the tape.

"Fair. Pretty good when you consider he was really more interested in that farm of his than in the job here. Do you know who hit him yet?"

"We're not even sure when it happened. But the OHP says his shift here at the shop ended at six."

B.J. Slater snorted smoke again. "He sure didn't work until then, if they found his body at six-fifteen. It woulda taken him forty-five minutes to drive down to Holton, with the roads the way they've been."

Sam nodded. "Did he keep a time card?"

"Yep, but I don't know when he left." B.J. Slater pulled a batch of cards out of her top desk drawer and fanned them out. "I don't have a big enough operation to justify puttin' in a time clock. The guys just fill out cards and turn 'em in every other Friday. They're supposed to fill 'em in every day, but—" She shrugged. "I'm not too picky, as long as the work gets done and they don't try to sneak in unjustified overtime."

"Pretty informal. You have any trouble with that system?"

"Not usually. So far the wage and hour boys haven't called me on it." She took another deep drag and snorted smoke. "Our work's hot and cold. We'll be real busy for a while, then things'll be slack. The guys know that if they get through they can go home early—I'm sure as hell not going to hang around and check up on them in the middle of the night! They make it up when things are busy."

B.J. Slater's eyes narrowed. She sat down on the edge of the desk, lifted a foot wearing a four-inch heel, and put it on a chair. She was wearing slacks, but it was not what my mother would have called a ladylike pose.

"I can tell how long they were here by lookin' at the work," she said. "But Joe was real reliable. I read his writing wrong once, paid him too much. He came in and told me, made me write him a check for less." She blew smoke through her nose. "I hated to do it."

Big Sam would have said she was tough as a boot heel. I sure wouldn't have tried to falsify any time card she was going to check over.

"How many people work on that ten P.M. to six A.M. shift?" Sam asked.

"Last night? Only two. Joe and Bubba James. We have a contract to put new armatures on electric motors for a repair outfit. Last night they were cutting keyways."

Sam nodded, but her explanation was as murky to me as the atmosphere in the room. She exhaled another enormous cloud of smoke into the warm air. I unzipped my jacket and tried not to cough. It was thick.

B.J. Slater waved her cigarette toward the telephone. "I just got hold of Bubba. He'll be here in five minutes or so."

Sam nodded and continued the casual conversation he uses so effectively when he's extracting information. Joe Pilkington had worked at the shop five years. Slater's biggest contract was to make parts for a small manufacturer, but they did all kinds of welding and other machine-shop work. Joe had asked for the ten P.M. to six A.M. shift because he liked having days to work at the ranch.

"Hell, I didn't care," B.J. Slater said. "Joe wasn't one you had to watch every minute."

When Sam finally asked B.J. Slater about Joe's gun rack, she arched her eyebrows again. "Did he carry a gun in it? To tell you the truth, I never noticed," she said. "Since he'd been working that late shift, sometimes I didn't see him for a couple of weeks at a time." She crushed her cigarette butt into a heap of similar debris in a giant metal ashtray. "Only unusual thing that happened about Joe lately was that call from the bank."

"About Joe? What bank?"

B.J. Slater scratched a stick match on the underside of her high-heeled shoe and lit another cigarette before she answered. "The Holton bank, whatever its name is. They wanted to talk to him. A'course, I told them Joe wasn't here days. That seemed to surprise 'em."

"Do you know who called?"

She shook her head. "Some fellow."

Sam blinked behind his glasses and seemed to study that information.

Her information was pretty interesting, if you knew about the operations of the First Bank of Holton. We had our account there, and either Sam or I went in there a couple of times a week. We also heard a lot about the bank from Big Sam, who was on the board. So I knew there was only one male member of the bank staff, the president, Brock Blevins.

Rosemary Murphy handled personal accounts; she'd call if Joe Pilkington had been overdrawn. Dayna Kittridge handled personal loans; she'd call if a car payment was late.

Brock handled larger loans. But Pilkington was a small-time rancher—really a machine-shop employee who ranched on weekends. He certainly wouldn't have been a major customer for the bank. Yet if a man called from the bank, it must have been Brock. So that call was probably more interesting to Sam than B.J. Slater realized.

Sam was speaking again. "Did Pilkington have a locker? Where did he put his stuff around here?"

The unnaturally dark eyebrows shot up again, and B.J. Slater puffed out a cloud of smoke before she answered. "All this for a traffic accident?"

Sam blinked innocently and shielded his thoughts with his glasses. "We try to be thorough."

B.J. Slater shrugged and led us out of the office and into the shop. As Sam had predicted, the shop itself was cold and drafty, not to mention dusty and loud. A smell that wasn't quite like motor oil permeated the air. Racks holding metal rods of various sizes lined one wall. Machinery, boxes, metal worktables, and giant orange or black canisters were strewn through the cement-block building. Steel curls that would have made a cute wig for a robot Shirley Temple littered the floor.

Five men, all wearing coveralls or heavy jackets, were scattered among the equipment. Each of them appeared intent on his work, isolated by the noise of his machine and the shield of his safety glasses. Yet each managed to look us over as we walked through.

B.J. Slater gestured toward a heavy machine as we walked along, buffeted by sound. A giant black man was positioning a steel rod on it. "That's the mill where Joe worked last night," she yelled.

"Anything unusual there this morning?" Sam yelled back.

She shrugged to indicate lack of knowledge and waved at the operator until he stopped, removed his safety glasses, and spoke to us. When B.J. Slater repeated Sam's question, he shook his head.

"Nothin' out of the ordinary," he said. He didn't look very friendly. Sam thanked him, and we walked away. But when I looked back, he was staring after us, still grim. I couldn't tell if he was looking at Sam or at his boss.

I decided B.J. Slater needed to be boot-heel tough if she was going to tell these men what to do.

B.J. Slater led us to a door in the back of the shop and banged on it with her knuckles. "Comin' in!" she yelled.

Behind it was a small, windowless room, where another gas heater took the chill off the air. An open door showed a toilet and sink, none too clean. A wooden bench sat along one wall, and a row of lockers was against the other. The lockers and bench looked as if they'd been salvaged from an abandoned school gym.

B.J. Slater closed the door, and the noise faded. "Most of the men just store their coveralls and lunches here," she said. "They don't usually change clothes or anything. They can lock stuff up if they want, but most of them don't bother."

Sam nodded. Each locker was marked with a first name written on a broad strip of masking tape. Sam crossed to the locker marked "Joe." It wasn't locked.

The locker held almost nothing. An old pair of work gloves was on the top shelf and a worn pair of shoes in the bottom. The only thing hanging in the locker was a light gray satin jacket. It said "Dallas Cowboys" across the back. Sam reached into the top shelf and pulled out two pencil stubs, a ballpoint pen, and an empty envelope with a Slater Machine Shop logo in the upper lefthand corner.

"I leave the paychecks in those," B.J. Slater said.

Sam nodded. He pulled the last item from the locker's shelf. It was a small and crumpled piece of paper. One end was jagged, as if it had been ripped unevenly off a pad.

I looked over Sam's shoulder. The paper looked as if it had been wadded up, then smoothed out. Two words and a number were written on it in red. "Brock Blevins," followed by the phone number of the First Bank of Holton. Beneath that, in a different writing, the words "Interest by March 1" had been scrawled.

I was trying to give Sam a significant look when the door into the machine shop flew open. Noise flowed in, and all three of us turned toward the sound. A huge and woolly man—at least two hundred and fifty pounds of fat, muscle, hair, and beard—stood in the doorway.

"What's this crap?" he shouted. "Who's poking in Joe's business? The guy's dead! Let 'im alone!"

Then he stepped into the room, slammed the door behind him, and sank onto the bench. He dropped his head into his hands, and his shoulders shook.

I realized that he was sobbing.

I didn't know how to react, and I didn't think Sam would know either. The Titus family lived by a standard of stoicism, and one of their tenets was don't inflict your own grief on others. I'd discovered this when Sam's brother died—only twenty-six and leaving two small children. I saw Sam's mother cry only once. She spent a lot of time excusing herself and going into her bedroom. She grieved, but she did it in private. The whole family was like that. So Sam had little experience in dealing with violent emotion on a personal level.

I didn't know what to do with a sobbing giant, for that matter. And certainly the boot-heel-tough B.J. Slater wouldn't know what to do.

But B.J. Slater was the first person to move. She stood in front of the hairy man and put a balled-up fist on each hip. "Bubba!" she said. "Bubba, stop this!"

The man's only reaction was to yank off his billed cap—it advertised beer—and throw it violently across the room. He kept sobbing.

"Bubba!" This time B.J. Slater's voice cracked. She looked wildly across the locker room. Then she shook her fists in the air.

"God damn it, Bubba! Now you've started me off!"

And the boot-heel-tough B.J. Slater began to sob, too.

I looked at Sam. He was standing like a pillar, with the note telling Joe Pilkington to call the bank still in his hand.

I saw a box of heavy red commercial rags in the corner. I pulled a couple out. They were clean. One I handed to B.J. Slater, who was patting at the edges of her eyes, apparently trying to keep her mascara from running down her cheeks. She took it, then turned and staggered out the door.

I sat down beside Bubba and stuck the other in front of him. He didn't take it, and in a minute I realized he had his eyes closed and couldn't see it. I put my hand on his shoulder. He yanked away from me.

"Here, Bubba," I said. I poked his hand with the rag, and this time he took it.

He put it over his eyes, sobbed a couple of new sobs, then used the rough rag to wipe the part of his face that stuck out of that forest of hair.

"Thanks," he said. Then he blew his nose loudly. "Sorry." Then he looked up at Sam, glaring. "It just seems like some fellas never have no kind of luck but bad! They work hard and try to do good, just like anybody else. But they get sick, marry the wrong people, get in debt, lose jobs, have car trouble—all through no fault of their own. To have a hard-luck guy like Joe just get out of his truck to open a gate—and get killed over it—well, it stinks! And then when I hear you're a'pawin' through his traps—well, that stinks, too!''

Sam nodded calmly, and now I remembered that he'd met lots of grieving people in his professional capacity. He sat down beside Bubba. ''I know just how you feel, Bubba. I'm in the business of clearing up messes, but sometimes I have to make a bigger mess before I can get on with the cleanup.''

Bubba was still glaring. ''Well, what are you doin' here, anyway? Joe got killed down south of Holton. I been down there. Where were you?''

Sam straightened his glasses and said his line about assisting the Highway patrol.

''And they've asked me to find out two things. The first is, when did Joe leave here this morning?''

Bubba blew his nose again. I got up and handed him another red rag.

''Well, we looked out around four A.M. and saw that it was startin' to snow pretty good,'' he said. ''Joe said he believed he'd knock off and go on home, because he didn't want to get stuck here and have nobody to feed his cattle.''

''So he left at four?''

''Mebbe four-fifteen. The snow didn't last long, but by the time we woulda known that, Joe was long gone.''

''Okay.'' Sam nodded. ''The other thing is Joe's gun. He had a gun rack in the truck, but it was empty. Did Joe have a gun in it last night?''

''Yes!'' Bubba jumped to his feet. ''Yes, by God! Joe always carried that gun. It was a Ducks Unlimited commemorative model. He was real picky about that shotgun—never fired a shell without cleanin' it afterward. If it wasn't in the rack, then the goldurned guy that kilt him musta stole it!''

Sam was still calm. ''Then you saw it last night?''

"Yes!" Bubba shouted. Then just as quickly he spoke again. "No!"

Sam looked at him and blinked.

Bubba put a hand to his bushy head. "He always had it," he said. "I'da noticed if it was gone."

A new voice, a woman's voice, entered the conversation. "If it was gone, Bubba won't likely know anything about it."

We all turned. A woman was stepping into the locker room. Her hair was somewhere between blond and red, and it curled elaborately. Her make-up was thick but perfectly applied, and the hand she was resting on the doorjamb sported long nails that matched her hair. She wore a long electric-blue leather coat over black slacks. When she spoke again her voice was as chilly as the weather outside the shop.

"If something's missing from my husband's truck, Sheriff, I'd ask the man who found his body."

FIVE

IT WAS MRS. PILKINGTON.

And she was talking about Johnny Garcia. Our Johnny, who helped Big Sam without hurting his pride, who showed Billy how to work with his calf, who gave Brenda a ride to classes when the weather was bad, who kept the Titus ranch running.

How dare she! I took a deep breath, ready to annihilate her with a brilliant and witty defense of Johnny.

"Just what do you mean by that?" I said.

Mrs. Pilkington stepped toward me, and her well-painted mask crumpled. Suddenly a desperately unhappy woman was standing there. "Well, who had the best chance to take that gun? Who had—"

But another voice interrupted then, a voice I knew. "Now, now," it said placidly. "Let's not get excited and start saying things we don't mean."

Nora Rich, another neighbor from our end of Catlin County and a good friend of Sam's mother, was coming into the locker room, calmly unwrapping a lacy gray knitted scarf from around her lacy gray hair.

Nora was the last person I would have expected to see with Mrs Pilkington. She was as short and plump as Mrs. Pilkington was tall and slim. She was old enough to be her mother. Mrs. Pilkington looked as if she lived on diet cola, and Nora on homemade cookies. They simply had nothing in common.

"Nora!" I said. "What are you doing here?"

Nora laid the scarf over the arm of her sensible flannel coat and reached over to give Mrs. Pilkington's arm a pat.

"This lady doesn't have any close family, Nicky. We couldn't let her deal with the arrangements all by herself."

I realized then that another of Nora's specialities was neighborliness. She'd probably had a casserole at the Pilkington's back door within ten minutes of hearing that Joe was dead.

When I turned back to Mrs. Pilkington, she did look like a grieving widow. She had uncrumpled her face, but the hand she was putting to her forehead was trembling.

"Nora came over here to go to the funeral home with me," she said. "I didn't know how to handle it."

Over here? Did she mean a Lawton funeral home was handling Joe's funeral? I was surprised. Every Catlin County funeral I'd attended had been arranged by Carl and Tonette Redding at the Holton Funeral Home.

Sam put on his wooden look, an expression that can indicate astonishment. "Then the Reddings won't be handling Joe's services?" he asked.

Mrs. Pilkington laughed bitterly. "Tonette Redding and I had a little artistic difference of opinion on hair, back when I was stupid enough to try having my own shop in Holton. If she got hold of any of my folks, they'd probably be displayed with their tongues sticking out."

Nora frowned, but she didn't speak. I was a bit shocked by the rude insult to the Reddings, and Sam became even more wooden. "Will the services be in Lawton?" he asked.

"Oh, no!" Mrs. Pilkington's voice grew shrill. "I couldn't do that to Joe! He loved Holton! That dump! The goddamn farm! The mud and the dust and the dirt. He rolled in it like a hog! He didn't care what I thought, where I'd like to live! He didn't care if the gossips in that stupid Podunk closed my business up. He didn't mind me having to drive sixty miles to work!"

Nora was trying to speak, but Mrs. Pilkington brushed her aside and kept screaming.

"He didn't care if we never saw each other, if I was gone all day and he was gone all night! And weekends he was out on his shitty tractor! Oh, no! I couldn't have Joe's funeral in Lawton. It will be right there in Holton, America! The center of his teeny-weeny little universe! I wouldn't inconvenience Joe's fellow farmers, just because he died! Those people were a lot more important to him than I was."

Then her face crumpled again, and the apricot head bowed. "But I didn't want anything to happen to Joe," she said. "I didn't want that. All I wanted was for him to pay me some mind."

Nora put her arm around Mrs. Pilkington, and this time the woman let it stay. Then Nora spoke to Sam. "She's really upset. I'm going to drive her on home."

Mrs. Pilkington raised her head. "I came to clean out Joe's locker and get his last paycheck! I'm not leaving until I get that done."

Bubba's voice rumbled. "I tol'ja I'd take care of that, Athena."

Athena? Mrs. Pilkington's name was Athena? The idea was surprising somehow.

But Mrs. Pilkington didn't object, so I gathered Bubba had called her name right. "I've got to take care of myself now," she said angrily. "I can't depend on anybody! Sheriff! Are you finished poking around in my husband's belongings?"

"Yes, Mrs. Pilkington," Sam said. "He didn't have much in his locker. I haven't taken anything as evidence."

"Well, that's a miracle! The way things disappear!" Athena Pilkington turned her back on Sam and yanked the locker's door open. "I repeat, Sheriff. I don't know if Joe's shotgun's missing or not, but you'd do better quizzing the guy who found him, rather than wasting time here with Bubba."

She'd pulled my chain again, and I inhaled, ready to let her have it. But Sam nudged me. "We won't overlook any possibilities," he said. "I believe we're through here." He turned to Bubba. "All I need is a daytime phone number for you."

Athena took a deep breath, then let it out raggedly. "I fail to see what Joe's locker has to do with a hit-and-run driver. Or how Bubba can help you." Her voice rose with each word, and she almost screamed out her final sentence. "How much more prying are you going to do?"

"We'll do as much investigating as it takes," Sam said. "We don't intend to let your husband's killer get away."

Athena's face grew stony. "I hope the rat that killed Joe rots in hell."

NEITHER OF US SPOKE until we had fought the wind across the parking lot, dodging ice thrown up by some guy in a pickup who suddenly decided to speed away, and were in the truck once more.

The wind had not cooled my opinion of Athena Pilkington, but I made an attempt to be fair. "Was that really a grieving widow, or just a bitch?"

"A little of both," Sam said. "I do think she's genuinely shocked and sorry about what happened to Joe. I guess she's lashing out at everybody because she's upset."

"But that remark about Johnny!"

Sam started the motor. "Yeah. That was pretty interesting."

"Interesting? You're not thinking of taking it seriously?"

"Nope." He turned the heater's fan on high. "No, I don't believe Johnny would steal a shotgun from a dead man. But her remark is pretty interesting on top of the rumor I got from Buck."

"You mean the rumor you aren't going to tell me?"

"Well, it's such an interesting rumor that I might have to share it after all."

"Golly gee! That good, huh? Just what is it? I know! Athena Pilkington's been sleeping with Bubba!"

Sam didn't laugh. "Not far off," he said. "Buck claims to have seen Johnny's truck parked over at the Pilkington place. Nights. A lot of nights."

It took a moment for that one to soak in. Johnny? At the Pilkington place? Nights?

Joe Pilkington had worked nights.

Good heavens.

I gulped. "Johnny? And Athena Pilkington? No way!"

Sam shrugged. "Well, you hear a different lot of gossip from the news I pick up around town. Have you heard anything about this? Does the Holton news network ever mention Johnny?"

"Not in my hearing. Of course, they might not say anything to me. I'm still something of a stranger to a lot of folks, I guess. And there's the connection with the Titus ranch. It seems they'd be more likely to tell you."

"The connection with Big Sam might stop some people from passing on speculation to me. Most people know we're partial to Johnny. Neither Big Sam nor I would take it kindly if anybody reported bad news about him."

I knew that was true. "The only talk I ever heard about Johnny came when he broke up with that girl from Frederick."

Sam nodded. "That was months ago."

I thought it over. Johnny had dated the Frederick girl, whose name escaped me at the moment, for a year. Then she had taken a job in Oklahoma City and moved up there. Oklahoma City was only a two-hour drive, but Johnny had never hinted that he'd been to see her. Johnny hadn't seemed very upset over the breakup. It was certainly possible that he had developed interests closer to home.

But surely not Athena Pilkington.

"Athena's probably ten years older than Johnny," I said.

"Right," Sam said. "On the other hand, she sure might be—available."

We let it drop. I thought Johnny had better taste than Athena Pilkington, but I don't always understand how men look at women. Availability can certainly make some women attractive to some men.

Sam carefully backed the truck over the icy lot, then drove off down the state highway, headed toward Holton. We'd gone about a mile before he spoke again.

"I wonder who that is," he said.

He pointed ahead casually, and I saw a white pickup stopped on the right-hand side of the road. The cab appeared to be empty, but the exhaust pipe was emitting a thin fog.

"Could be anybody," I said.

Sam slowed down. "How come it's sitting here empty?"

"Car trouble? I mean, pickup trouble? The driver got out because something went wrong mechanically?"

"Yeah, but if the driver got out, where is he?"

I looked around. "Good question," I said. The state highway between Lawton and Holton is not noted for its hills and heavy woods, and this particular spot was particularly barren. A few trees were scattered along the fencerow, but they were all completely lacking in leaves. The grass and weeds in the bare ditch had been flattened by the snow and ice. That was no place to hide. The truck sat up high on big tires, and I could see that even the ground under the truck was bare, and no one was standing in front of the truck unless he was hiding behind the right front tire. In fact, I could see at least two miles in every direction, and nobody was in sight anywhere.

"It looks as if the driver got out and walked off over the horizon," I said. "Or else he got a ride."

"Then why did he leave the motor running? Maybe I'd better check this out."

"This isn't your county."

"But that truck's from my county."

"How do you know that?"

"Because from where I'm sitting, I can see the logo on the side. And it's not only from Catlin County, it belongs to Catlin County. That's some Catlin County employee driving that truck." Sam pulled up fifteen feet or so behind the truck. He zipped his jacket up under his chin, put his gloves on, and got out.

I watched as he strode up to the pickup and looked in the driver's window. He stared a moment, then rapped on the glass. Immediately a head popped into view. It was a bald head balanced on burly shoulders. The head leaned toward the window, and I could see Sam talk. The head shook and nodded in response.

The driver had been lying down in the seat, and Sam had roused him, I decided. Since they seemed to be talking calmly, and the driver didn't get out of the truck and look under the hood, the situation didn't seem to be an emergency.

The bald head seemed familiar. After two and a half years in Catlin County, I knew a lot of folks. Who was it? The bald head turned, and I got a glimpse of a snout the size and shape of an Idaho potato. I immediately put a name to the nose.

"Otis Schnelling," I said. "What the heck is he doing here?"

Otis Schnelling was the caretaker at the Catlin County Fairgrounds. I remembered him from the county employees' Christmas party. Although the party punch hadn't been spiked with anything more potent than 7-Up, Schnelling had been drunk. He was one of the good old boys who kept sliding down the hall for a nip.

But I'd seen him more recently, too. He'd been at the livestock show earlier that day. He was the heavyset man Billy had bumped into in the crowd.

Sam gave Schnelling a casual wave and came back toward me, his head bent against the wind. Schnelling's truck drove slowly off.

Sam got into our truck fast. "Awful out there," he said. "It's getting colder than ever."

"What was wrong with Schnelling? Was he drunk?"

Sam turned toward me. His glasses had fogged up again, and it was like looking into a muddy pool.

"I wouldn't have let him drive off if I'd thought he'd been drinking, Nicky."

"Oh, I know. But why on earth had he stopped and lain down like that?"

Sam pulled the glasses off and polished them with an old, very soft blue bandanna he carried around for that purpose. "He didn't really give me a reason," he said. "He said he'd been to Lawton to see about getting a fence welded."

"A fence welded? Welded?"

"Yeah. One of those metal fences from the fairgrounds. Apparently he went in and talked to B.J. Slater about it."

I thought about that. "You mean he was at Slater's? The place we just left?"

Sam nodded. "Yeah. I guess that was his truck that left just as we came out the door."

I recalled that a truck had pulled out about that time, hitting us with ice. I hadn't noticed it particularly, since I'd been more concerned with keeping the north wind from blowing my stocking cap off.

"I guess it's nice to know where he'd been," I said. "But what was his explanation for stopping his pickup out in the middle of nowhere and lying down in the seat?"

"He didn't seem eager to discuss that."

"That's weird!"

Sam resettled his glasses and put the truck into gear. "Lots of weird things have been happening today. And I still have to tackle the weirdest one of all."

"What's that?"

"I've got to track down Johnny and ask him nosy questions about his sex life."

I didn't envy him the job, although I was curious to hear what Johnny had to say.

After we got back from Lawton, Sam dropped me at the house, then put on his insulated coveralls and went to work with Johnny as they fed and checked on cattle.

The day's high had been less than twenty degrees. As soon as I got inside our house, which is a remodeled country church, I kicked the thermostat up. Then I looked out the east window, toward the gate where Sam was turning the truck onto the road. The scene filled every corpuscle in my body with a fear I refused to name.

The reason I refused to name it was that the name would be awfully close to agoraphobia, and the dictionary says that is "an abnormal fear of being in open places." What I felt was not abnormal; any sensible person would feel uneasy when facing several thousand acres of nothing.

I had had this feeling off and on ever since I'd come to southwest Oklahoma. I'd had therapeutic reasons for taking my prairie sky pictures, the ones that had earned me a place in the big Houston show. I'd had some idea that dealing directly with the images that frightened me would make them less fearful. It hadn't worked completely.

I shuddered as I looked out the window.

To the south and east of the house, the ice-covered plains stretched away like Arctic tundra. They never seemed to reach the horizon, but merely turned into a matching gray sky at some indistinct point, then folded over themselves and climbed up to loom over my head.

These views explain why this part of the country is called "the plains." It was the plainest vista I'd ever seen—no trees, no houses, no hills. And this year's ice, snow, and dismal skies had washed away even the usual pale tints of the season and had hidden much of the one brilliant color that was present in the icy landscape, the vivid green of winter wheat fields.

I called this sight "the great American desert," in the words of early explorers.

Sam, however, referred to it by a later slogan, "the breadbasket of America." The dull scene actually was a view of the most fertile land on the Titus Ranch. If the ranch had good winter pasture and a bumper wheat crop year after year, it was because of those "plain" fields on the south and east sides of our house.

I reminded the agoraphobic side of my personality that Sam's version was right, then I whisked the draperies shut. Those level fields might keep us economically healthy, but they still scared the dickens out of a city slicker like me. I quickly went to the west windows, which overlooked the mountains. Even the snow couldn't mar their massive shapes. Then I turned to the north window and looked at the grove of pecan trees that began in our backyard and went down the hill to the creek. Those two views usually were comforting enough to overcome my unease about the south and east views.

But dusk was coming on, and tonight the bare branches of the pecans whipped in the awful north wind, becoming the grasping fingers of monsters or the tentacles of weird beasts. We'd put storm windows and insulation all over the house, but the cold seemed to seep through the very walls.

I pulled the north draperies shut, too, then built a fire in our freestanding fireplace. I'd get out the card table, and we'd eat dinner beside the fire, I decided.

The scene should have been cosy, but somehow the steeply pitched ceiling, left over from the old sanctuary, made the living room seem like an ice cave. Even the cherry-red rug and flag-blue couch failed to warm it up.

I rushed into the kitchen and pulled down the red, white, and blue plaid roman shade. I considered yanking the quilted wall hanging Marty had designed for us right off the wall so I could wrap up in it, but the fireworks it depicted looked cold; they seemed to represent snowflakes, rather than skyrockets. I hated to open the freezer looking for something to thaw for dinner. Even spaghetti sauce didn't seem warm, but I put it in the microwave to thaw.

SAM DIDN'T HAVE much to say during dinner, and I deliberately kept the conversation away from ranching, rustling, and death. After the dishwasher was loaded, I huddled in the corner of the couch, pulled an afghan over my knees, and reached for the television guide. I was almost settled when Sam tossed me an audiocassette and said, "Do you suppose you'd have time to transcribe this tomorrow?"

I must have looked amazed, since Sam doesn't usually ask me to do secretarial-type stuff. His office manager, Nadine Webster, is much more efficient at it than I am, and he's even been known to demonstrate his own knowledge of the touch system.

"It's the interview with Johnny," he said. "Nadine won't be in until Tuesday. Johnny and I need to move cattle tomorrow, and I want to pass this on to Greenburn and the OHP as quickly as possible."

Greenburn is the area agent for the Oklahoma State Bureau of Investigation.

I dropped the TV schedule and picked up the cassette.

"Wow! This might be hotter stuff than the featured presentation on HBO," I said.

"Listen and see." Sam shrugged. "I'm going to get in the shower."

I took the cassette and the tape recorder to the desk in the corner of our living room and flipped the tape on. Judging by the background of heater fan and the occasional moo, Sam had quizzed Johnny in the pickup.

"A tape? I don't mind, Sam, but it sure makes the whole thing seem official."

"It's just a sort of shorthand for me, Johnny. If I need an official statement, I'll get Nadine to type one up, and we'll call you to come in and sign it."

"Sure. But I don't know anything."

"How'd you happen to be on Split Creek Road this morning anyway?" Sam's deadpan voice barely sounded interested.

"I wanted to check on those cattle in the east pasture. I spent the night at my mother's house." I knew that Johnny's mother lived in Holton, within walking distance of the school where she cooked. "She had some pipes freeze up, and I went over there last night to help get them thawed. My brother came by, and we got talking. She fixed dinner. It got so late I just stayed over."

"I see. What did you see when you came on the scene of Joe's death?"

"The first thing was that old pickup of Joe's, standing there with the door open."

"The door was open?"

"Right. That made me slow down. Of course, at first I just thought he'd gotten out to open or shut the gate. But I got closer and closer, and nothing moved. Joe didn't seem to be around. That's when I realized something must be wrong. So I pulled up across the road and stopped. As soon as I walked around Joe's truck, I saw his body."

"Did you touch him?"

There was a long silence before Johnny answered. "No, Sam. I'm not very proud of it, but I couldn't make myself touch him. His neck—" There was another long silence. "Well, his head was at such a funny angle, I knew his neck was broke. I was afraid I'd make things worse. And the way he looked—man, I knew right away that he was dead."

"Right. What did you do then?"

"I got out of there, looking for help. Oh, first I shut off the motor of his truck. And I put that raincoat over him, that long one Big Sam calls my 'cowboy suit.' I left the headlights on. It didn't seem right to leave him there in the dark.''

"Did you see a gun in the truck?"

"No. There might have been one. Down behind the seat or someplace. I didn't look around much. Just reached in and turned the key, then slammed the door."

"Was there a gun anywhere around Joe?"

"You mean outside of the truck? I didn't see one. I didn't see anything around. Just Joe."

"How well did you know Joe?"

"Just to speak to. Didn't know him at all."

"How about Athena Pilkington?"

There was a little pause on the tape before Johnny answered. "I didn't really know her either. I'd run into her at the Co-op a few times."

"Then you never visited with them?"

"Nope."

I could hear Sam sigh deeply. "Well, Johnny, I had somebody tell me that you'd been hanging out over there a lot."

"Huh? What would I go over there for?"

"Well, the story was that you went to see Athena Pilkington."

There was another pause. Then Johnny's laugh boomed over the tape. "That old gal! You gotta be kidding!"

"She's probably ten years older than you, true, but I hear there's a lot to be said for experience."

"I'll bet she's had plenty of that." Johnny laughed again, but this time the sound had become contemptuous. "I'll tell you, Sam—" He broke off in the middle of his sentence. "I'd better shut up."

"If you've got something to say, you'd better spit it out."

"I don't want to bad-mouth the woman. It might have been my imagination."

"What happened?"

Three deep moos were recorded on the tape before Johnny answered. "Well, I ran into her down at the Co-op, like I said. This was last fall, right after I broke up with Shannon."

Shannon. That was the name of the girl from Frederick. Now I remembered.

"I was just picking up a block of salt, when Mrs. Pilkington came up to me. We were back in that corner..." His voice trailed off again.

"Yeah, I know where they stack the salt."

"Yeah. Well, as I lift the block, she reaches over and puts her hand on my arm. She says, 'Feel that muscle.'" Johnny made his voice simper and squeal as he repeated Athena's words.

Then he went on. "That embarrasses me, so I kind of laugh and move away, and she follows me down the aisle. 'Hey, I hear you broke up with your girl,' she says. And I say, 'Yeah, I guess so.' And she says, 'You won't be lonely long, Johnny. Lots of us girls like Latin lovers.' And she pats me again. On the back this time. Then, as I'm putting the salt on the counter, she says, 'I guess I better stop at the IGA and get a case of beer. Somebody might drop by and have one with me.' Then Joe comes out of the office, and they get in her car and drive on off."

Sam snorted. "It doesn't sound like your imagination to me. It sounds pretty much like an invitation."

"Well, I never took her up on it."

"Lots of guys would have been tempted."

"Maybe so. And I guess I'm not any holier than the next guy, in spite of my mother draggin' me to the Iglesia de Dios three times a week the whole time I was growin' up. But that Mrs. Pilkington—well, she's just not my type."

"Too old."

"That. And too married! She pulled all this when her husband was right inside the store, in the office. She wanted him to see what was goin' on!

"Sam, that was too kinky for me. I've got enough problems with my love life without gettin' mixed up in some kind of sex triangle. I'd probably be the one who wound up shot. I am not interested in that situation."

"Very smart."

"I don't know if I'm smart or chicken, but I'll swear on the biggest stack of Bibles in Oklahoma that I'd never been near the Pilkington house until this morning, when I went over there at six-fifteen after I found Joe."

I heard a thump coming from the tape, and I pictured Johnny rapping the truck's dashboard for emphasis.

"I've never been there but that once," he said. "And there was nobody home then."

SIX

I WAS TAPPING AWAY on my old electric portable when Sam spoke from the stairs.

"You don't have to do that tonight," he said.

I whirled around. "Where was Athena Pilkington?" I asked.

"You mean when Johnny went by this morning to tell her about Joe?"

"Yes! Where was she? Did she have a good explanation for being gone at six-fifteen in the morning?"

"She didn't mention leaving the house. She could have been asleep and just not heard Johnny. Or she could have been in the shower."

"Is that what she claims?"

"She doesn't claim anything," Sam said. He crossed the room and stood with his back to the fireplace. He had put on his favorite pair of jeans, the ones with the patches on the seat, with a sweatshirt and a pair of fleece-lined moccasins. "Nobody's asked her about it."

"Nobody asked her?"

"Right. The wife of an accident victim doesn't usually have to account for her whereabouts."

"Oh. And you're still pretending this was an accident."

"Yep. And I just got Johnny's statement a couple of hours ago, so nobody's talked to her since I found out Johnny says she didn't answer her door at six-fifteen. But it makes things look sort of funny."

"Why?"

"When we went by to break the news she volunteered the information that she'd slept uneasily and 'just knew' something might have happened to Joe."

"Oh! Volunteering information could be a sign of a guilty conscience."

"It could be a sign of nervous talking, too. When you bring people the word that somebody's been killed, you get all kinds of reactions."

"But if she didn't come to the door when Johnny knocked—"

"That doesn't prove she wasn't there. She could have a dozen reasons not to come to the door. And a dozen more not to admit she wouldn't let him in."

"Will you quiz her again?"

"Not right away. First, we'll see if any garage around here has a customer bring in a truck with the window shot out. Or a vehicle with a dent in the hood. We'll give the garages until Tuesday. We'll talk to Mrs. Pilkington again after that."

So the weekend passed. On Saturday Sam had a long telephone conference with Greenburn, the OSBI man. Then he and Johnny loaded steers into a trailer and moved them from a pasture to a wheat field. I worked in the darkroom, developing and printing the pictures I'd taken Friday. They were pretty good. And Big Sam, Marty, and Brenda took both Billy and Lee Anna, Brenda's four-year-old, back to Lawton for the final session of the Heart of the Great Plains Classic Steer and Heifer Show. In a few years Lee Anna might be showing a heifer, too. Big Sam liked to start the indoctrination into ranching early.

On Sunday Brenda dropped by to borrow a videotape and told me Mike Mullins's Hereford heifer had been named grand champion. Two Circle M steers took their classes as well, so it was a winning weekend for Buck and Mike Mullins. Dr. Mullins had beamed and whammed Buck on the back, she said.

Brenda's voice had a pensive quality as she reported this news. I wondered if she was trying to sound noncommittal about Buck. They'd had three dates that I knew about.

I tried to be noncommittal, too. I didn't want to influence Brenda. "Buck seems like a real nice person," I told her.

"Well, he's very gentlemanly. Not grabby or anything," Brenda said. "I never dated anybody but Bill before, really. I don't have much of an idea of what to expect."

Brenda had been only eighteen when she married Sam's brother, Bill. They had been high school sweethearts. She'd given birth to Billy when she was twenty.

I knew Brenda had been invited on dates only weeks after Bill's death. I'd been a bit surprised that she'd waited two years to begin going out.

She smiled at me. "I guess I'll have to ask you for some pointers on adult dating, Nicky."

I'm less than a year older than Brenda, but my life has been very different from hers. I'd been away from home six years, at college and later working in New York and Paris, before I married Sam. Sam hadn't been the first man in my life, and I hadn't been the first woman in his. When we started getting serious, he and I had discussed the past as deeply as either of us wanted to, but we tacitly agreed to drop the subject of our previous love lives at the altar. And I certainly wasn't going to talk to Brenda about anything I wouldn't discuss with Sam. My cheeks felt a little hot.

"My only advice is don't do anything you don't feel like doing," I said. "It's your life."

"Oh, I know it is." Brenda's cheeks looked a little hot, too. Maybe she was sitting too close to the fireplace. "But that's kind of hard to grasp, when I shared my life with Bill for six years. And the kids. If I make a wrong decision, it would be awful for them, too."

She looked up at me then, and for a moment I thought tears were about to appear. "I sure have appreciated you and Sam and Marty. Big Sam, too. If you hadn't been around for me to hang on to, I might have made a big mistake long before this.''

We might have both teared up, but right at that moment Lee Anna fell down the stairs that led up to our sleeping loft, and we both de-sentimentalized.

I appreciated Lee Anna's intervention. I'm not as frightened of emotion as Sam can be, but sometimes we say things in the heat of the moment that embarrass us later. I don't like scenes.

I guess that's one thing that makes me hate going to funerals. But I went to Joe Pilkington's, either out of neighborliness or out of curiosity.

The Pilkingtons had lived in Catlin County five years. Joe knew most of the other farmers and ranchers, but Athena had kept to herself. Brenda had told me that the Maids and Matrons, Holton's biggest women's club, had invited her to join when she was new in town, but she had refused. She had also snubbed the neighborhood home demonstration organization and the Catlin County Cattle Growers Auxiliary.

And neither Athena nor Joe seemed to have much family. When Sam and I were ushered into the Community Church, where the service was held, I saw that only one row had been set aside at the front left, the traditional spot for the family to sit. The right front row, usually the spot for the pallbearers, held two couples I recognized from the Catlin County Farmers Co-op meetings. I'd heard there would be no graveside service, so I concluded there were no pallbearers either.

Big Sam, Marty, Sam, and I were seated on the right-hand side, too, directly behind three women with rather extreme hair styles. I wondered if they weren't a delegation from the Wichita Falls beauty shop where Athena Pilkington worked. I saw Buck Houston across the aisle, beside the Circle M hand, Daniel, and Dr. Mullins. B.J. Slater was behind them, and Bubba was with her, anchoring the row in a powder-blue western-cut suit. The president of the First Bank of Holton, Brock Blevins, was at the other end of that row.

A few more neighbors, Holton tradesmen, and members of the Community Church were ushered in while the organ played softly. Then the funeral director escorted Athena down the aisle, followed by a thin blonde and a heavyset man, and the service started.

In the two and a half years I'd lived in Holton, Sam and I had attended half a dozen funerals for neighbors. This seemed to be a lot, and Sam blamed it on demographics—the population of rural Oklahoma is aging, he says.

I'd learned the routine for small-town funerals. There were often two ministers, for example. That was because the family is likely to be friends with more than one, and they don't want to leave an acquaintance out. The music tends to be old-timey hymns—"Rock of Ages" or "Blessed Assurance," although the family of one old rancher requested "Wagon Wheels." For some reason I hadn't yet divined, Baptist funerals tend to be more emotional than services led by ministers of other churches. It's something in the tone of a Baptist preacher's voice.

But Tink Dawkins, minister of the Holton Community Church, was leading this service. He stuck to Bible verses and innocuous comments. He didn't make any reference to the fact that, as far as I could tell, Joe Pilkington hadn't entered the door of this or any church from the time he was baptized as a baby until he was rolled down the aisle in a coffin. Joe's age was in the little folder we'd been handed at the door. He'd been forty-two. Seven years or so older than Athena, I guessed.

The weather was still miserably cold, so I was glad we got to skip the trip to the cemetery. "The family" would receive friends in the church parlor following the service, Tink announced.

The gathering wasn't like a wake, and there hadn't been any wake before the funeral either. Wakes, at least as formal events, are not the custom in Oklahoma, Sam had told me. People take a cake by the family home and sign the guest book, or they go by the funeral home if they want to view the body, but there's usually nothing like a formal reception.

In the parlor we found that someone from the church had made coffee, and there were a few plates of cookies. Katherine Dawkins, Tink's wife and my best friend in Holton, murmured to me, reporting that Athena had turned down the church women when they offered to serve lunch for the family.

"Well, there's hardly any of them," I muttered back. The only family members present were the faded blonde, identified as Joe's sister, her husband, and Athena.

I turned away from Katherine, planning to introduce myself to Joe's sister, but instead I found myself facing Daniel of the Circle M, whose last name I still hadn't remembered.

He smiled sadly and gave a shake of his ash-blond ponytail. "A sad occasion, Miz Titus," he said. "It's sure too bad."

"Yes, it is," I answered. "Did you know Joe well?"

"Just as a neighbor." He gave a wide-eyed grin. "I'd wave at him on the road, see him out in the pastures. He was a hard-working man. He worked two jobs, like me."

"I thought you worked for the Circle M full time."

Daniel nodded. "Sure do. So I have to use my off time for my real career."

"Career? Oh, your singing?"

"My singing and songwriting. I'm making a demo next week."

Behind Daniel I saw that Katherine Dawkins's conversation with Joe's sister had apparently run out of topics.

"That's good," I said. "But excuse me a moment. I wanted to meet Joe's sister."

"Certainly, Miz Titus." Daniel smiled broadly. I hadn't expected him to be sobbing, but he certainly was carrying the stiff-upper-lip type of funeral behavior to extremes.

I had just introduced myself to Joe's sister when I heard Bubba's voice boom out.

"You oughta know," he said. "You're the expert on dealin' misery."

I turned to find the hairy giant standing jaw to jaw with Athena. Both were glaring, and their body language hinted that they were thinking of punching it out. Silence fell over the group, and I heard Joe's sister whisper, "Oh, dear. Oh, dear."

"Misery!" Athena's voice was shrill. "You're the one who knows how to hand out misery, Bubba! Fillin' Joe's head with junk! Stupid ideas about what's goin' on when you don't have the slightest idea about anything! You make me sick!"

I could see Daniel move slightly, so that Buck's bulk hid him from the irate widow. The only one who didn't seem to be suffering from paralysis was B.J. Slater. She stepped purposefully toward the two. Bubba barely had time to roar "You little b—" before his boss had him by the arm and headed for the door.

"Come on, Bubba," she said. "I want you to drive me back to Lawton."

Athena yelled after them. "Actin' so sweet to me now, when you bad-mouthed me to Joe all the time!" Then she seemed to realize that she had become the center of attention, and she glared around the room, looking the rest of us over contemptuously.

"What a bunch," she said. "Every one of you hassled Joe over something. Fences. Money. Stupid cattle. Nosy neighbors and their foul mouths. Why the hell did Joe insist on living in this dump anyway?"

Bubba stopped in the door and turned, but Athena faced him and yelled again. "Go on and leave! Nobody's helped me before, and I can get along without your help now!"

I saw a distressed-looking Tink moving toward Athena, but Buck Houston reached her side first.

His voice was very soft. "Athena, you're all upset. Why don't you let me take you home?"

Athena's head swiveled toward him. Her eyes were fiery, and for a minute I thought she was going to roast Buck, too. Then she gave a most unattractive laugh.

"Oh, you're here, are you? Some nerve. After you—"

"I'm concerned about you."

Buck took her hand, but Athena yanked it away. She glared at him a long moment, then she whirled toward Joe's sister. "Come on, Edith," she said. "Let's let this bunch have their coffee and chitchat. I'm goin' home."

Nobody argued with her, and she made only one more comment. After she stalked out into the church foyer, I heard "And you stay out of this, buster!" echo back into the parlor.

I couldn't tell who had drawn the final shot. I hesitated a moment, but curiosity won. I looked out the door to see who was there.

The bulky shape of Otis Schnelling was near the main door. Schnelling was scratching his bald head and looking after Athena.

Sam passed me and joined Schnelling. "Don't let her bother you, Otis," he said.

The bald man looked around slowly. When he saw Sam, he jumped like a startled bull. "Wha—wha—what's goin' on?" he said.

"Mrs. Pilkington's a mite upset," Sam said. "I didn't see you at the service."

This comment seemed to throw Schnelling even further into confusion. "Wuhdent there," he muttered. "I jes come by to ketch Buck.'' He managed to stretch the name into two syllables. ''Buh-uck.''

''Buck?''

''Yeah. Buck. I got to ask 'im sumpin' about that show nex' week.'' Schnelling threw his head back and rolled his eyes. Now he looked like a frightened bull. ''It ain't nothin' important,'' he said. ''I din't think 'bout you bein' here.''

''Come on in,'' Sam said.

''Naw, I'll wait out here,'' Schnelling said.

''Come have a cup of coffee.''

But Schnelling shook his head again. ''Naw. Naw, ah'll jes ketch Buck later.'' He took a step away from the parlor.

''If you won't come in, I'll send Buck out,'' Sam said.

I moved back into the parlor and talked to Katherine Dawkins until Sam had sent Buck out to Schnelling. Sam joined Katherine and me, and Dr. Mullins trailed along.

''What a scene,'' the doctor said. ''I can't believe I came to pay my respects to a neighbor and was insulted for my trouble.''

''The insults got pretty general,'' Sam said. ''I wouldn't take it personally.''

''Oh, I know. She'll say that she was just upset. But I'll admit that crack about fences got to me.''

''Did you have trouble with Joe Pilkington over fences?'' Sam said.

''Well, yes. When I bought the Circle M, we got a new survey, of course. For title purposes.''

Sam nodded.

''Well, one section of the boundary between his property and mine was out of line about ten feet. Apparently some previous owner had used trees as fenceposts. Got everything all messed up.''

The doctor cleared his throat. ''Joe wasn't happy about having to move the fence. But we didn't quarrel about it. He agreed that it needed to be done, and he did it, but he said it came at a real inconvenient time.''

"I've never known a convenient time for workin' on fences," Sam said. "That's my least favorite job."

Buck joined us then, shaking his head. "Sometimes I wonder about those guys you hire to work for the county, Sam."

"If you mean Otis, you'll have to blame him on the commissioners. I just hire for the sheriff's office. What's Otis up to?"

"Oh, he needed to know how we want the stalls set up for the Sooner State cattle show next week. He just doesn't seem real bright."

"I know," I said. "Sam and I ran into him on a back road south of Lawton yesterday. He had stopped out in the middle of nowhere, and he was lying down in the seat of his pickup. I thought he must be sick, but he told Sam he wasn't."

Buck frowned and looked seriously at Sam. Then he crumpled his Styrofoam coffee cup. "Odd," he said. "Well, I guess Daniel and I better get back to work."

Sam and I turned toward the door, too, but this time Sam was stopped by Brock Blevins, Holton's banker. As usual Brock wore a spiffy suit in a gray that was only a few shades off from his hair. He put his head close to Sam's and spoke in a low voice. "What's the situation with Joe's death?"

"It looks like a hit-and-run, Brock. Why?"

"I didn't like those ugly remarks Mrs. Pilkington made, that's all."

"She's just upset."

Brock fiddled with the silver tie bar that immobilized his black, red, and gray tie. "I know she was getting at me with those cracks over money. I guess I can't blame her for being upset."

"Joe didn't leave her in very good shape?"

"No. He'd been one of our problem loans for a year or more. If your dad hadn't stood up for him, I imagine we would have foreclosed last fall."

"I'm not too surprised," Sam said.

"He just had a marginal operation, Sam. Those little outfits simply can't let their debt pile up, or they're sunk. You know that."

"I know that from sad experience," Sam said. "I spend quite a few hours up in the middle of the night, wondering what's going to happen to the Titus Ranch if the price of cattle stays this low."

Brock looked around the church parlor, and his voice became a low murmur. "Listen, compared to Joe Pilkington, you're blue chip. Big Sam has always been very cautious about debt, and I'm glad to see he drilled that into you, too. And neither you nor your dad takes a big salary from the ranch. But Joe—" Brock stopped talking abruptly. He gulped a couple of times, then turned toward the door. "I've got to get back to the bank," he said.

We followed Brock out, but neither of us said anything until we were in the patrol car. Then Sam chuckled. "Ol' Brock nearly forgot himself and gossiped about bank business."

"There's going to be plenty of gossip around after that funeral," I said. "What did you make of Athena's outburst?"

"Pretty interesting. I wonder what brought it on."

"I imagine she's just trying to blame her grief on somebody else," I said. "It was such a general attack."

"A general attack?" Sam looked at me vacantly.

"Yeah. She let us all have it. Everybody there either was related to Joe's money problems, or his ranching problems—or gossiped."

But Sam shook his head. "I didn't mean that," he said. "I was thinking about what she said to Otis Schnelling."

"Otis Schnelling?"

"Yeah. She yelled something like 'Stay out of this, buster.' Just what did that mean?"

"Did it mean something special? I thought she just wanted him to get out of her way."

"Maybe so." Sam looked at me and shrugged. "I guess I'll have to ask him," he said.

Sam tried to talk to Schnelling that afternoon, but the caretaker was away from the fairgrounds and hadn't showed up at the house the county provided him by the time Sam came home at seven. Sam said he'd try to catch him the next day.

That morning, Tuesday, I had to drive to Lawton for a breakfast meeting. I'd become fairly active in a photography club over there. The membership is about half professional and half amateur, and the group was planning a show in April. Their show the year before had started me on my way to the big Houston event, so I owed the club a lot.

Since most members of the show committee had regular jobs, we'd finally agreed to hold our meetings over Egg McMuffins and Breakfast Burritos at one of the Lawton McDonald'ses. So I got up when Sam did and left in my antique Volkswagen about the time he headed out to feed cattle.

My Volkswagen was nearly twenty years old, and Sam shook his head about it, but I hung on to it for sentimental reasons. My father and I had rebuilt it the year before I went away to college, working in the hobby shop at Fort Leavenworth. Its soft red color and rotund shape had inspired my mother to suggest naming it after her favorite variety of tomato, and Big Boy had seen me through four snowy years of college at Ann Arbor, Michigan. The next year I'd lived in New York, and Big Boy had lived at the Connecticut home of some family friends. He'd taken me on many a ski trip and weekend jaunt before I moved back to Germany. Then Big Boy had been shipped over to revisit his roots, and I'd driven him all over Europe. Sam and I had exchanged our first kiss over Big Boy's hand brake, in the shadow of the Eiffel Tower.

Big Boy and I had been through a lot together. I wasn't going to give the VW up as long as we could find a mechanic to keep him together.

The overnight low had been just above zero. But Big Boy loves winter weather, and he chugged confidently as we left our home in the pecan grove at six-fifteen A.M. that Tuesday, headed for Lawton. The roads weren't bad, so I was buzzing right along when I came to the intersection with Split Creek Road.

I stopped at the stop sign that gives the Split Creek Road traffic the right of way, and I saw headlights approaching. I sat there, motor chugging, as a dark-colored pickup pulling a gooseneck trailer roared up to the intersection.

As it approached, the chugging of the Volkswagen seemed to fade away. It was being drowned out by the sound of music.

Music? Ultra-loud music?

I stared at the oncoming truck in amazement. A farm truck equipped with a boom box? Wouldn't that scare the livestock it normally carried?

Then I realized what music was playing.

It was the Queen of the Night's aria, by Mozart.

Mozart?

It could be the same music Dr. Franklin Mullins had claimed he had heard the morning Joe Pilkington was killed by a hit-and-run driver. And it was being played just as loudly as he had reported.

The truck and trailer flashed by me and roared through the intersection, heading south on Split Creek Road.

I took one deep breath, then spun Big Boy's steering wheel.

I headed down Split Creek Road after the truck.

SEVEN

THERE'S AN OLD JOKE about the dog who always chased cars. When he finally caught one, he scratched his ear with a hind foot, then barked, "Why did I want this thing?"

I thought briefly about that dog as I headed south after those faint taillights, but I was perfectly clear about why I was chasing that truck and trailer.

My purpose was not to catch the cattle thieves. No, sirree, bob. I was alone and unarmed and untrained in law enforcement techniques. I had no radio to call for help. Whoever was driving that truck was likely to be a dangerous criminal. I was not dumb enough to try to catch him. I was simply going to see where that rig went, and maybe get its license number. I would chug gently along—staying at least a quarter of a mile back. But when that truck and trailer turned off the road, I'd know which way they went.

If Sam was too busy to take an interest in my work, okay. I could still take an interest in his. If I got a line on the cattle thieves, he would be really proud of me.

The taillights were growing even more dim, so I put my toe down. I didn't want to get too close, but I didn't want the truck to get away from me, either.

I looked at my speedometer. Big Boy was hitting fifty as he tried to keep up with the truck. That was a pretty fast rate for a pickup on a gravel road, and I deduced that the trailer was empty. Then I saw brake lights glow, and I realized the driver was slowing for the crossing one mile south of where I had started the chase.

It was Thomas Jefferson who first ordered government surveyors to mark off the United States, including southwestern Oklahoma. They did it by laying a giant grid over the continent, using longitude and latitude lines as guides. On the Great Plains, where there are few natural obstacles, this is easy to see. A map of Catlin County could be used as a checkerboard. All the roads, fences and property lines run north and south, or they run east and west. The farms and ranches are rectangles. The county is cut up into squares, with county roads every mile.

It's common for a farmer to give directions by saying, "We live two south and three and four-tenths east of Holton," for example. He means that if you start at the high school on the south edge of Holton and drive two miles south on the state highway, then turn left on the road that intersects the highway there, you'll come to his home in three and four-tenths miles.

So when that truck slowed, I knew it was crossing the county road a mile south of where I had picked up its trail. And my heart beat a little faster, because just a couple of miles straight south of that intersection was the Pilkington farm.

The truck barely slowed, then went through the intersection without turning. It was headed back to the scene of the crime.

I tried to picture the road between me and the point where Joe Pilkington was killed. Catlin County may be laid out on a basis of squares, but there are lots of variations. Prairie road builders didn't completely go along with the surveyors' foursquare plan. There are creeks to be crossed, for example, and these follow the rule that water seeks its own level. There are rock outcroppings that road builders detoured around. There are areas where the roads dead-end into wheat fields or pastures for no apparent reason, and a fence line carries on the pattern.

I tried to picture the next two miles of gravel. It wasn't a route Sam and I took very often. I'd explored around this area, taking pictures, but my memories were vague. Did the road run straight until it got to the Pilkington place? What was coming up?

The Anderson Creek crossing.

That was it. A low-water crossing that at dawn in February would be a sheet of ice. Damn.

Anderson Creek was dry much of the year. Usually Big Boy could swoop down its steep banks on the gravel road, then scoot through its cement-lined bottom with merely a stomach-turning dip. But our bitter winter had been preceded by a wet fall, and the Christmas freeze had caught the Anderson Creek crossing full of water. It hadn't had a chance to thaw out since.

I hadn't been through the crossing that winter, but I remember Sam and the Highway Patrol had worked an accident there a week earlier. A hay truck had gone out of control on a patch of ice and had landed crumpled against a tree. The driver wound up in the hospital.

I slowed Big Boy to forty.

Ahead, the brake lights of the Mozart truck had dimmed again, so it was gaining speed. I paused at the stop sign and went on through after it.

I felt fairly confident that I wouldn't lose the truck and trailer if I slowed down to get ready for the Anderson Creek crossing. For the next half-mile the road went through open fields, so I'd be able to see if the truck turned off. A grove of trees surrounded the curve that led down into the creek bottom, but their limbs were bare, of course. The truck would have to slow down when it hit that curve, because it would have to creep through the crossing, just as I would. I'd worry about catching up with it after I got up the other side of the creek bed.

Just as I expected, the truck went straight on for half a mile. Then the trailer's brake lights brightened, and headlights bounced off the bare trees as it swung left into the curve. It started down the hill into the creek bottom, and the lights became reflections on bare branches.

I slowed as I approached the curve, too. I didn't want to wreck Big Boy. I crept around the bend and into the woods. There was ice and snow on the road here, where the shadows of the creek bank and of the few scrub cedars had prevented the weak winter sunlight from hitting the gravel road. They made the road treacherous. Big Boy groaned as I downshifted to third.

We started down the hill, and I braked gently as Big Boy tried to gain speed. Then I shifted down to second. This was a steep incline even when the road was good. The truck and trailer had gone slowly down the bank and—

"Good Lord!" I said. "What happened to that truck?"

Because right at that moment it occurred to me that I hadn't seen the lights of the truck go up the opposite creek bank.

I braked harder, and Big Boy lurched toward the ditch.

"Oh, no!"

I yelled, but the words were drowned out by a swelling sound of Mozart. The truck and trailer loomed into my headlights.

The driver had stopped in the creek bottom. He was parked diagonally across the road, with his lights out.

Big Boy seemed to be barreling down the hill. I remember thinking fatalistically that there was no way I could keep from smashing into that truck.

I spun the wheel, and Big Boy began to skid toward the right side of the road. I turned the wheel in the direction of the skid, and the tires caught. I plunged onto the shoulder, parallel to the gravel road. This tipped me sideways, since the right-hand wheels were in the bar ditch. It was still headed downhill. Brush and branches whipped the passenger's side of the car. Trees flashed by in the headlights. Rocks and boulders tossed Big Boy up and down, and the steering wheel jerked back and forth in my hands. If I got any farther off the road, I'd be in the trees. But the truck and trailer in front of me was so long that it blocked the entire road and hung over the edges. I was still headed straight for it.

I tried to yank the car sideways, but the ice kept the tires from climbing the little incline. I had shoved the brake pedal clear to the floor, and the tires seemed to have stopped turning, but the car kept on slipping, sliding down the hill on a sheet of ice.

The truck and trailer were getting closer and closer, and Big Boy was completely out of control.

Then, suddenly, the little car spun. I was thrown to the right, and only my seat belt kept me behind the wheel. My shoulder belt clutched my neck. Then the whirl ended, and I was sitting still. Big Boy gave a shudder, and his motor died.

I wasn't hurt.

Mozart was pounding against the car, and I could see the truck not ten feet away from me.

I had to get out of there. Strapped into the car I was a sitting duck, and if the guy in the truck cared enough about me to wreck my car, he might have other plans in mind for me as well.

I fumbled with my seat belt, but as it clicked open I realized that the truck was moving. It backed up slowly, then turned slightly and moved forward, away from Big Boy and me.

It lumbered placidly up the other side of the creek bank. Mozart's Queen of the Night let out a final shrill, raucous trill. She seemed to be laughing at me.

The truck and trailer disappeared over the top of the hill. For a few minutes I could hear the music echo back; then I was alone in the silence.

I pushed in the knob for the headlights and turned off the ignition, then leaned against the steering wheel, trying to understand just what had happened.

The truck driver had obviously realized that he was being followed and had been willing to risk being hit in order to stop whoever was after him.

That was very incriminating, when you thought of it. It more or less proved that I had been on the trail of the thieves' truck, not some innocent truck driver who happened to be a Mozart freak.

I could hardly wait to tell Sam that the truck was still in the area. Even if I hadn't gotten the license number. Heck, the light had been so bad I wasn't even sure what color it was. Black? Or maybe dark green?

But once I had caught my breath, I realized I was in a mess. I was a long way from a phone, on a back road with a crossing so dangerous all the drivers in the neighborhood would be avoiding it. The nearest house I could think of was the Circle M, nearly a mile south.

And the temperature on the thermometer outside my kitchen window had been four degrees just before I left the house. The wind was blowing at least fifteen miles per hour, pushing the windchill factor way below zero.

Should I stick with the car, running the heater just enough to keep from freezing before help came? Or should I wrap up in my ski jacket and heavy cap and hoof it to the Circle M?

Or could I get Big Boy out of the ditch and back on the road without help?

I decided to survey the situation before I tried to move the car. I fished my woolly cap and gloves out of the backseat where I'd tossed them after the car warmed up. I zipped all the zippers and hooked all the Velcro on my jacket. I put the cap and the gloves on and tied a long scarf around my face. I got my flashlight out of the glove compartment. I wiggled my toes inside my storm boots, took a deep breath, turned on Big Boy's headlights, and got out of the car.

It was horrible out there. Even though Big Boy and I were pretty well sheltered from the wind by the creek banks, the temperature was bitter. I fought the desire to jump back inside, restart the motor and turn the heater up. Instead I looked at how much traction Big Boy had. I didn't really understand why we'd stopped before we hit the truck. According to the law of gravity, we should have slid right on down and smacked into its side.

Hay. The ditch was full of hay.

I realized that Big Boy had come to a halt at the spot where the unlucky truck driver had slid off the road a week earlier. Sam had told me his load had been giant cylinders of hay, the kind that are five feet long and five feet in diameter. Two or three of them are as big as an old-fashioned haystack. Ranchers in southwest Oklahoma favor that method of putting up hay over the traditional rectangular bale, even though the monsters must be handled by specially equipped trucks.

But the huge rolls had apparently spilled over the road and bar ditch. Even though the giant cylinders had been scooped up—hay was too valuable to waste—enough had been scattered in the bar ditch to stop the car.

Sam had said the hay-truck driver was still in the hospital. I resolved to send him flowers.

Maybe the hay he'd left behind meant I would be able to get the car out of the ditch. I got back inside and started the engine. Big Boy roared, but he didn't want to move forward. I put the car in reverse, and he moved back slightly. But when I slid into first again, his back wheels tried to spin, and I couldn't rock the car.

Well, maybe I could put more hay under the back wheels.

I got out again, wishing I had some sort of a shovel, and began to grab up handfuls of hay and pack it behind the wheels. The breeze blew it away immediately.

After a few minutes I quit trying. I stood there staring at the blowing hay, feeling the cold creep through the soles of my boots. Big Boy was going to have to be hauled out of that ditch. I had to think of another plan.

Walk? Or wait? Go for help? Or stay there until it came?

At that moment, lights flashed through the branches over my head, and I heard a motor. Someone was coming.

Was it a good guy? Or a bad one? Did I dare try to hitch a ride?

At least the vehicle wasn't playing Mozart. The headlights came over the hill across the creek and began to inch down the roadway. I stepped into Big Boy's headlights and began to wave my arms.

The vehicle came on down the hill and stopped in the crossing, just about where the truck had been blocking the road. It was a pickup truck with a tire affixed in the center of the hood, a setup used for pushing equipment. The driver's door swung open. Thanks to the headlights of both vehicles, I could see a Circle M logo painted in its center.

"Buck?" I called out.

"No, m'am." The voice was male and extremely mellow, but I didn't recognize it. A hulking figure stepped down from the driver's seat, a shape so bundled that the driver might as well have been a walking igloo.

The human igloo came closer, slipping once on the ice, and Big Boy's headlights hit his face. "It's me, Daniel Bibb, Miz Titus. I hope you're not hurt."

It was Buck's hired hand. I felt a little surge of relief, and I made a mental note of his name. Bibb. It wasn't a hard name, just sort of country. I pictured him wearing bib overalls instead of tight blue jeans. Maybe that would help me remember his name.

"No, I'm all right, Mr. Bibb. But my car's wedged in that ditch, and I can't get out. I don't suppose you've got a rope."

"Sure thing. I got a towing cable in the back. I'll get you out of there in a hurry." Daniel Bibb's voice rolled over me like warm syrup. He had a mellow baritone.

He dug through a tool box in the back of the Circle M pickup and came back with an old blanket over his shoulder and a cable looped over his arm. The cable had large hooks in each end. Sam and Johnny kept similar ones in both Titus Ranch trucks for impromptu towing chores.

"I reckon I can haul you out of that ditch quick as a jackrabbit," Daniel said. It occurred to me that his accent was folksier today than it had been at Joe Pilkington's funeral. He dropped to his knees in front of Big Boy and spread out the blanket.

He looked up at me and smiled blandly. "How'd a pretty lady like you wind up in such a predicament?"

I didn't have a ready answer. I certainly wasn't going to tell him I'd been chasing a truck that might have belonged to the cattle thieves. I decided to play it innocent. Like a real accident victim.

"It was really weird," I babbled. "I was headed for Lawton, for a breakfast meeting of a club I belong to over there."

Daniel nodded, then lay down on his blanket and slid under the car. I squatted beside Big Boy's left front fender and looked under, as if I couldn't wait to tell my story.

"Anyway, I realized I'd forgotten some papers I needed to take, so I turned back there at the stop sign and thought I'd go home this back way. There was nobody on the road but some idiot"—I repeated the word for emphasis—"idiot! ahead of me in a truck. And when he got right down in the bottom of this crossing, the stupid jerk came to a dead stop."

Daniel slid out from under the car. He lay on his back, his eyes wide. "He stopped?"

I gestured with my ski gloves. "I guess he couldn't get up the other side, maybe. Though the road doesn't look that icy to me. Anyway, I came down the hill, and there he was, right in the smack middle of the road. Right where you're parked."

"Right there?" Daniel sat up, and his nose was suddenly only a few inches from mine. "Did you see who it was?"

"I sure didn't. I couldn't see in the cab, and the truck was nothing special. I don't think I'd ever seen it before in my life," I said. That was the truth. I stood up. "I don't see how I kept from hitting him. I slid off the road when I hit the brakes, but it could have been a lot worse. And then"—I shook my fist for emphasis—"then the idiot drove off and left me!"

Daniel stood up. "You're one lucky lady, Miz Titus. Why don't you get on in the truck, and I'll pull up where I can hook onto your car."

I slipped once on the ice as I walked to the Circle M pickup, and Daniel quickly reached out and grabbed my arm. I shook his hand off. I didn't feel uneasy about accepting a ride from him, but I didn't want to encourage him either. His manner was a little past neighborliness and into excessive gallantry.

The cab of the truck was warm, but I didn't unwrap. Daniel pulled Big Boy back to the top of the hill, then we both got out and looked him over. A deep scratch ran the length of his right-hand side, but when I got in, his engine purred right into action.

"Good boy," I said, patting his dashboard. I looked up at Daniel, who was leaning in the door. "Looks like I'm okay."

But he shook his head. "I think you're leaking something," he said. He pointed down the hill. "You left a trail. I'll tow you someplace."

I got out and inspected the road. He was right, but I felt uneasy about moving Big Boy. "I think we'd better leave the car here," I said. "If you can give me a lift—"

We rolled Big Boy off the road, and I climbed into the warm cab of the Circle M truck once more. Daniel took off his gloves and pushed back the hood of his padded jacket, revealing his ash-blond ponytail. I unwrapped my scarf and yanked my hat off.

Daniel Bibb turned on the dome light. He grinned at me and gave me a long look. I saw that his eyes were a vivid blue. "I got coffee," he said. He pointed to a thermos in the floor of the truck.

"No, thanks. I'm not much of a coffee drinker."

"Okay." He gave me a sultry look from under his lashes as the truck moved off. I decided to assume his manner was just a habit, the habit of a man who's used to coming on to women without it having any serious meaning.

"You're out early," I said. "Am I making you leave cattle hungry?"

"No." Daniel's voice was abrupt. "No, ma'am. I don't go feedin' cattle in the dark if I can help it. I was takin' some stuff over to the fairgrounds for Buck." He grinned in my direction again. "For the stock show."

"Oh. This weekend."

"Yes, ma'am. Buck, he's real busy workin' on it. Keeps me busy, too. Today I'm haulin' a bunch of extra groomin' chutes and old blow-dryers and stuff over."

"I'm sure glad you came along. I guess I shouldn't have tried that crossing."

Daniel flashed me a brilliant grin. "It ain' so bad. You just gotta hit it right. But I'm gettin' used to picking people up off the road."

"Oh, that's right! You were one of the first people at the scene when Joe Pilkington was killed."

"I found that accident back there at the crossing, too. That guy in the truck."

"I didn't know that."

"Well, I guess I shouldn't have tole it. I tried to stay out of it, and here I've shot my mouth off to the sheriff's wife."

"Oh, I don't have any connection with law enforcement." I looked at him closely. The sun was coming up now, and I could see his face fairly clearly. "Why didn't you want to be involved?"

"No reason, I guess."

He clipped the words off short. I thought about his answer. Why wouldn't he want to report an accident? Maybe he didn't want to draw the attention of law enforcement officials to himself. That could be interesting.

"I made sure we got help for the guy in the hay truck," Daniel said. "I got Buck to call the cops, then we went down there and got the guy out of the truck. It was jus' his leg was busted." He gestured again. "Now Joe—that was another situation. There wasn't nothin' to do for him."

I remembered what Johnny had said about the angle of Joe's head. Apparently Daniel agreed that the rancher had been killed instantly.

"Yes, that was awful." I wondered if Daniel had heard or seen anything about Joe's death. If he was trying to avoid attention from law officers, he might not have told anybody what he had seen. I decided to pump him.

"Did you see anything that morning, Mr. Bibb? You live close to where Joe Pilkington was hit."

"No, ma'am. Din't know a thing until your man— Johnny—banged on the door of the trailer." It was lighter now, and I could see Daniel's jaw clench after he finished speaking.

I opened my mouth to ask if he'd heard anything, but Daniel turned his head toward me and gave a rather insinuating smile. "I liked that red dress you were wearing at the funeral, ma'am. You looked real pretty."

His comment came as a surprise, and I began to stammer. "Oh. Well. Uh." I felt like a complete fool. Damn. Maybe I shouldn't have accepted a ride with Daniel. "That dress isn't really red. Sort of wine," I said. "Nobody wears black to funerals in Holton." And what did that have to do with anything?

Daniel dropped his lashes, then looked back at the road. "Yes, the funeral was very plain. They didn't even have music."

"Well, there was the organ, of course."

"No singing. That's what I like." He gave me another dose of eye contact. "I've been a musician too long, I guess."

I looked straight ahead. "Yes, we enjoyed your performance a lot at the county Christmas party. I particularly liked it because you sang in a variety of styles. What kind of music is your favorite?" And if he says Mozart, I'll jump out of this truck, I thought.

"Country," he answered. "Me and Garth Brooks."

Garth Brooks? I'm not much of a fan, but I knew Garth Brooks was an Oklahoma native who had made it big in country music by building an image as a sex symbol. Was that how Daniel Bibb saw himself?

"I certainly hope you do as well as he has," I said.

"Well. I'm better lookin' than he is." Daniel gave a throaty laugh.

Uh-oh. He seemed to think he was irresistible. "Do you play an instrument?" I asked.

"Guitar. But I mostly sing. I worked in Nashville for two years."

"How wonderful!" It didn't seem tactful to ask what he did in Nashville. It could have been washing dishes. "How did you wind up at the Circle M?"

Daniel laughed. "Got stranded on the road. I was a backup singer for the Barn Burners. Their manager stole all the money and left the whole bunch of us broke and stuck with the motel bill in Wichita Falls. I heard of this job, so I took it to get a new stake. After I save up, I'll try the Austin scene."

"A ranch job seems like pretty hard work."

Daniel waved a hand dismissively. "Buck ain' too hard to work for. I get lots of time to work on my songs."

"Practicing?"

"Writin'. Words and music."

"Oh, you're a songwriter! Where do you get your ideas?"

That question annoys many creative people, but it turned out to be the right one to ask Daniel Bibb. From there until our road Daniel stopped flirting to lecture me about the creative process. You can't count on inspiration, he said. You have to work every day, whether you feel like doing it or not. His only way of forcing inspiration was to listen to tapes, he said. He immersed himself in music—and not necessarily country music.

"I listened to nothin' but John Philip Sousa for three weeks," he said. "Than I wrote a song called 'American Chariot.' It's a truck-drivin' song with a 'buy American' message. I sent it off to a big Nashville producer last week."

I was delighted to see Sam's truck in the shed when Daniel pulled up behind our house. Sam was back from feeding cattle and was getting ready to go to the office. After he'd made sure I wasn't hurt, I told him about my adventure.

As I'd anticipated, he found the Mozart truck interesting. "I'll look for it around there," he said, "but they might have been taking it out of the county to get it fixed. We'll pass the word in Wichita Falls. They could have been headed there."

I had to miss the photography club meeting, and Sam had to go to work as sheriff, looking for Otis Schnelling among his other chores. It was afternoon before we could go back to the Anderson Creek crossing to check on Big Boy. In the daylight we decided that the car could be towed by the farm truck, and we'd just hitched it to the pickup when the two-way radio Sam uses to keep in contact with his dispatcher called for Catlin One.

"This is Catlin One," Sam answered. "What's up?"

Nadine Webster, office manager and dispatcher, sounded excited. "We've got a death, Sam. Sounds like an accident."

"What happened?"

"It's out at the fairgrounds. The caretaker. Otis Schnelling. He's been electrocuted."

EIGHT

WE HEADED FOR the fairgrounds, dragging Big Boy along.

He had to be hauled into town to the garage anyway. In fact, we passed Holton's one garage on our way through town, so Sam stopped and unhitched the Volkswagen as we went by. The garage was closed, but we left Big Boy in the driveway with the car keys under the floor mat. One of the advantages of small-town living.

But even with the stop, it was only twenty minutes from the time Nadine called until the moment we pulled into the Catlin County fairgrounds parking lot in Holton and saw Buck Houston waving from the door to the cattle barn. Sam parked the truck next to the big blue metal building.

The sun was nearly down, and as often happens in this part of the world, it had come out from behind the clouds for the first time all day. Its rays slanted across the top of the mountains on the west side of Holton, making Buck squint as he walked over the gravel toward us. He was bareheaded, and he was holding something blue wadded up in both hands. He'd twisted it up like a dishrag, but I finally identified it as a cap by the stiff bill that stuck out one side.

His voice almost shook. "Helluva thing, Sam. It's a helluva thing. I found him."

Sam nodded. He got out of the truck and headed toward the door to the cattle barn. I jumped out on my side and trotted behind.

For once Buck forgot to be chivalrous. He cut in front of me, still talking to Sam. "He must have been standin' in a wet spot and—"

But this time Sam held up his hand. "Let me look around before you tell me about it, Buck. Is the power off?"

"Oh, yes. I pulled the breaker as soon—"

"Wait here." Sam motioned Buck and me to a halt just inside the door. It was dark inside, after the sunlight outside, and Sam strode away into the murk at the back of the building. In a minute my eyes adjusted, and I saw the white jackets Holton's volunteer ambulance crew members wear as uniforms. All the Holton ambulance crew members are women. Two were kneeling over a hump of olive green, and a third was holding a giant light over their heads.

Buck was right. This was a helluva thing. I looked away, around the building. Anywhere but at the emergency workers.

This building at the Catlin County Fairgrounds should some day be renamed the Big Sam Titus Memorial Barn. Before his injury incapacitated him, Big Sam was a county commissioner, and he ran for office on a platform that included improving facilities at the county fairgrounds, particularly for livestock shows. To give him credit, at the same time they built the new barn, they remodeled the original building into an exhibit hall for sewing, crafts, vegetables, and flowers—the categories traditionally known as the womanly arts.

Not that the new fair barn Big Sam had ramrodded through was any architectural wonder. It was a blue metal building with concrete floors. But Big Sam had been to a lot of livestock shows, and he'd insisted that the building be convenient. It had plenty of restrooms, for example, and the hot water in them worked. It had water faucets everywhere in the area where cattle were kept, and it had bays where old bedding and dung could be pushed aside.

It also had an overhead power system that was state of the art. If Otis Schnelling had been electrocuted, I couldn't believe it was because of any problem with the county's equipment.

Buck and I were both silent as we watched Sam. He spoke to the ambulance volunteers, but they didn't look up. Then he stared overhead, at an electrical cord.

The power system for the cattle barn—and for the buildings designed for sheep and for swine—was designed to allow exhibitors to use anything they might come up with in the way of equipment and to use it anywhere they wanted to.

A show barn must house rows and rows of cattle during competitions. And the cattle don't just stand around chewing their cuds. They must be groomed. The drying and the clipping are done with electrical equipment. In addition, the exhibitors may want to use special lights and giant fans. And each outfit wants this stuff arranged according to its own pattern.

So much electrical equipment is used, in fact, that most exhibitors own gasoline-powered portable generators to run it. But these were rarely used at the Catlin County show barn, because of the flexible overhead power system.

It relied on heavy-duty electrical cables on reels that hung from the ceiling. The reels moved along on tracks. Then the cables could be pulled down like giant extension cords, which I guess is what they were. They were like portable electric plugs. I'd often wished I had such a flexible system at home, if it could be had without a lot of cords hanging from the ceiling. Then Sam's coffeepot could be moved to the breakfast table, and he wouldn't be getting up and down all the time, and the whole downstairs could be vacuumed without having to stop to unplug and replug four times.

The cattle barn is around a hundred and twenty-five feet long, so I couldn't see exactly what Sam was doing down by the ambulance crew, but he seemed to be looking the equipment over. Then Dr. Thomas, Holton's only doctor, came in. He paused a moment near us, maybe because it was dark in there when you came in from the sunlight. I pointed to the group at the other end of the barn.

"God! God!" Buck said. He fished a big bucket out of the stall nearest us, turned it over, then sat on it. "This is all so useless," he said. "He's dead!" He put his head between his hands and stared at the floor.

He was still sitting there when the west door opened again, letting in one last shaft of sunlight. Daniel came in. He nodded solemnly at me, then stood behind Buck, leaning against the wall.

About then Sam turned the lights back on in the barn. He beckoned me to the opposite end of the barn and asked me to take some pictures of the scene. I don't do that too often lately, but I had my camera equipment along, and it saved a trip for Sonny Blacksaddle, the deputy on duty. He would have had to leave what he was doing and bring out the Sheriff's Department's point-and-shoot camera.

Since the first-aid crew had moved the body, I didn't have to look at Otis. Sam had me photograph a cattle blow-dryer, a vacuum cleaner tank with a long hose. It looked curiously innocent for an object that had just taken part in a killing. He also had me take pictures of the electrical system and of a puddle, plus some overall shots of how the objects related to each other.

When we came back to Buck's end of the barn, the cattleman was still sitting on his bucket, staring at the floor, with Daniel leaning against the wall behind him. Buck must have heard Sam's boots echo on the cement, because he looked up, then jumped to his feet.

"God, Sam, I'm never going to forgive myself for this," he said. "But I warned him. I warned him!"

"Warned him about what?"

"That dryer! I told him not to touch it. Daniel heard me."

Daniel nodded. "That's right."

Buck gestured helplessly. "But you know Otis! Not real bright. I guess he fooled with it anyway."

Sam sighed gently. "Just what do you think happened, Buck?"

"Isn't it obvious? I brought that dryer up here to use as an extra at the show. I knew it had a short. I'd gone down to the hardware store to get the part to fix it, and I swear I told Otis to leave it alone. But when I came back, Otis was plastered over that grooming frame. His body was still shaking." Buck ran his hands over his face. "Sam, it was a pure-dee accident. But I killed him."

Buck went on like that for some time, blaming himself. I didn't understand why. He'd warned Otis not to touch the dryer, and he'd left the dryer unplugged himself. It was hardly his fault. It was almost as if Otis had committed suicide.

Sam tried to be reassuring. "Buck, like you said, it was just an accident. If Otis hadn't been wearing those leather-soled shoes, if he hadn't been standing in that puddle, none of this would have happened. There's just one thing I don't understand."

Buck's face looked pinched. "What's that?"

"Why the heck would Otis turn that dryer on anyway?"

"That I can't tell you. Except—Did you know Otis at all?"

"Just to speak to."

"I got to know him over this show. The fellow was a tinkerer. You know, always fixin' something, always working on some gadget. The kind that takes the sink apart, then has to call a plumber to get it back together."

Sam nodded.

"All I can figure is that I told him the dryer was broken, so he got curious about what was wrong with it."

Sam agreed that that would be a fairly sensible explanation, if there can be a sensible explanation of an unsensible accident. The OSBI mobile lab came and began a technical investigation. Sam assured Buck this was merely routine, then he sent Buck home.

By the time he waved the mobile lab on its way, it was after six o'clock. It was dark outside, and the temperature had dropped into the teens. The unheated barn was freezing cold. I had pulled my stocking cap down around my ears and zipped up my ski jacket. A few more people had showed up, some of them county officials and the others just gawkers. The ambulance crew had taken Otis away.

"I've got a couple more chores to do around here," Sam said. "Do you want to take the truck and go on home? I could get Sonny to bring me home later."

"I hate to turn a deputy into a chauffeur," I said. "I'll hang around. I'm still a paid-up member of the Sheriff's Reserve. Maybe I can help."

Sam smiled, and I knew he'd wanted me to stay. "Well, maybe you can run down to The Hangout and get us a couple of hamburgers," he said. "I'll look around a little more, then lock up and go over to search Otis's house."

I left Sam with Harley Bolinger, the county commissioner who was officially designated to oversee the fairgrounds, shooing the spectators out. When I got back with the hamburgers, the cattle barn was dark and all the trucks and cars were gone, but there were lights in the caretaker's house, a small, square frame building at the back of the fairgrounds.

When I had parked outside the house, Sam came out of its front door. He climbed into the passenger side of the truck and laid several evidence bags behind the seat. "Do you mind eating here?" he asked. "I'd rather not disturb anything in the house until I've had a chance to look around more thoroughly."

"Then you think this was more than an accident."

Sam shrugged. "I sure 'nuff do hate coincidences."

"And?"

"It's a mighty funny coincidence when I spend two days trying to find a guy I want to question and never can track him down. Then when I do find him, he's dead. It doesn't sound just all that accidental."

We sat there with the truck's heater running and wolfed our cheeseburgers and Dr. Peppers. I inherited enough southern genes from my mother to make my taste buds clap their hands at a sip of Dr. Pepper. Then we put our greasy napkins and empty cups in the sack that had held the goodies, and Sam dug two pairs of thin plastic gloves out of his pocket.

"I could call Sonny to help me with this," he said, "but there are no secrets in Holton. Everybody in town will know I called Sonny over and we did a complete search. If I let you come, maybe I can convince folks I just made a routine check of Otis's house."

"I take it you want me to bring my camera in."

"Right." Then he grinned broadly. "Besides, I'm eager to hear what you think of Otis's decor."

I followed him across the wooden porch. Sam opened the door, then stepped back for me to enter.

"Good Lord!" I said. "Now I know why they call television the bug-eyed monster."

The living room of the tiny house wasn't more than twelve feet square, but the entire side wall seemed to be taken up by an enormous television screen—I'd guess a thirty-five-incher.

"Otis must have been some TV fan," I said. "This room's sure not laid out to encourage conversation."

The room did have a worn vinyl couch, a floor lamp with its shade askew, and a couple of unmatched TV trays. Heat came from a big space heater in the corner. I could see the blue and gold gas flame reflected on the floor.

But the only other piece of furniture that competed for attention with the television set was a recliner. It was covered in purple crushed velvet, and it still had the store's protective plastic draped over the headrest and the footrest. A tag dangling from the arm proclaimed "Sale."

"I guess I hadn't really expected Otis Schnelling to have a gracious life-style," I said.

"Yeah, but the Circle M cattle live better than this."

"The Circle M cattle live better than any of us."

The walls of the room had been painted a dull green, now touched here and there with stains I did not want identified. The wooden floor was scuffed and bare, unless you count the dust and actual dirt—the kind Sam kicks off his boots outside the back door—drifted in the corners.

But it was a crowded room. The vinyl couch, the purple recliner, an old dining chair, a rippled vinyl hassock, the teetery floor lamp, two TV trays, and a discount store smoking stand were crammed into a dinky space. The giant television screen still managed to dominate the room visually, though the piled-up cigarette butts in the smoking stand dominated the atmosphere.

I held up my hands and wiggled my fingers inside their plastic gloves. "Are the gloves to protect the evidence from us? Or to protect us from the evidence?"

"The place does give you the feeling you could pick up a serious disease by walking across the floor."

"On the other hand, the mold spores would probably cure you."

I wandered to the door beyond the television set. "Good night! He's got a water bed!"

"Yep," Sam said. "Too bad he never put sheets on it. And look in what we decorators call 'the dining area.'"

No table or chairs furnished the end of the kitchen that had been planned for eating. Instead, the area contained a portable dishwasher. Like the chair, it still had a "Sale" tag attached to the door. I could see the connections for it at the kitchen sink.

"New TV, recliner, water bed and dishwasher. Looks as if Otis has just been on a spending spree," I said.

"Yep. Pretty interesting."

"Pretty pitiful, too." I gestured around the room. "It's sad to think of poor old Otis sitting around here watching his big screen TV with his head resting on plastic. Washing his dishes in a new dishwasher when he didn't even have a table to sit at.''

"And sleeping in a new water bed on sheets that don't fit it," Sam said. "That's how I'd live if you hadn't taken me in.''

"Sure! I saw your BOQ. Leather easy chair and Parson's table. And that Navajo rug now hanging on our bedroom wall didn't come cheap.''

"I was just trying to impress you.''

"You did. Southwestern decor, but no coyotes.''

"When you're raised on a ranch, it takes more than a bandanna around the neck to make a coyote look attractive. Did you see Otis's artwork?''

He gestured at the wall over the couch, and I turned to look at a picture at least two and a half feet by three feet in size. Light from the ceiling fixture reflected off its slick, cheap surface, almost hiding the sentimental scene of bird-dog puppies. They were surrounded by a wide gilt frame I suspected wasn't as heavy as it looked.

I tried to make a cynical remark. "A blue-light special?'' But my voice sort of gave out on the last word. I looked down at my camera bag and blinked rapidly.

"Like you said. Pretty pitiful," Sam said.

He hugged me then, and in a moment I was back in control.

Then we searched. Sam looked through the messy drawers. I checked the pockets of the work pants and shirts in the closet. Sam muscled the television set away from the wall to see what was behind it. I went through the kitchen cupboards. Sam looked behind the couch and under all the cushions. I checked the bathroom and found nothing but mold.

The things we didn't find were papers. There were no magazines, no books, no letters. There wasn't even a box of legal papers or tax records. We found an envelope of paycheck stubs, and one pamphlet touting hearing aids. That was it.

The house wasn't that large. It only had a tiny living room, the bedroom that was wall-to-wall water bed, the kitchen with room for a table, and a small bathroom off the bedroom. After forty-five minutes, we were nearly out of places to search.

I went into the living room and stood with my back to the big heater. "Actually, if it weren't for the dirt, this isn't that bad a house," I said.

Sam looked up from the floor, where he knelt to check under the recliner. "No, it's a good, tight house."

"I lived in lots worse in New York."

"Right." Sam nodded, but he seemed to be staring at my feet.

"There's even an air conditioner on the back porch," I said. "I guess he installed it in the kitchen window in the summer. At least, the 220 plug is in there."

"Uh-huh." Sam squinted. He was still looking at my feet.

"What's the matter with my feet?" I probably sounded a little irritated.

"Nothing," Sam said. "Except that I wish you'd move them from in front of that stove."

I stepped to one side and he crawled across the floor, keeping his head low. When he reached my feet, he lay flat and looked under the heater.

"Yeah," he said. "Yeah."

I dropped to the floor beside him. "What is it?"

Sam pointed silently at two items resting on the floor under the stove. Even without pulling them out, I could identify them: a pair of fencing pliers and a rope.

I gave a startled gasp, and Sam sat up on his knees.

"Well, well," he said. "This may solve one minor mystery."

"Which one?"

"I've been trying to figure out how the cow manure got in the sheep barn."

NINE

COW MANURE in the sheep barn? What was Sam talking about?

I understood why he got excited about finding a pair of fencing pliers and a rope. These were ordinary objects on a ranch, and they'd be vital tools for a cattle thief.

But the manure stumped me.

"What's going on here?" I said. "What's all this about cow manure in the sheep barn?"

"I'll tell you as soon as we tab and bag these things."

I took a couple of pictures of the rope and pliers, then Sam pulled them out from under the stove and slid them into paper evidence bags. He made out tags identifying when and where we had discovered them.

"Now I want an answer," I said as he marked the final figure. "What's the deal on the cow manure in the sheep barn?"

"Harley Bolinger gave me a set of keys to the fair barns, and I walked through them while you were out gettin' our supper. The sheep barn hasn't been used since last fall, in theory, but I found a cow patty in there."

I thought a moment before I spoke. "Is that really so odd? Couldn't it have fallen off a truck? Don't most ranchers use trucks and trailers for whatever kind of animal they need to move? A sheep trailer could have held cattle on its previous trip."

"Sure. But according to Harley, no truck or trailer should have been in there recently. He seems to keep a pretty close eye on operations down here. And this particular piece of evidence didn't appear to be more than a week or so old."

Sam raised his eyebrows. "I bagged it. That's what I left in the truck."

"Terrific. I hope the bag is well sealed." I considered his report. "Then you think that Otis hid the cattle thieves' truck and trailer in the sheep barn?"

"It would sure be a good place. The fair barns get used fairly often in the spring and summer, but this time of the year nobody would notice if he kept the sheep barn locked up. Harley said he hadn't been in there in weeks himself."

"So even before you came down here to search his house, you suspected Otis was mixed up with the cattle thieves."

"Right." He held up the bags with the rope and pliers. "If we ran across a cattle prod, we'd have poor old Otis pretty well tied up."

"And it was the cow manure that made you suspect he was involved with the thefts?"

"Well, after you proved at least one of the culprits was very likely to be a Catlin County resident—"

"I proved it? How'd I do that?"

"By wrecking your car."

I blinked blankly, and Sam went on. "When he passed you on the road this morning, that cattle thief had no particular reason to think you'd recognized his rig, right?"

"I suppose not."

"Yet when you turned and followed him, he reacted by blocking the road and causing you to hit the ditch."

Sam reached over and caressed the back of my neck with his plastic glove. "By the way, have I mentioned that I'm real glad you didn't break this particular neck when you pulled that stunt?"

"You didn't mention it in so many words, but I got the idea when I told you I'd wrecked the Volkswagen, and you yelled, 'Are you hurt?' It was much more romantic than 'How bad is the damage?' would have been."

"Yeah." Sam rubbed my neck again, then dropped his hand. "Well, if that truck driver had thought he was being followed by some purely innocent red Volkswagen, he would have ignored you. Split Creek Road is a public thoroughfare, after all. But he caused you to have a wreck. Therefore, he knew you were following him. Or at least he suspected it.''

"So?''

"So how did he know? The only way I can think of is that he had some reason to suspect you had a connection—however remote—with law enforcement." Sam adjusted his glasses, then nodded wisely. "It was too dark for him to see who was driving, so I believe he recognized your car.''

"He recognized Big Boy?''

Sam nodded.

"But Volkswagens are not that unusual.''

"They're not all that ordinary, either. And Otis and I are both county employees. You and Big Boy would have crossed his path now and then.''

I thought about it a minute. "At the Christmas party. I drove to the courthouse and met you there. Otis parked right beside me. He pulled up just after I did, and we walked in together. It was the only time we ever exchanged two words.''

"Right. Or he could have seen you at the Co-op buying gas. Or at The Hangout. Or the grocery store. Holton is a small town, Nicky. After I had a chance to think about that crazy wreck this morning, I became convinced the truck was driven by somebody who recognized your car.''

"But that didn't mean it was Otis.''

"Right. But Otis had already attracted attention from the law.''

"By his odd behavior when he lay down in the seat of his truck.''

"And Athena Pilkington singled him out to yell at at Joe's funeral. For that matter, I may have caused poor ol' Otis's death by asking around for him. Somebody knew the law was trying to find him, and that person got nervous about what Otis would tell.''

I backed up to the heater again. All of a sudden, I was shivering.

"So you think he was murdered."

"I may not be able to prove it. But, yes, I think he probably was."

"But who?"

"It could be anybody. The fairgrounds is a public place. Anybody could have driven in there, rigged the dryer—"

"It was Buck's dryer—"

"Yeah, but if Otis's accomplice had already decided to rig an electrical accident, he would have just grabbed up some object that happened to be there. It'll take some time to get an answer from the lab on that one. Maybe Otis even told him the dryer had a short. No, if this wasn't an accident, it was arranged by the second cattle thief, and I don't see Buck in that role."

"You might as well suspect Big Sam, I guess. The financial rewards would be pitiful to a guy who rakes in a good salary from the Sooner State Association and another one from the Circle M. It would be stupid. Buck's not stupid."

Sam put a hand on each of my shoulders and caressed them. "Nicky, whoever these guys are, they're playin' rough. I don't want you to go off chasin' after any more trucks or trailers."

"I didn't intend to catch that one!"

"I know. But we've had two 'accidental' deaths. You're too important to the world to risk being a third."

I suppose that as a modern woman, completely conscious of her own capabilities, I should have objected to being told to butt out. But because I'm conscious of my own capabilities, I'm conscious of my incapabilities, too. As a photographer, I'm hell on wheels. When it comes to law enforcement, Sam's the detective.

I took some courses in law enforcement so I'd understand a little about Sam's profession. The main thing I learned is how little I know. Even if I found out something useful, I might blow the case for Sam—either by letting the bad guy see what I knew too early or by spoiling the evidence. Lots of times law officers "know" something, but it's even more important to be able to prove it in court. "Knowing" isn't very satisfying, if you can't find enough admissible evidence to send the criminal to jail.

So I try to stay out from under Sam's feet. And I sure try to stay alive.

I leaned forward and rubbed his nose with mine. "Yes, sir, Sheriff. Believe me, I do not want to be any further involved in this case."

Sam rubbed my nose back. "Well, actually I might be able to use a little help. I just don't want you goin' off on your own."

"I'll stay right by your side." I patted that side, or something close to it. "What do you need?"

"From the direction that truck was travelin' when it ran you off the road, I figure there might be some traces of it further on down in the southern part of the county."

"And?"

"Since I've publicly handed the investigation into Joe Pilkington's death over to the Highway Patrol, I need an excuse to drive up and down those roads looking at tracks."

"And?"

"Do you think you could feel inspired to do a winter photography project down that way?" He puckered his lips just a little.

I puckered up, too. In a few minutes I answered his question. "There's nothing as beautiful as the pattern of fences in the snow. I'd sure appreciate it if you'd take me down that way in the pickup. Especially since Big Boy's likely to be in the garage a couple of days."

"It's a date. The county owes me a day off. How about tomorrow?"

"Sounds good."

"Sonny can spend the day asking around about Otis's family and friends."

"And I can pray for good photography conditions."

Actually, I didn't pray for good weather. It seems irreligious to me when people try to interfere with the way God has the weather planned, asking Him to change things for human convenience.

But miracle of miracles, the sun came up the next morning anyway. I suppose that doesn't seem too unusual most of the time, but that winter had been so gray and horrible that I'd about forgotten there was something big and bright behind those clouds.

When Sam got back from feeding the cattle, the sun was definitely up over the broad and uninterrupted horizon on the east side of our house. There wasn't a cloud in the blue prairie sky, and the snow and ice were sparkling the way Las Vegas wishes it could sparkle. By the time we'd eaten our bacon and eggs, the snow on the east side of the machine shed roof had even begun to turn into water and drip off the edge.

I loaded my camera bag while Sam stuck his coffeepot in the dishwasher. "If this thaw keeps up, I may get some great shots of mud," I said.

Sam checked the indoor-outdoor thermometer. "Still below twenty," he said. "But I need to stop and see Buck before we really get started. Maybe you can get some artistic shots of dripping icicles."

When we pulled past the mini-mansion Dr. Mullins calls his "ranch house," one of the doors to the four-car garage was up. I could see the doctor's Land Rover inside.

"Looks like Mullins is takin' a day off," Sam said. "I think he's usually in Oklahoma City on a Wednesday."

He drove on by the house and stopped at the barn, which was king-sized, like everything else at the Circle M. A sapphire-blue pickup with the Sooner State Cattle Growers' Association logo on the door was parked on the gravel outside.

"I guess Buck is here," I said.

"Yep. And there's the doctor." Sam opened the truck's door and called out, in accordance with Catlin County etiquette, "Sure is good to see the sun again!" Polite conversation in Oklahoma seems to require an opening discussion of the weather, no matter what the real topic at hand.

But Dr. Mullins ignored the local custom. "Well, Sheriff," he said, speaking through neatly pursed lips. "I certainly hope your visit doesn't indicate trouble."

"Just wanted to talk to Buck a minute," Sam said. "How's it goin'? I'd sure like to see this sunshine stick around."

Dr. Mullins was still frowning suspiciously, but he admitted it was a better day than we'd had recently and accompanied us into the barn, if you could call the building a barn. It really was a miniature show ring.

The metal building seemed to have no real use as far as ordinary ranch work was concerned. It held no hay, no feed, no tractors or plows. But it did have two spacious stalls, several grooming chutes, and a whole wall of storage for halters, scissors, clippers, bottles, and cans. Everything was very neatly put away. It was brightly lit. In one corner was a curbed concrete bay for washing cattle.

Mike Mullins, wearing brilliant yellow waterproof pants and jacket and matching knee-high rubber boots, was inside the bay, spraying a middle-sized heifer with a hose. The water was swirling into a drain.

The contrast with the stall where Billy and Johnny Garcia washed Dogie was striking. Billy and Johnny did have a hose and a concrete floor, but Dogie's bathwater drained along a trench and out into the barnyard. Dogie's bath corner was lit by a trouble light on an extension cord. The Titus Ranch grooming chute was kept set up in a corner of the barn, but when show time came the same chute would be packed up and hauled to the show barn to be reassembled and used there.

Buck was shoving aerosol cans back and forth on a shelf. He looked up as we came in. "Hi, Sam, Nicky. I'm not sure I want to see you folks, after the events of yesterday."

Sam smiled. "Don't worry, Buck."

"Just a minute, and I'll be through here."

"Sure. No hurry." Sam walked over to the washing bay and rested a boot on the lowest of the pipes that fenced the area. He watched as Mike turned off the hose, then picked up a bottle of dishwashing detergent and squirted a string of it on the heifer's side.

I thought I recognized the animal Mike had been showing at the Heart of the Great Plains Classic. She chewed placidly. Mike rubbed her forehead and looked solemnly into her eyes. "Soo, Mary," he said. "Sweet Mary."

Sam grinned. "I can see you're a real good hand with cattle, Mike."

Buck joined us. "He sure is," he said. "Best hand I've ever had."

Mike ducked his head. "Proud Mary's easy to handle," he said. He rubbed hard, lathering up her neck.

"Congratulations on her win last week," Sam said. He turned his back on Mike and the heifer. "Buck, I just dropped by to tell you that Otis's death appears to merit only routine treatment. I'll make a report to the district attorney in a few days."

Buck looked relieved. "I told you it was just a crazy accident."

Sam nodded. "That's sure what it looks like."

Dr. Mullins broke in right then. "Mike, you've missed a spot there."

"It's all right, Dad." Mike's voice had become sullen.

Dr. Mullins frowned at his son. Then he turned to Sam. "It seems to me that the county should not hire people who don't respect others' belongings," he said stiffly. "My insurance is bad enough at my office. I certainly don't want to be worrying about getting sued here at the ranch."

"I don't see any possibility of that," Sam said mildly. "Buck here says he had warned Otis not to touch the dryer, and Daniel backs that up. Besides, we haven't been able to track down a next-of-kin for Otis. Who would sue?"

"Well, I've got good lawyers, if somebody decides to try," Mullins said. "Mike! You still haven't scrubbed that heifer's back!"

Mike's shoulders hunched defiantly, and he ducked his head.

Dr. Mullins's remark had called our attention to the boy and the heifer again, and Sam turned back toward the two. He leaned his elbows on the top pipe and rested his foot on the bottom one.

"I can tell you've taken good care of Proud Mary, Mike," he said. "She's a real pretty little heifer."

"Well, she ought to be." Dr. Mullins used his strutting voice. "She's a daughter of Red Rover, and her mother was from the Gillespie Ranch line."

Sam nodded. "That Gillespie line is good. Good conformation. And docile. Billy's calf is out of that line."

Mike picked up the hose again and began spraying the calf's side, and the doctor gave a start. "Mike, you haven't washed her nearly well enough! You skipped the whole back."

Mike shot a lethal glance at his dad. "You said I had to hurry, or I'd be late for the orthodontist."

Sam cleared his throat. I could tell he wanted to smooth the situation over. "We've got a dozen cows from the Gillespie Ranch line," he said. "We've never lost but one calf out of a cow from that line."

"I remember," I said. "That poor little Skunky, the one the wild dogs got."

Buck nodded. "That sure was too bad," he said. "That was the farthest east that pack came. I checked the Sooner State records on that." He sounded defensive, almost as if as the Sooner State Cattle Growers' regional representative he should have been able to halt depredations by feral dogs.

Plenty of city folks think it's kind to abandon unwanted dogs in the country. They seem to believe that kindly farmers will take them in. The truth is that the dogs usually starve. If they survive, they do it by becoming stock killers—raiding henhouses and pastures, sometimes in packs. Those dogs are eventually shot or poisoned by farmers and ranchers trying to protect their livelihoods. The animals die much more painfully than dogs in shelters.

Buck shook his head, and Sam reached over and ran his hand down the side of Mike's heifer.

Then he gave the ultimate cattle raiser's compliment. "All the cows from that Gillespie Ranch line are good mamas."

"Huh!" Dr. Mullins made a noise like a chimpanzee. "This one's mother was no good. She rejected this calf. Buck and Mike had to raise her on a bottle."

Buck resettled his hat. "It was a good experience for Mike," he said easily.

Mike looked around at his dad. His face had become pinched and angry. "Yeah! It was good for me!" He cut the water off and angrily threw the hose down. "Proud Mary and I get along fine. Neither of us has a mother!" Then he began to untie the rope that held the heifer calf's head.

Dr. Mullins stared at the floor, looking angry and crushed by his son's behavior. Big Sam would have said that Mike had taken a nail to his dad's inner tube. But his words made me wonder what had become of Mike's mother.

When the doctor raised his head, his mouth was a thin line. "Guess I'd better get a few things done before I have to take Mike into Lawton. I had to keep him out of school

for the morning, but I want to get him there after lunch.''
He swiveled on one of his high-heeled boots and marched
out of the barn.

I felt a bit sorry for Dr. Mullins. He wasn't a likable person, but I supposed he couldn't help some of his personality traits. It must be awful to know that your own son
doesn't like you very well. Of course, fifteen years earlier I'd
been the age of Mike. As I recalled, neither I nor any of my
friends liked our parents very much. And our parents
sometimes didn't seem to like us either. I decided not to read
too much into the episode.

"Well, now I've done my duty," Sam said easily. "I'm
going to take the rest of the day off."

"Day off? What's that?" Buck's voice was tight.

Sam chuckled. "No days off on the ranch, right? But the
county owes me a day, the ranch is halfway caught up, and
Nicky wanted to go photographing today."

"I'm hoping there's some pretty snow left," I said. "Sam
said he'd take me down into the southern part of the
county."

"You want snow pictures?" Buck frowned. "You ought
to try over on the west side of the mountains. I was over
there making Sooner State Association calls last week. They
had a lot more snow than we did."

He followed us out to the pickup.

"Sam, I been wanting to ask you somethin'."

"What's that?"

"What about these cattle thieves? Do you have any leads
on them?"

Sam paused.

Buck kicked the pickup's left front tire. "I don't want to
interfere, Sam, but the association's board . . . well . . ."

"I thought they might be thinkin' about hiring their own
detective."

"Right." Buck looked relieved as he nodded. "Would
you mind?"

"Nope," Sam answered. "All help appreciated. We don't really have any leads more conclusive than a few tire tracks. Of course, I'm not the only sheriff involved."

"Yes, but I've talked to a lot of the others for the Sooner State Association, and I think they'd follow your lead."

Sam chuckled as he opened the passenger's door for me. "I don't know about that. The other sheriffs I know don't seem to want to follow anybody. Independent as a whole herd of hogs on ice."

"Think about it," Buck said. "We don't want to do anything uncooperative." Then he focused his attention on me. "Nicky, Brenda thought y'all might be interested in going down to Wichita Falls to eat dinner some night. Maybe catch a movie."

My stomach gave a little lurch. Would Sam want to double-date with his brother's widow and her new boyfriend? But Sam didn't let me see his reaction to the suggestion. He just started walking around the front of the truck, toward his own side. So I decided to play it straight.

"Sounds good," I said.

"I'll leave it up to you girls," Buck said. "So long." He slammed my door before I could think of a reply that would let him know I resented being called a "girl." I decided to skip it.

Sam got in the driver's seat without a word, gave Buck a wave, and drove off. Neither of us spoke until we were out on Split Creek Road and headed south.

"Well, what did you think of that suggestion?" I asked.

"About dinner? I'll think about it," Sam answered. "On the face of it...well, I don't know. I don't want to interfere with Brenda. She's got to make up her own mind."

"If it was her suggestion—"

Sam nodded. "Yeah. That's pretty interesting by itself. I'd think you and I would be the last people she'd want hanging around on a date."

"Does she see us as protection maybe? She told me Buck wasn't...'grabby,' she called it. Maybe she doesn't want that kind of a relationship right away."

"I don't think sex is at the top of Buck's list when it comes to Brenda," Sam said.

"Why do you say that?"

Sam didn't answer for a long moment. "I'm speaking out of turn. It's just that he's past thirty, and he's never been married, never seemed to date anybody seriously in the two years he's lived in Catlin County."

"Buck seems pretty normal to me. You don't actually believe there's anything kinky about him, do you?"

Sam hesitated. Then he grinned. "Maybe I'm just nervous about somebody who knows a lot more about cattle than I do moving in on the ranch."

"We'd better start on that photo project. How about turning in at the next gate? It's got those trees over by the creek. Could be cover for a truck and trailer."

We turned in at the next gate. I took a couple of pictures, and Sam looked for tracks in the snow, near the road and over toward the trees. Then we drove on to the next road that seemed to have likely access to some sort of a cover for a truck and trailer and repeated the process.

In the next four hours we covered a lot of square miles of the southern half of Catlin County, and we looked at a bunch of barns, groves of trees, and creek beds. I even took quite a few pictures.

Sam compared a lot of truck and trailer tracks with the photos of the cattle thieves' tires. But the only match he made was at the gate where Joe Pilkington had died, and we already knew the guilty truck had been in that pasture.

There were a bunch of tracks at that gate, and Sam pointed out one particular small patch. The snow hadn't messed them up, he said, because Joe's body had landed on them, and because Johnny had draped his raincoat over Joe.

Sam believed that these tracks were from the truck that actually hit Joe.

"Oh! Then the thieves' truck didn't run Joe down?"

Sam shook his head. "We don't think so. Near as we can tell, Joe was hit by a truck that came from the south. Maybe he was facing toward the pasture, and he got hit from the side. The cattle thieves must have come in two vehicles."

"What kind of truck was it?"

"Well, we're speculating that it was white, judging from a smear on Joe's coveralls. It's going to take a couple of months to get that official paint analysis, but I'll bet it was a standard make. If we track down the perps, we may match it up. But with the number of white pickups around—and the number of them that have dents in the front fenders or the hood—" He shrugged. "We're not pinnin' our case on that."

At twelve-thirty Sam parked the pickup at the top of a little rise, and we took a break to drink the last of the hot chocolate we'd brought in his heavy stainless-steel thermos bottle. The temperature had reached something like thirty degrees, but it was still pretty cold, unless you stayed in the sun.

"Guess I'll check in with Nadine while we're sitting up high." Sam picked up his radio, and I reminded myself that this wasn't a real day off for him.

The only news from Nadine was that Sonny had checked in on his way to lunch at The Hangout. "He said to tell you he hadn't had any luck," she said. "He said social life appeared nil. Whatever that means. Base out."

Sam put his portable radio back in the seat.

"Sonny was checking on Otis's friends?" I asked.

"Right. Apparently he didn't have any." Sam sighed. "I was counting on getting a line on Otis's fellow thief by checking up on who he hung out with. They must have gotten well acquainted with each other before they showed up in the pasture with the cattle prods." Sam leaned his head back into the corner of the truck's cab, took off his glasses, and rubbed his eyes.

Sam was very discouraged, but I wasn't sure how to cheer him up. He was terribly tired, physically exhausted by the hard work and long hours the bitter winter required of a rancher. And now he had to concentrate on being a lawman. Frankly, I wondered if he was physically ready to deal with two deaths in his jurisdiction. He sure did need a vacation.

It wouldn't do any good for me to point that out. Again.

I sipped my hot chocolate and stared off down the road. And a baby-blue dot of hope appeared on the horizon.

I watched it come closer for a couple of miles before I spoke. Then I nudged Sam. "Is that your dad coming?"

Sam put his glasses back on and looked. "Yeah, that's him. Wonder what he's doin' down this way."

He flashed his lights as the blue pickup came closer, and Big Sam first waved, then pulled up beside us. He and Sam both rolled their windows down.

They spoke at the same instant, and they both said the same thing in the same accent and with the same pitch to their voices. They sounded like a choral reading.

"Wha' cha up to?"

I hid a grin. Sam thinks he's nothing like his father, and Big Sam thinks his son is "hard to make out," which is Okie for "difficult to understand." Sam's mother and I go hide in the kitchen and giggle about them. Big Sam talks more than Sam does, but their attitudes and values and reactions are what Big Sam would call "beans from the same hull."

Sam answered the mutual question first. "Nicky's taking some pictures. Where're you headed?"

Big Sam laughed. "Well, don't tell your mom, but I thought I'd go down to Crawdad Corner and comfort ol' Otis's girlfriend a bit."

TEN

COMFORT OTIS'S girlfriend?

I stared openmouthed. Who was Otis's girlfriend? And what did Big Sam mean by "comfort"?

He couldn't be giving it a double meaning. The idea of Big Sam even looking at a woman who wasn't Marty, his wife of thirty-five years, was ridiculous.

Even more ridiculous was Sam's reaction. He laughed.

"Well, I didn't know that Otis hung out down there," he said. "But I guess I shoulda figured it out." Then he shook his head. "But I won't need to tell Mom you've been there. One sniff and she'll know."

Big Sam laughed again. "I can't fool that woman. But sometimes a man just needs a little spice in his life, no matter what it does to his innards. Y'all want to come down with me? I'd be better off with a chaperon."

"If I wear a badge in the front door of that place, a bunch of folks will run out the back."

I couldn't stand it any longer. "What are you two talking about?"

Big Sam grinned widely. "Crawdad Corner," he said. "I'm goin' on. Be happy to have your company." He drove off.

"Huh?" I said. "What is all this?"

Sam started the motor and swung the truck around to follow his dad. "Haven't I ever mentioned Crawdad Corner? It's that beer joint right on the county line."

"The one where they sell pot, but you can't prove it?"

"That's the one."

"I didn't know it was named Crawdad Corner."

"It's not. I don't think it has a name at all. Maybe 'Bud-weiser.' Or 'Live Music Saturday Nights.' But way back when, maybe back in the twenties or thirties, the ol' boy who ran it had a still on the creek back behind it. Whenever he went out to the still to fill a fruit jar, he'd tell any by-standers he was going out to hunt crawdads. I guess his moonshine tasted so bad people got to joking about him flavoring it with mud bugs."

Creeks in southwest Oklahoma abound in crayfish, known as crawdads. Because of their resemblance to in-sects, Sam and his dad called them "mud bugs." Children catch them, I knew, because Billy and his best friend had brought quite a collection up to our house once. But unlike their cousins, Louisiana gourmet-variety crayfish or Gulf Coast shrimp, Okie crawdads are not considered particu-larly good eating. Big Sam had told me they were "too muddy." Of course, he won't eat catfish either.

"I should have realized ol' Otis might have been hangin' out down there," Sam said. "It's just so far from town, I didn't think about him coming all this way to socialize. The folks down there aren't very reliable witnesses anyway."

"Why not?"

"Because that place has been owned by a long line of crooks. A regular dynasty. At least four generations."

"Who's this 'girlfriend' your dad was talking about?"

"I assume he meant the ol' gal who runs the place. Queen Anne Tudor."

"Queen Anne Tudor! Nobody could have a name like that!"

"Well, that's the name on her birth certificate. Or it would be if she had one."

"You've got to be kidding."

"Nope. I guess her mother figured out that Tudor was a royal dynasty, so she picked a royal name. But most of the customers call her 'Queenie.'"

I thought that over before I asked the next question. "Just what is the 'spice' Queen Anne Tudor offers?"

Sam looked over at me and grinned. "Queenie makes the hottest, greasiest—meanest—chili in the state of Oklahoma. No, make that the United States."

"Oh, I see." I knew that Sam's mother, Marty, was very careful about Big Sam's diet. He'd always had a tendency to be heavy, and since he had been disabled and gotten less exercise, he struggled with his weight continually. Nobody can keep a cattle rancher from eating beef, but at least Marty made sure most of their dinners were lean beef, and she never served fried foods. And dessert was likely to be poached apples with artificial whipped cream. She made delicious chili, but she used ground turkey or the leanest possible ground beef as the main ingredient.

"Queenie's chili requires a stomach as tough as the cast-iron pot she cooks it in," Sam said. "It just about puts Big Sam to bed for two or three days, and one whiff of it will elevate your cholesterol ten or fifteen points."

He gestured down the road, toward a couple of small frame structures that had appeared on the horizon. "If you breathe deep, you'll be able to smell Queenie's chili already. The customers leave there in a fog of peppers, grease, and garlic. After this lunch you'll have to wash everything you're wearing, including that lacy bra I admire so much." He reached over and squeezed my hand.

Crawdad Corner, or whatever its real name was, was a dilapidated, paintless one-story frame building. It actually had a false front that pretended to be a second story, just like the Old West. An equally dilapidated two-story building stood behind it. As we pulled in I saw that the three upstairs rooms of the two-story building opened onto a rickety porch, like some antique motel. I decided not to ask if the rooms were available by the hour.

The place looked like a holdover from pioneer days. From the muddy parking lot to the hound sleeping on the steps of the wooden porch, it would have been right at home on the "western" street of a Hollywood back lot.

But the buildings weren't on any kind of street. Crawdad Corner sat all alone, out on the bald prairie, and this section of the prairie was extremely bald. We were out of sight of the mountains, and the land around Crawdad Corner didn't roll the way the northern part of Catlin County did. This section barely rippled. I'd have called it completely flat.

There were no houses nearby, either. If four generations of crooks had run Crawdad Corner, as Sam claimed, it was likely the law-abiding majority of Catlin County residents had shunned the area from the time it was settled back in 1901. There were no neighbors to pop in for coffee—or to call the sheriff about the aroma of moonshine.

A half-dozen pickups stood in the slushy parking lot. Most of them looked like farm and ranch trucks, but one was marked with the electric co-op's logo and was loaded with reels of wire. I saw Big Sam sliding out of the driver's seat of his blue pickup. He balanced himself against the door, then reached back into the seat for his cane.

Sam pulled up beside him and got out. Without seeming to hurry, he managed to be standing right beside his dad when Big Sam got to the tricky business of slamming the door. He and Johnny Garcia had become experts on salving Big Sam's pride.

We talked about the weather as Big Sam struggled across the slushy parking lot, pretending we were all three walking slowly just to enjoy the sun, not because of Big Sam's cane and gimpy leg. He paused on each of the three porch steps, declaring this winter the hardest in Catlin County history. At times like this I had to admire Sam's dad. After an active outdoor life, he'd been forced to accept limitations that were bound to be frustrating. But he never took his frustrations out on others.

Sam opened the door, and I went in. It was so dark inside that for a moment I thought the only light came from the neon beer signs over the bar. After the brightness outside, the room was a cave.

I stopped, afraid to step forward. The possibility of finding a pit or an open trapdoor right under my feet seemed all too likely. Then my eyes began to adjust, and the shapes of tables and chairs began to be visible through the murk.

The floor, I was glad to see, appeared solid, although it had been scuffed and scarred by generations of boots and farmers' brogues, just the way years of rainstorms and snowstorms had scuffed and scarred the outside of the building.

A dozen old kitchen tables, most of them the Formica-topped kind with metal legs, were scattered around half of the dim room. The unpainted walls were covered with newspaper clippings, posters, and bumper stickers that said things like "When guns are outlawed, only outlaws will have guns" or "Yes, I do, but not with you."

Nearly everything looked old, worn, and dingy, but there was one big exception. A pile of electronic equipment was stacked on one side of the room. Speakers, mikes, and a keyboard synthesizer were piled up on a little platform along the wall, with a clear space in front of them. I realized that the little platform was a primitive bandstand. So the clear space must be a dance floor. That was unexpected.

"Let's get away from the air comin' in that door," Big Sam said. Then he began clumping his way toward the back of the room, stopping at nearly every table to pat shoulders. "Hey, Jack. Howdy, Bob. You frozen yet?" Naturally, he knew nearly every man in the place, and he spoke to the others with the usual Okie friendliness.

I knew a few of the men. Jack Rich, whose spread was next to the Titus Ranch, was sitting at a table with Harley Bolinger, the county commissioner. Jack ducked his head before he spoke to us.

"Don't tell Nora you caught me down here," he said. His grin looked shamefaced.

Big Sam took off his heavy jacket and hung it on the back of a chair, then planted himself at the end of a table and propped his elbows on its green Formica surface.

"Howdy, Queenie!" he yelled.

As I sat down, a swinging door popped open in a back corner of the room, and a blond head appeared from behind it. "Waal, I do believe I hear Big Sam Titus a'bellerin' out there," a voice said. "Howdy yores'f. Am I gonna be able to sell you a beer this time, or you still on the wagon?"

"Ice tea for me!" Big Sam said.

Sam's whole family, and nearly everyone else in Oklahoma, drinks iced tea no matter what the weather. And they want it with plenty of ice, too, even if there's a blizzard outside. Sam and I sat down, and I began to try to decide on what to drink with "the hottest, greasiest—meanest—chili in Oklahoma."

Sam spoke up before I could decide. "This is my day off," he said. "Queenie, you got any Coors? You want one, Nicky?"

I felt surprised. It was extremely rare for Sam to have anything to drink at lunch. Then he blinked behind his glasses, and I caught on. It was all part of the campaign to get information on Otis from a person who might not want to give it.

"Sure," I said. "Coors Light?" Certainly hot, greasy, mean chili calls for a tart and tasty beverage like beer.

But for a moment I didn't think we were going to get anything to eat or drink. Queen Anne Tudor came out from behind the swinging door and glared at Sam, hand on hip. Her mouth pursed up so tightly it almost disappeared. She didn't speak as she walked over and stood beside our table. I stared at her in amazement.

Now that she was out in the dim light, I could see that she had a strong resemblance to the photos of Queen Victoria in middle age. She had a plump, jowly face with that fine, beautiful skin sometimes called the English complexion, the one that is sometimes conferred on natural blondes. Not that Queenie was a natural blonde. Her hair was strictly out of a bottle, a home bottle at that. It could definitely have used some toner, but she wore it puffed up on top and swooped back over the ears in a style that was highly reminiscent of the Widow of Windsor in her later years.

I guessed Queenie's age at middle sixties. She had an ample, comfortable figure, and her erect, graceful stance added to the regal effect. She wore blue jeans and a king-sized T-shirt in a vividly royal purple. The sleeves of the shirt were pushed up. Her forearms were like Popeye's, but her wrists were delicate and her hands tiny.

She stood staring at Sam for a minute, then slapped a dainty hand on the tabletop. "You're askin' for a Coors, Sheriff? You sure you didn't really come down here lookin' for my grandbaby Charles?"

"Not today, Queenie. I just wanted my wife to try your chili. Have you met Nicky?"

Queenie turned a baleful pair of blue eyes toward me. I tried to follow Sam's hint and act as if this were simply a social call. I smiled and nodded. "Hi. I have it on good authority that you serve the hottest chili in Oklahoma," I said. I left out the "greasiest" and "meanest" parts.

Queenie cut her eyes back to Sam, over to Big Sam, then back to me. "That's all I serve," she said. "Chili and catfish. An' Big Sam here—he never eats fish."

"Now, Queenie—" Big Sam's voice was almost conciliatory.

But Queenie ignored his attempt to speak. She leaned toward me. "You know why he won't eat it, don't you? That's because fish is brain food."

"Brain food?" My voice may have sounded a bit weak.

"Right. He's afraid that if he puts a single solitary morsel in his mouth, his IQ would double. Then he'd see the error in his ways and have to change his whole method of doin' business."

She smiled then, leaning across the table to whack Big Sam on the shoulder.

She ignored Sam as she turned back to me. "What do you want, honey? Beans, macaroni, or plain? A high dip or a low?"

I sure didn't know the answer to that one, but Sam spoke. "Why don't you try a low dip with beans, Nicky? And I'll have the same."

Big Sam ordered a low dip plain, and Queenie moved regally back to the swinging door.

"A low dip?" I asked. "What are we getting?"

"Real chili has a lot of suet in it," Big Sam said. "Since fat rises to the top of the pot it's greasier—not to mention soupier—at the top of the pot. Some people like it that way, but I like a meatier bowl myself. A low dip."

"And what's this about beans and macaroni?"

"Well, if you can't stand it plain—because Queenie's chili is crammed full of the real item when it comes to red peppers—you can tone it down with macaroni or with beans."

Queenie brought the beer and tea, then returned to her kitchen. Sam leaned over close to his father. "Do you know Queenie well enough to ask her to sit down?"

Big Sam looked insulted. "I told you I came down here to comfort her," he said, and when Queenie brought back the three bowls of chili—don't ask me how she carried all this in one trip, but she didn't use a tray—he gestured toward the fourth chair at our table.

"Have you got a minute? I haven't had a chance to talk to you for a dog's age. Be happy to buy you a beer."

Queenie gave a dignified shrug and turned back toward her inner sanctum. Big Sam busied himself handing out napkins from a dispenser, and in a minute Queenie came out with a long-necked bottle of beer in one hand and an ashtray with a lighted cigarette in the other. She sat down opposite Big Sam.

"Now, Nicky, you're about to get a lesson in judging chili," Big Sam said. Then he winked at Queenie. "Nicky's a sweet girl, but she's half Yankee."

Queenie laughed. "I'm half myself, or that's what my mama always claimed."

Big Sam smiled, but his grin had an embarrassed edge, and he turned back to me "Now, Nicky, here's how you do it. You just take one of these soda crackers"—he reached into a plastic basket in the center of the table, took out a package of saltines and ripped it open—"but don't crumble it. You drop it right in the bowl. Let it land flat."

I picked up a cracker and imitated his action. Then I stared at the bowl. "What am I looking for?"

"The color." Big Sam gestured at my cracker. It had turned a rich reddish orange, as if it were soaking in liquid paprika.

"See that?" Big Sam said. "A really good bowl of chili turns a cracker red immediately, the second you drop it in."

I picked up the spoon Queenie had brought in on the plate that held the chili bowl, used it to break up the soggy cracker, and filled it with the reddish-brown mixture. The thick chili heaped up in the spoon, and I moved it toward my mouth.

"Be careful!" Sam's voice was sharp.

I looked at him, holding the spoon in midair.

"Queenie's chili is powerful stuff," he said. "I advise you to start with a smaller bite."

I emptied the spoon, filled it with a smaller amount, and put it in my mouth. It was fine, until I swallowed. Then I choked and reached rapidly for my Coors Light. Big Sam, Sam, and Queenie all laughed.

"Went down your Sunday throat, did it?" Big Sam said.

"Actually, it's good," I said, after I'd gulped the beer.

"It's terrific," Sam said. "It's just surprising. I always go slow until my tongue gets used to it."

Big Sam crumpled a handful of crackers into his chili and took a big bite. "Dee-licious," he said. "It makes my heart sad to think that poor ol' Otis won't be comin' down here for a bowl of this anymore. You heard what happened to him?"

"Sure did." Queenie shook her head sadly. "Hard to believe. A'course he didn't come down here too often. Just Saturday nights. For the music."

I nodded. "Yes. I saw your sign. You have live music every week?"

"Most weeks. Otis, he really liked the Biscuit Boys, my grandbaby Charles's bunch. He usta come every time they played. But he liked all the bands, I guess. Wild about 'em. He was a pretty good customer."

"I thought you all were pals," Big Sam said. "Seems like you were talkin' to him once when I came in here at noon."

"He'd come in the middle of the day now and then." Queenie shrugged. "I'd sit with him if I weren't too busy. Couldn't nobody talk to Otis, much. He was deaf as this table, you know."

Sam made one of his expressive "Huh" noises. "Wonder why he came for the music then?"

"All he could hear, I reckon," Queenie said. "It's damn loud, you know. Sometimes I think the walls of this ol' place are goin' to fall right out flat from the sound, and the roof's just goin' to descend on us all."

We all laughed appreciatively and ate chili, and Queenie took a deep drag on her cigarette.

"Poor ol' Otis," she said pensively. "It's a funny way for him to die."

Big Sam gulped iced tea. "Funny how?"

"Electrocution," Queenie said. "As much as he'd worked with electricity, you'd think he'd of known better."

Big Sam frowned. "Did Otis know anything about electricity?"

"Sure. He was an electrician's mate in the navy. Served in Korea."

I glanced at Sam, but he'd dropped his eyes to his plate. He looked just a little smug, and I knew it was because his opinion on Otis's accident had been strengthened. He swallowed another bite of chili and turned to Queenie. "We can't find anybody to release the body to. Did Otis ever mention having any relatives?"

"Not to me. I know he didn't go anyplace Christmas, so I guess he didn't have any folks around close."

Sam scowled. "Well, the county can bury him, of course. The county health insurance plan includes enough life insurance to pay for it. But it'd be nice to at least find a friend to make the arrangements."

Queenie shook her head. "Don't look at me. He was just a customer down here. The only people I ever saw him talkin' to was those country musicians." She stood up and gestured toward the door, where Jack Rich and Harley Bolinger were standing beside the cash register. "I got to take these fellers' money. I don't know a thing about Otis's friends or relatives."

She took a step toward the cash register, then paused. "The only person he was ever in here with was that other guy that was killed this week."

"Joe Pilkington?" Sam almost let his voice get excited.

"Yeah. Joe and that wife of his come down to dance one night, and Otis bought them a beer. Made quite a show of it. You could tell it was a big deal for him to treat someone." She shook her head. "Poor old codger. That bitch Athena Pilkington laughed at him."

She walked away.

ELEVEN

I PICTURED Athena Pilkington, with her artificial hair, face, and mannerisms, sitting at the same table with Otis Schnelling, all overalls and earthy fingernails. Talk about incongruous.

Of course, Joe had been at Crawdad Corner, too. Otis and Joe might have known each other. For that matter, Otis might have joined the Pilkingtons simply because their table offered the only seat in the room. Crawdad Corner wasn't large; even a small audience would fill every table.

This wasn't the place to ask Sam what he thought about it, so I took another bite of chili and tried to keep my face straight and my windpipe clear.

After he'd paid his bill, Jack came over to our table. "How's it goin'?" he asked Big Sam. "This weather sure makes the cattle business rough."

"Sure does," Big Sam answered. "I've got three men stealin' cattle and two stealin' feed, and I'm still about to go bust."

We all chuckled appreciatively, then Jack leaned close to Sam. "Speakin' of stealing cattle, you got any new ideas about these cattle thieves?"

"Nothing I'd call new, Jack. What do you think about them?"

I had the feeling that Jack had some opinions he'd been dying to share. "Well, did it ever occur to any of you law officer types that those fellers must have a lookout?" he asked. "Somebody's figuring out just which herds to go after."

Sam nodded. "Yes, we figured that out, but we haven't been able to learn who it might be, Jack. You got any ideas?"

"No strangers seen around?"

"Not so far as we can tell."

Jack frowned. "Well, how about people who'd be around anyway?" He jerked his head toward the cash register. A thin man in a cap marked with a bolt of lightning was putting his billfold away. "How about him?"

"The electric co-op man? How'd you pick on him?"

"Well, I know he was workin' over in Cotton County ten days ago, and that was right around the time that twenty-five head disappeared from the Phillips place."

Sam nodded. "We'll check him out, Jack."

Jack leaned closer. "It makes sense, Sam. It's gotta be somebody with a reason to be hither an' thither in the area, an excuse to drive around lookin' at cattle."

Sam looked amazed. For a minute I thought he had choked on his chili, but then I saw that he was grinning.

"My God, Jack!" he said. "Are you accusing my own father?"

We all laughed. "He might be the one at that," Jack said. "He's the most conscientious Sooner State Association board member we ever had. Really keeps up with the members. Maybe he's got an ulterior motive for all this visitin' around he does. If I was you, I'd sure check him out."

He stood up, but before he left, he leaned his head down beside mine. "Now, Nicky," he said in a low voice, "don't you go tellin' Nora you saw me down here."

"Of course I won't, Jack. If you don't want me to." Then I turned to Sam. "Are you sure you should have brought me to this place? Maybe a respectable woman shouldn't be in it, if both Big Sam and Jack are so bent on keeping their visits a secret from their wives."

Big Sam and Jack chuckled, and Sam gave a mock frown. "Just don't come down here alone," he said. He patted his hip, where his jacket hid his handgun. "Make sure I'm along to protect you from the wild and woolly cholesterol."

We all laughed, and Jack Rich left. But he hadn't really explained why he wanted the visit to be a secret, and as soon as we were back in the truck and headed toward home, I asked the question again.

"How come Jack doesn't want Nora to know he goes down to Crawdad Corner to eat chili? A skinny guy like that shouldn't have to watch his diet, should he?"

"Jack's diet has nothing to do with Nora's objections."

"Then what is it?"

"Nora wants him to stay away from her family, I expect. Queen Anne Tudor is Nora's sister."

I gaped as I pictured Nora Rich—house proud, domestic to the teeth, and thoroughly respectable. She was president of her home demonstration organization and the leading light of her church circle and neighborly enough to help Athena Pilkington make funeral arrangements.

"Queenie is Nora's sister?" I could hear the incredulous tone of my own voice. How could two such different people as Nora the Neat and Queenie the Quirky be related?

"Well. Maybe half sisters." Sam shrugged. "I think maybe both their fathers were guys named John."

I gasped at that news. "You can't mean their mother was a prostitute!"

"I doubt she was ever convicted of it, though her marital status was pretty questionable and her sex life pretty interesting, according to Big Sam. But I do know Nora and Queenie's mother served time for bootlegging, back in the thirties."

"But how did the two sisters come out so different?"

"The bootlegging conviction, I think. When their mother was sent to the pen, people took the children in. Queenie stayed with relatives, but Nora was shifted to some other family. She found out about the joys of respectability, and she never went back to Crawdad Corner.''

''It's really strange. Nora and Queenie certainly have nothing in common.''

''They're both good cooks. Maybe that's a hereditary trait.'' Sam looked at his watch and pressed his foot on the accelerator. The pickup shot forward, skidding slightly on the slushy road.

''Whee!'' I said. ''Where are we headed?''

''If I hurry, we may have time to talk to Athena Pilkington before I have to head home and help Johnny feed. I need to find out what Athena knows about Otis Schnelling.''

The sun had cleared most of the snow and ice from the gravel road between Crawdad Corner and the Pilkington place, so we got to Athena's gate within twenty minutes. Sam slowed down before he turned in.

''Do you want me to do anything?'' I asked.

''Just act casual. I'll offer to help her with the cattle. Let her think that's why we've come.''

Athena opened the door to her small house while we were still picking our way over the muddy clay between the truck and a cement walk that led to the front porch. I tried to step in the bits of snow; they were less muddy and slick than the slush, and they kept my boots cleaner.

Athena's eyes were wary. ''What have you found out?''

''Nothing new. I haven't talked to the Highway Patrol today,'' Sam said. ''I'll call over there as soon as we get back to the house. We were out this way and wanted to drop by and see if you need any help with the cattle.''

Athena picked nervously at her green sweatshirt. ''Dr. Mullins has been sendin' Daniel Bibb over to feed for me. I don't know anything else you could do, unless you want to make an offer for the whole bunch.''

Sam frowned and sort of winced. ''I'll think about it, but we're having trouble buying enough feed to keep our own stockers goin'.''

Stockers are yearling steers that are pastured until they're ready to fatten up for market. Although the main business of the Titus Ranch is its "cow-calf" operation, the ranch usually buys stockers in the fall to keep on wheat pasture over the winter. In the spring, when the native grass and Bermuda pastures green up, all the cattle are moved to regular grass. The wheat pasture then ripens, heads out, and is harvested early in June. This double use of wheat—first as pasture, then as a cash crop—is what makes wheat farming and ranching complementary operations.

But this year's icy winter had left grassland and wheat pasture in bad shape and had made all ranchers fall back harder than usual on stores of hay and on purchases of commercial feed. It made cattle more expensive to raise.

Sam cleared his throat. "And I don't know a darn thing to do, with the price of cattle still going down."

Athena brushed her hair back with a hand that almost trembled. "I guess the bank's going to wind up with Joe's herd. I guess they'll take the ranch, too. At least I've got a job. I'd better start lookin' for an apartment in Wichita Falls."

"It's sure too bad," Sam said. His Okie accent can get quite strong when he thinks such speech will help his line of questioning along. "You've had real bad luck. And now losin' a friend."

"A friend? What do you mean?"

"Otis Schnelling. Wasn't he a friend of yours?"

"Otis Schnelling?" Athena looked mystified, then she blinked. "Oh, do you mean that old fart that works for the county? The one who showed up after the funeral?"

Sam nodded.

"I didn't really know him. He sat at our table once when Joe and I went down to Tudor's for a dance. He made some personal comments, and Joe took it amiss. He sure wasn't what I'd call a friend. What about him?"

"You heard he was killed in an accident?"

She shrugged. "Too bad. But it's no skin off my nose."

She hadn't asked us in, and it didn't look as if she planned to. Sam and I were still standing in the snow, and my feet were getting cold. Sam looked down and shifted from foot to foot. "Well, I guess we'll be on our way, then."

"We'll see you soon, Athena," I said. "We're thinking of you."

"Thanks." She was still wringing her hands nervously. She didn't sound grateful.

I turned and stepped toward the truck, but Sam grabbed my arm. "Watch it, Nicky! That looks slick."

He led me around in a circle—right through the mud I'd been trying to avoid. "Sam!" I said. "What are you doing?"

"Just trying to keep you from falling." His fingers tightened on my arm, and I realized I was getting a signal of some sort. Unfortunately, I didn't understand his code.

I waved at Athena and climbed into the pickup. The widow took her apricot-colored hair into the house before we'd pulled out of the yard.

"What were you up to back there?" I asked. "I was trying to keep from getting mud in your truck."

"Didn't you see the tracks?"

"Tracks? You can't mean the tracks of the thieves' truck? I didn't see any tracks with the right tread."

"No, these weren't Kellys. But I'll have to get the OHP over there right away. These tracks were from some kind of a pickup, I'd guess."

"A pickup's tracks? What pickup?"

"I think"—he repeated the words—"I think maybe it might be the one that killed Joe."

"What? In Athena's yard?"

"Yeah. It was a pickup with Goodyear Wrangler tires. The tread was half worn down, and one tire had a big hunk gouged out of it. I think I saw the same pattern back there."

"Wait a minute," I said. "Did I spend the whole day looking for tracks from a stock trailer and pickup when I should have been looking for tracks from a pickup by itself?"

"Nope. We went down that way looking for traces of the cattle thieves' rig, to see if we could figure out where they had moved it. The tracks I saw in Athena's yard might be from the second truck, the one that killed Joe. These tracks are something like fingerprints. If you have a suspect, they're useful. But there are too many pickups in southwest Oklahoma to go checking all their tires. If we come across those tracks, it would be by chance."

"Like stepping in them in Athena's drive."

"Right. And eyeballing them, like I did back there, is no use. The OHP will have to compare them with the casts and the photographs from the scene."

Sam drove in silence for half a mile. "Listen," he said. "I'm going to stop at Brenda's and use her phone. It's closer, and I want to see if I should go back and take new casts myself or if I can get the OHP out there this afternoon."

"Can't you radio them?"

"I don't want this on the air. Too many people listen to the police channels."

He turned into Brenda's drive. Her red-brick one-story house was its usual neat self; even the slushy drive and snowy fields surrounding it couldn't ruin its cared-for atmosphere. The front porch still had too many white pillars for my taste, but it looked cheerful. Winter cabbage filled the barrel halves Brenda used for planters, and a grapevine wreath decorated with wooden hearts stained red hung on the front door. Lee Anna, Brenda's four-year-old daughter, was building a tiny snowman under the bare branches of one of the two small trees in the front yard. She peeked out of her blue hood and waved at us.

Brenda's car was in the machine shed behind the house, along with a small bicycle and a tricycle. A familiar pickup stood between the shed and the barn.

"Johnny's here," I said.

"Yeah, he's probably working with Billy." Sam stopped the truck beside Johnny's and got out. "Tell Johnny I'll be out in a minute." He headed for the house at a lope. "Soon as I get hold of the OHP."

I was wearing my boots, of course, but I picked my way toward the barn, once again trying to step in the snow, not the mud. The wind was picking up, the sun was moving into its late afternoon mode, and I could feel a hint in the air that the warmth of the day was about to fade. The mud was getting hard and icy again.

The big main door of the barn was closed, so I went to the side door. I could smell hay, manure, and dish detergent as I stepped inside, and I could hear the whir of the blow-dryer. I stood still, waiting for my eyes to adjust to the dimness.

"Hi, Aunt Nicky!" Billy's voice came from my left, piping higher than the blow-dryer's noise.

He was wearing his miniature insulated overalls, just like Johnny's, and was drying Dogie after her bath.

"Hi, Billy." I could feel a grin coming on as I watched him manipulate the hose that blew warm air over Dogie's furry mahogany-red side and pretty white face. It was impossible to see Billy and Dogie together and not grin. Billy was so serious and grown-up about his calf, and the little heifer accepted his attentions so placidly. The two of them were—well, I hate the word, but they were cute together.

Billy had apparently inherited the Titus genes for height, and he was one of the tallest children in the first grade. At almost eight months, Dogie was almost exactly the same height as Billy, but we all knew she'd soon be taller than he was.

Dogie's mother, one of Big Sam's mother cows who went by her ear-tag number, No. 78, had been one of the last cows to give birth the previous year. In fact, Sam and Johnny had been concerned that she was having problems, and they'd decided to move her to Big Sam's barn. I'd gone along on the June morning they'd gone to the pasture near Brenda's house to get her. Johnny had roped No. 78 and tied her to a fence post, ready to load her into the small trailer.

No. 78 had been furious and had bawled mightily, protesting the move. She was usually fairly docile, and Big Sam, Johnny, and Sam had stood by the fence speculating about what ailed her. She'd been dripping milk for days, a sign that she was ready to give birth. But nothing had happened, as late as the evening before. Now they were reassessing the situation. These things aren't always easy to figure out, even for an experienced rancher.

Then Billy had come tearing across the pasture. "Uncle Sam! Granddaddy! Johnny! Come see!" he'd yelled.

He'd grabbed Johnny's hand and pulled him along. Sam and I followed, but in a minute Billy turned and made an imperious, pure Titus gesture at me.

"Stay here, Aunt Nicky," he commanded.

I stopped and watched, listening to No. 78's angry bawling. Dancing with excitement, Billy led Sam and Johnny over to a clump of sumac. They all knelt, and in a minute Sam stood up and pulled a Hereford calf to its feet. He and Johnny both touched its muzzle and rubbed it gently, then Sam waved at me. "It's okay. You can come on."

Big Sam came, too, and Billy ran to meet us. "It's a dogie, Grandaddy!" He yelled. "I thought it was a doggie, but it was a dogie!"

His pun seemed to delight him, and he hopped around gleefully.

Sam grinned at his dad. "Number 78's done it again," he said. "She's dropped a nice little heifer calf, just when we decided she'd changed her mind about the whole thing."

Behind me No. 78 wailed in anger because those awful human beings were touching her baby after she had carefully hidden it from dangers like people and coyotes.

"I knew not to touch her, Uncle Sam!" Billy said. "When I saw her under the bush, I thought it was a doggie. But then I looked, and I saw it was a dogie!"

"How come you call her a dogie?" Sam asked. I had been wondering, too. "Dogie" was a historic term for a calf, I knew, but I'd never heard a real live cattleman use it. It seemed to have gone out of fashion about the time the railroad replaced the Chisholm Trail.

"Oh, we sang about it in school," Billy said. "'Git along, little dogie'!"

We all laughed. Big Sam, Johnny, and Sam assured themselves that the calf was fine—they'd felt her muzzle for dried milk, just to make sure she'd already nursed—and put her back where No. 78 had hidden her. Then we all climbed through the fence before Johnny turned the irate mother loose.

Then, of course, No. 78 wandered off in another direction. "She won't go near that calf while we're still watching," Big Sam explained to me.

Billy was still excited. "I hope that someday I can have a calf just like that little dogie!" he said. He ran toward the house. "Wait'll I tell Mama about her!"

Johnny, Big Sam, and Sam exchanged glances, then stared into the pasture. "She's a nice little heifer," Johnny said. "Be a good start."

"You'd have to fool with him," Big Sam said.

"Johnny hasn't got time," Sam said.

Big Sam took off his hat and scratched his head. "I don't want to keep you from your studies, Johnny. Think you could handle it?"

"Oh, sure." Johnny grinned. "And a heifer's best."

"I don't know," Sam said. "If I get real busy—"

Big Sam spoke firmly. "Johnny can handle it, if you turn into a Rexall rancher on us."

I'd grown accustomed to laconic cowman talk, so I'd understood the conversation. They were saying that this calf might be a good one for Billy to have as his own, his first calf. But if the calf were really given to Billy, Johnny would have to spend extra time teaching him how to care for her and train her. Between college and work, Johnny didn't have much extra time. Sam didn't think he had enough.

On the other hand, Billy had a close feeling for this particular calf, she appeared to be healthy, and she came from a good line. Big Sam thought it was a good idea. He had overruled Sam. As usual, Sam tightened his lips, but he didn't argue.

A heifer calf was ideal if a child was going to be given an animal to raise. Because a heifer calf usually isn't slaughtered.

Thanks to western movies and cowboy ballads, it's easy to romanticize the ranching business. But in real life, "business" is the key word. People don't raise cattle as pets. Beef cattle would become redundant to the scheme of the world if they weren't sent to market, then slaughtered, butchered, packaged, and stacked in the supermarket meat department as hamburger, pot roast, brisket, and steak.

And that's what happens to most bull calves. They're castrated—turned into steers—to make them more manageable and to encourage their growth. They're pastured a year and a half or so, fattened in a feed lot, then sent on to the slaughterhouse to become beef.

Ranch kids learn the family business by raising calves. A likely heifer calf will grow up to be a mother cow who will live out her life producing more calves. But a steer can't breed. Its only function is to be made into beef. So a kid who takes a steer to raise has to understand from the first that eventually it will be slaughtered.

Frankly, I don't see how the kids who show those prize-winning steers stand it. They may spend a year or more washing, brushing, training, and showing an animal. And if they're really successful, this beast they've loved and cared for is chopped up into prime T-bones.

Sam says he cried like a baby every time he sold one of the steers he raised for 4-H and Future Farmers. Then he grins.

"Of course, as I got older I cried all the way to the bank, especially with the one that was Reserve Grand at Tulsa."

That calf earned Sam $5,000 at the premium sale, meaning a restaurant paid big bucks for it so it could advertise that it served prize beef. Many a farm boy has put himself through college on money earned by prize show cattle.

And the system teaches the future ranchers and farmers not to be sentimental about livestock. Farm animals have to be regarded dispassionately. A ranch is a beef factory, not a cattle refuge. If the rancher can't sell cattle for more than it costs to raise them, he'll wind up in another line of business.

But this is a pretty tough lesson for a six-year-old. For a young child, most ranchers agree, a heifer calf is best, because she can be added to the family herd, or at least to someone's herd. Heifers who are unsuitable for breeding are slaughtered, of course, just as old cows who have passed their breeding prime are. But a "good mother" will be part of the ranch herd for as long as a dozen years.

So that morning, as soon as Big Sam got Brenda's okay, No. 78's calf was given to Billy, who naturally named her Dogie. Big Sam watched Billy softly patting her.

"Fifth generation," he muttered. "Fifth generation."

Sam gave a snort.

His dad looked over at him. "Only if the boy stays interested," he said defensively. "Only if he stays interested."

The original quarter-section of the Titus Ranch is on land Big Sam's grandfather homesteaded in 1901. Billy is a great-great-grandson of that pioneer—the fifth generation of

Tituses to live on that land, and now the fifth generation to run at least one cow there.

Although Big Sam's father lost the farm during the Depression of the 1930s, Big Sam was able to buy it back in the early 1950s, and he worked hard to indoctrinate both his sons on what my Sam sneers at as "the sanctity of the Titus land."

Sam may scoff at the idea, but when Bill died, and he was needed to help run the ranch, Sam immediately trotted back to Oklahoma to help out. He hangs on to his law enforcement work as a symbol that he doesn't buy the "sanctity" idea wholeheartedly.

But he grins when he watches Billy caring for Dogie, too. The calf has a sweet and placid personality, and she simply loves being washed, blown dry, combed, and generally pampered by a little boy who coos in her ear and sings "Git along, little dogie" to her in a high, squeaky voice.

By the time Sam came over to the barn, Billy had finished drying Dogie and was walking her around in a circle, tugging her along by a long strap snapped to her leather halter. He clutched his show stick in his left hand, trying to keep it perpendicular to the floor.

Dogie likes this part of being a show animal much less than she likes the grooming. Billy walks in a circle, but Dogie comes to a halt anytime she takes a notion. And she poses any way she wants, not necessarily in the position that Billy wants her to hold.

If Billy taps her hoof with his show stick, which is nearly as tall as Billy is, Dogie is likely to pick the hoof up and move it left when Billy wants it to go right. If he wants her to face west, she's just as likely to turn north, mooning the imaginary audience.

Billy kept concentrating on Dogie as Sam came in. Sam grinned at him, then looked at Johnny. "How're they doin'?" he said quietly.

"Pretty good for beginners," Johnny said.

"Mind if we hang around a little? A guy's supposed to come by and see me."

Johnny looked at Sam. "Mind? You're the boss, Sam. Hang around any time you want."

"Huh-uh," Sam said firmly. He gestured at Billy and Dogie. "This is your project. I haven't held a show stick in nearly fifteen years." He turned to me. "I've got to wait for a while. Bubba's coming by."

"Bubba?" I felt blank for a minute, then I remembered. "You mean the hairy guy from the machine shop?"

"Right."

"Why's he coming out here?"

"Too impatient to wait for me to get to the office. When I checked in with Nadine he'd been pacing a hole in the tile for two hours. As soon as he found out where I was, he took off. Nadine couldn't stop him and tell him to wait for me to come there."

Johnny spoke, his voice quiet, but firm. "Watch out! Keep your show stick down."

I looked back at Billy, and I saw that he was struggling to switch his show stick to his right hand and hold on to Dogie's lead at the same time.

The show stick is a thin pole with a hook on one end and a padded grip at the other. It's held in the left hand while the exhibitor leads a heifer or steer and in the right when the animal is being encouraged to take the correct stance for judging. Using it requires a certain amount of manual dexterity, sort of like learning to use a twirler's baton.

And Dogie got jumpy if a show stick was raised in the air like a weapon. If Billy didn't hold his stick exactly the way he was supposed to, dropped down by his side, she'd give an unexpected jump. And a jump by a 650-pound calf is very likely to leave even a big first-grader on his face in the barn floor.

After Johnny spoke, Billy quickly lowered the stick. He readjusted his left hand's hold on Dogie's lead and took a new grip on the show stick with his right hand. He tapped her left hind hoof, which she had planted too far forward, in a position that didn't show off her shapely hindquarters to their best advantage.

Dogie moved the hoof—even farther forward.

"Dogie!" Billy said in a voice that combined whining, pleading and fury. "Dogie! Move your stupid hoof back!"

"Keep it cool, Billy," Johnny said. "Dogie doesn't speak very good English. She hasn't been to cow-lege."

That made Billy laugh, and he tapped the hoof again. This time Dogie moved the hoof backward, true, but she moved the other three hooves, too.

Billy sighed, shifted the show stick, and tried again. I stood by helplessly, knowing he had to do it himself. I lurched from foot to foot, trying not to be obvious about the body language I was using to help him.

I was concentrating so hard on Dogie and Billy that I barely heard the slam of a car door. Sam turned toward the sound, but before he could head for the barn's door it flew open.

Bubba the hairy and huge burst in. "Sheriff!" He roared. "I got to talk to you! I just can't keep shut no longer!"

His next remark got lost in a tangle of noise that involved a boy, three men, a woman, and a heifer calf.

"Dogie!" That came from Billy.

"Stop!" That was me.

"Watch out!" That was Sam.

"Keep that stick down!" That was Johnny.

"Moooaaaaa!" That was Dogie.

"Aaaah!" That was Bubba.

Hooves thudded across the barn floor, and Dogie went by me, running more like a horse than a Hereford.

Billy landed on his face with an "oof."

And Dogie knocked Bubba back out the door, on his back in a heap of snow.

Then she ran right over him.

TWELVE

SAM AND JOHNNY DASHED for the door, getting tangled up in the opening like two of the Stooges, then disappeared outside after Bubba and Dogie.

I went for Billy, though I could tell by the angry wails that he wasn't hurt seriously. But having your very own heifer calf drag you into the dirt is extremely humiliating to a six-year-old rancher.

Especially when the little rancher knows the heifer did this because he himself forgot and raised his show stick in the air.

I helped Billy up and dusted him off. I found a tissue in my pocket for his eyes and nose. By then Johnny came back in, leading Dogie, who was once more her placid little bovine self.

"I'm sorry, Johnny." Billy had almost quit crying. "That man yelled, and I looked at him. I didn't even know I had raised the stick. I didn't mean to scare Dogie!"

"She's forgiven you," Johnny said. He was matter-of-fact, and I was glad to see that he didn't urge Billy to be a little man or quit crying or any of that macho stuff. He just rubbed Billy's back gently.

Billy put his arms around Dogie's neck and buried his face in her furry shoulder.

"Is Bubba hurt?" I asked Johnny.

"He's on his feet."

I went to the door and saw Bubba standing in the snow. Sam was brushing mud off the beer logo that embellished Bubba's billed cap.

"I didn't think about y'all keepin' an attack cow out here," Bubba said.

"I'm just glad you're not seriously hurt," Sam said. "Why don't you come on over to our house? It's just a mile on down the road. We can give you some coffee and a chance to get that snow out from the back of your neck. Maybe a hot shower. That would keep you from getting stiff."

"Naw! I mean, thanks, but I ain't got the time. I got to get to work at four. I just wanted to talk to you a minute."

"Sure. What can I do for you?"

"I feel kinda like a jerk for bein' here at all."

Sam didn't answer. Just waited.

Bubba scowled. "I guess you ought to know a couple of things. But they're things told me confidential, see. I hated to let 'em out."

Sam nodded. "Things Joe told you."

"Right." Bubba kicked a lump of snow. "Just the two of us, working all night like that—we talked. On our breaks and such."

"What did Joe have to say?"

"Well, he was real concerned about that wife of his. She hated the ranch. Kept wantin' him to sell out and move to Whisky-taw Falls."

Sam didn't blink at the slang term. Lots of southwest Oklahomans use that nickname for Wichita Falls, Texas. For a long time after much of Texas approved the sale of liquor, Oklahoma still had Prohibition. So southwest Oklahoma drinkers made regular trips across the Red River to Wichita Falls to buy booze. Or else, Big Sam says, they called a bootlegger for home delivery.

"Athena claimed Joe could get a better job at one of them plants down there in Texas," Bubba was saying. "But mainly she just hated living on the ranch."

Sam nodded. "I got that feeling from her myself. She seems dissatisfied."

"Dissatisfied. Yeah." Bubba clamped his lips together. He stamped his foot, turning a lump of snow into mush, but he didn't go on.

So Sam spoke. "Did Joe think she was dissatisfied enough that she'd started seeing somebody else?"

Bubba looked up, and I could see tears in his eyes. He nodded miserably.

There was no surprise in that, of course. After the way Athena had come on to Johnny, I'd figured she was playing around with somebody, and Joe had probably figured it out, too.

Bubba was still kicking lumps of snow when Sam spoke. He kept his voice patient and noncommittal. "Did he tell you who he thought it was?"

Bubba's woolly chin moved, and I decided he was grinding his teeth. Then he took a deep breath. "That goddamn doctor!" he said.

I may have gasped. The only doctor he would mean was Dr. Franklin Mullins, and I found that idea ridiculous. Dr. Mullins annoyed me so much that I couldn't imagine any woman in the world being willing to go to bed with him.

But that was silly, of course. He had a son, who must have had a mother, so someone obviously had been willing to do more than shake his hand. But the idea of Athena and Dr. Mullins in the throes of passion made me want to fall down in a snow bank, laughing hysterically.

Bubba obviously didn't think it was silly. He looked crushed. "Joe thought that Mullins could give her stuff— presents and like that—that he couldn't."

"Did Joe have any evidence that she'd received such gifts?"

"Well, there was some kind of clothes. Real expensive. She told him she bought them used from a customer at her shop. Said she used her tips. But Joe said she'd always sneered at the idea of secondhand clothes. Claimed she grew

up wearing her sister's hand-me-downs, and she wasn't goin'
to wear such anymore.''

"Her story could have been true, though."

"Oh, that wasn't all! Joe found—in the bed—well—''
Bubba gave me a nervous glance, then leaned close to Sam.

"Hair," he whispered.

He obviously didn't mean hair from a head. But Bubba's
distress over the mention of hair—coming from someone
who was himself as furry as a sheepdog—was about to tickle
my funnybone. Sam looked at me, and his lip twitched. I
knew he was finding the situation humorous, too.

One more minute and he and I were going to start laughing. I decided I'd better retire before we both disgraced
ourselves. Besides, my presence was obviously embarrassing Bubba.

So I faded back into the barn. My absence apparently
made Bubba feel less inhibited, because he raised his voice.
I stood just inside the door, watching Billy and Johnny, but
I could hear every word Bubba said. Sam spoke more quietly, and I couldn't catch the next question he asked.

"Naw! Naw!" Bubba answered. "It wasn't that he could
tell one from another. He was just sure it wasn't Athena's
'cause it was the wrong color, and he had made the bed
himself, before he went to work. So he didn't think it had
been there when he got up that afternoon.

"That got him suspicious, see. So he looked in the shower
drain, and he found some gray hair—just like that doctor's.''

Sam spoke, but I still couldn't understand what he said.

"Huh-uh," Bubba said. "He didn't want to face Athena
down about it. He told me about it a few days before he got
killed. I tole him he ought to sling 'er out. But he didn't
want to do that. He was crazy about that bitch.''

This time I caught Sam's words. "Surely he decided to do
something.''

"Yeah. That's the real reason he decided to leave early the night he was killed. He thought he might catch 'em. He hadn't tried it before because that S.O.B. doctor hadn't been down this way 'cept on the weekends lately. But Joe happened to see that fancy vehicle of his as he drove by the guy's ranch, so he knew Mullins was around that night."

Bubba stopped talking, and Sam didn't speak either. I heard the snow crunching, and I decided Sam was pacing, the way he does while his mental computer is processing data. Then he took a deep breath and spoke clearly. "Bubba, had Joe ever left early before?"

"Nope. Why?"

"Just curious. He didn't take off and come back or call in sick or anything like that? Anytime this winter?"

"Huh-uh. Not until that night he got killed."

Another long silence fell, but this time Bubba broke it.

"I feel like shit tellin' you all this," he said. "But I just got to thinkin' that the law ought to know about it. This whole situation is dadgum funny."

"Funny how?"

"It just seems too downright coincidental that Joe would go home tryin' to catch some feller in his bed, and that same night he'd get killed in a hit-and-run. Especially when I got to thinkin' about that insurance."

"Insurance? Company insurance?"

"Naw. The company insurance probably just about buried ol' Joe. Five thousand in life is all. But Joe tole me he'd bought insurance at the bank, insurance to cover his loans, to leave Athena in good shape if anything happened to him."

What! I almost jumped back out the door, hollering in excitement.

After Athena had given us that sob story about the bank taking the ranch? And all the time Joe had had term life insurance to cover the value of his bank loans. She had lied to us. That was pretty interesting news.

I restrained myself, but I could hear Sam pacing again. I knew this had been news to him, too.

Bubba spoke. "I just got to thinkin' that the law ought to know about it."

Sam had his surprise under control. His voice was calm when he answered. "You're right, Bubba. I appreciate you telling me all this. And now I want you to forget it."

"I can't forget it!"

"I don't mean forever. The day might come when we need your testimony. But don't talk about it. It might get you in trouble, if the wrong people hear about it."

"Huh!" Bubba's voice was derisive. "That pipsqueak doctor don't scare me!"

"I guess he didn't scare Joe either." Sam's voice was quiet.

Bubba let that sink in before he answered. "I reckon you're right. There's nobody I'd tell about it anyways."

He said good-bye then. I came out of the barn and watched as he took off in a new Buick, throwing snow and gravel behind him.

"What did you make of that?" I asked Sam.

"Oh, I expect Bubba's telling the truth. The truth about what Joe told him."

"Insurance! Won't that leave Athena in a lot better shape than she's telling us?"

"Maybe. I'll run a credit check on Joe. That'll tell us where he stood with the bank. He may not have had insurance on all his notes. Maybe just on the cattle. Bubba could have misunderstood."

Then he cleared his throat. "And now I want to ask your opinion about something. Do you buy that stuff about Dr. Mullins and Athena? I'd like your opinion as a woman."

I tried to picture Athena and Dr. Mullins in bed together. Heck, even in my imagination he was still wearing that stupid cowboy hat over his gray hair.

"Well," I said cautiously, "I find Dr. Mullins pretty repulsive myself, but there's no accounting for tastes."

Sam blinked, but he didn't say anything. I decided he was using his silent treatment on me. He often does this to people he questions. He just stays quiet, and pretty soon they can't stand the silence, so they say something they didn't mean to. But he doesn't usually do it to me.

"Sam!" I said. "Cut it out! You don't have to trick me into talking."

Sam laughed. "I didn't mean to, Nicky. And you obviously know all my tricks anyway. I just didn't want to influence your opinion. I'm glad to hear that Mullins doesn't appeal to you, but do you think he'd appeal to Athena?"

I looked over my shoulder at the barn, where Johnny and Billy were still working. The door was closed, but I lowered my voice anyway. "If we take Johnny's story about her coming on to him at the Co-op as gospel—well, then I don't think she'd go for Dr. Mullins at all. Johnny is an entirely different type. His big attractions would be that he's a really good-looking, well-built, Latin lover type. And a lot younger than Athena."

Sam nodded. "And Dr. Mullins doesn't have even one of those qualifications."

"Right. Now, she might go for older men because she had some kind of screwed-up relationship with her father, I guess."

"But that would not make Johnny attractive to her."

I nodded. "So I think Dr. Mullins's age would be against him. And since he's not good-looking, well built, or a Latin lover, all he would have to offer Athena would be money."

"But Johnny doesn't have money."

"Well, Johnny could probably spring for a nice dinner and a motel in Wichita Falls, but I wouldn't expect him to come up with expensive gifts. And besides—" I looked over my shoulder and dropped my voice almost to a whisper. "Johnny wouldn't need to pay for sex. I bet there's a hundred girls over there at SOSU who'd be willing to go on a date with him. And at least fifty of them—"

Sam wiggled his eyebrows like Groucho. "I had no idea you felt so strongly about Johnny."

I slid my arms under his jacket and pulled him against me, so that our open coats met. I wiggled my own eyebrows. "You'd better stop working so hard, fella."

Sam cupped his hands on each side of my face and gave me a long, lingering kiss. Then we stood nose to nose. "Or maybe I'd better start working harder," he said.

I caressed his hip pocket. "Well, back to the current job. Neither of us believe that Johnny was seeing Athena. But we believe his story that she invited him over. So he evidently appealed to her. I'd interpret this to mean that she was more interested in a tumble with an attractive guy than in any financial advantages.

"If we take that as a given—and that's a big 'if,' because she might want Johnny for love and Mullins for money— then she doesn't think of sex as a financial transaction. And I don't see what else Dr. Mullins would have to offer her."

Sam nodded and kissed my forehead. Then he stepped back. "It sounds more like Joe was telling himself a story— convincing himself it was just the money that Athena was after."

"That might have saved his pride a bit, rather than thinking she was after a younger, handsomer guy. Are you going to ask her about it? Or ask Mullins?"

"I'm going to think about it before I do either thing." Sam stared at the mountains for a long moment. Then he sighed. "This started out looking as if Joe interrupted some cattle thieves, and they killed him. If we try to turn it into a crime of passion, it gets real complicated."

"Complicated?"

"Yeah. Joe didn't catch his wife screwin' with somebody in a ditch at five in the morning with a blizzard blowing. Nobody gets that eager."

I considered that. "They could have been in a truck or a car."

"If we were talking about kids, maybe. But Athena had a house with a comfortable bed. All to herself. So the crime of passion idea is out."

"Well, Joe might have gone home and caught them, and they killed him there and tried to make it look like cattle thieves—" I quit and considered some more. "No, it doesn't make sense, does it?"

"No, if they killed Joe at the house—or even at Dr. Mullins's house—they'd still have to carry him out to that ditch and run over him." Sam grinned at me. "Of course, we don't have an autopsy report yet, but there would be lots of easier ways to get rid of an inconvenient husband."

"Besides, they'd have left tracks."

"Right. And they'd have to have access to that truck and trailer the cattle thieves have been using."

"Yikes! That's more farfetched than the idea of Athena and Dr. Mullins in bed together." I zipped up my jacket. The afternoon was definitely getting cooler. "That whole idea makes me wonder."

"Wonder about what?"

"How come Joe picked on Dr. Mullins as prime suspect as his wife's lover?"

"Well, that gray hair, Bubba said."

"Sam, I doubt Joe Pilkington took those samples of hair and compared it microscopically with samples from Dr. Mullins. I'd bet a bunch of money that he had some other reason to suspect the doctor in the first place."

"That's sure possible." Sam nodded his head toward the road. "Hey. Here comes Buck."

Buck's sapphire-blue pickup was coming from the north. The magnetic sign that said "Sooner State Cattle Growers' Association" was slightly askew, and the truck was tooling along fast, slipping from side to side on the gravel road.

A beat-up blue pickup was close behind his truck, and I had a quick impression that it was chasing him. But that was silly. I felt in my pocket for my gloves.

"What's she up to?" Sam said softly.

I looked again and the old blue truck pulled forward and out to the side, coming up beside Buck. I could see someone inside, a flash of green.

The truck's driver did seem to be chasing Buck.

"What's going on?" I said. "Who's after Buck?"

"I believe it's Athena Pilkington," Sam said.

Buck threw on his brakes, and Athena shot ahead. By now Buck was nearly opposite Brenda's gate, and I could see him twist the steering wheel hard to the left. He was still going fast, but he made the gate. He barreled down the drive and stopped beside us.

Out on the road, Athena hit her brakes so hard the blue pickup swung into a U-turn I suspected she hadn't planned on making. The front of the truck seemed to come to a halt, but its bed was loaded with two huge round bales of hay standing on end, and their weight kept going sideways. Eventually the hay pulled the back of the truck off the road. Athena wound up facing back the way she had come, with her rear wheels in the ditch.

By now Sam and I were running toward the road, and I could see Athena slump over. Her head was on the steering wheel, and she was beating the dashboard with both fists.

Sam beat me to her door, and he yanked it open. "You hurt?" he asked.

Athena sat back and took a deep breath. She shook her head. "Stupid, stupid!" she said.

"I'll see if the truck's okay," Sam said, "then we'll get you out of this ditch." Athena nodded and climbed down from the cab. She seemed spent emotionally, and she looked so miserable I almost wanted to hug her and tell her she was going to be okay. Then I realized she wasn't wearing a coat.

"Athena, you're going to freeze," I said. "Come on into Brenda's house."

Athena was shivering, and she followed me toward the drive.

"Yes," Sam said. "You go on inside. It doesn't look as if anything is wrong with the truck. Buck and I will get you back on the road."

Athena's head swiveled at his last words, and her lips curled back. "Buck!" She spit the word out.

At this point we heard a scrunch in the snow, and Buck came walking up. Athena whirled toward him. Her body tensed, her fists clinched, and she took in an angry breath. "You—you—!"

Buck calmly returned her gaze. "Glad to see you're not hurt, Athena," he said. His booming voice was unusually soft. "That could have been a dangerous episode."

Athena gasped, then she exhaled, her breath panting out a ragged rhythm.

Buck patted the hood of the pickup. "Yes, ma'am. I reckon you've got good insurance," he said in that same soft tone. Then he went on around the truck, back toward Sam.

"I've got a tow chain," he said.

I nudged the shivering Athena toward Brenda's drive. When we got into the house, tears had frozen on her cheeks.

THIRTEEN

ONCE BRENDA AND I had settled Athena with a cup of hot cocoa and an afghan, and her tears had melted, I gave in to curiosity.

"What was all that about?" I asked. "It looked as if—well, as if you were chasing Buck."

"I'm not chasing that bastard!"

Brenda sniffed, and Athena cut her eyes toward her.

"Believe me, honey, you're welcome to him," she said. "And good luck to you." She obviously knew Brenda had been going out with Buck. Everyone knows who's dating whom in Holton.

Brenda handed Athena a box of tissues. "I don't really think we need to talk about Buck," she said. Her voice was cold.

Athena blew her nose. She gulped, trying, I guess, to gain control of herself. "Oh, don't get me wrong," she said. "I don't know him that well, and I'm probably speaking out of turn. It's just that he and Joe never got along. He's been a real pain in the ass as a neighbor."

I didn't know what to say, and Brenda wasn't talking either. Finally I came up with a platitude. "Maybe this is the time to let the past go, Athena."

"I wish! I wish!" Athena said.

Brenda left the room and came back with a heavy denim jacket. "Here," she said. "You can wear this when you go home."

Athena just shook her head.

"Suit yourself," Brenda said. She hung the jacket over the back of a chair. "Look, I've got to get Lee Anna into the bathtub, warm her up. She's been out in the snow all afternoon, and she's cold as a fish. Athena, stay as long as you want to." Brenda started for the door.

Athena looked after her for a long moment. Then she spoke. "Brenda! I need to—"

Brenda turned and frowned slightly. "What is it, Athena?"

"I just wanted to tell you—" We heard steps on the porch, and Athena's head whirled toward the sound.

She took a deep breath. "I just wanted to tell you thanks."

Brenda shrugged. "A cup of instant cocoa. Big deal. Forget it. I'm glad you weren't hurt." She gestured toward the door. "Nicky, the cocoa mix is there on the counter. See if the guys want some, okay?" She left.

When the back door opened, only Buck came in the house. Athena glanced up, but she bowed her head again while Buck knocked the snow off his feet in Brenda's mudroom.

She didn't speak when Buck came into the kitchen. "Looks like the truck's ready to go," he said.

Athena jumped to her feet, but she didn't look toward Buck or answer his remark. She turned her back on him and spoke to me. "Tell Brenda I'll bring her jacket back tomorrow. I'll be going now." She slammed the back door behind herself.

I offered Buck a cup of instant cocoa.

"Thanks," he said. "I'll fix myself some coffee."

Without any hesitation, he reached for the cabinet that held Brenda's heavy mugs, then opened a second cupboard and pulled out instant coffee. He took milk from the refrigerator. His familiarity with the layout of Brenda's kitchen surprised me. Maybe Buck really would turn out to be the answer to Sam's split professional allegiances. The idea was still rather scary.

But if Brenda married Buck, and he took over the ranch, maybe Sam wouldn't have to work so hard. You could get used to seeing more of your husband, I assured myself. But my cocoa kept churning around in my stomach.

"Brenda went to put Lee Anna in the bathtub," I said. "Buck, what was going on with Athena? I swear she was chasing you, maybe trying to run you off the road."

Buck shook his head. "I don't know why I caught it from her, but I think the thing she was really mad about was those highway patrolmen coming back. On my way over here I happened to drop by her house, just to see if Daniel was helping her with the cattle the way I told him to. That highway patrolman was out in the drive, lookin' at something in the snow. I guess she couldn't yell at a lawman, so she laid into me. Jumped on me about a minor set-to Joe and I had two years ago."

He sipped from his cup. "Fool woman! I wouldn't stand still for it, but I didn't want to argue with her. So I just turned around and left. But I guess she wasn't through lambasting me, because she jumped in the truck and came aroarin' down the road."

I heard Brenda call from the bathroom. "What's the Highway patrol doing here?"

"Probably just stopped to talk to Sam," I yelled. I got up and went into the living room to look out the window.

Athena was sitting in her pickup. Sam and a uniformed Highway patrol officer were kneeling at the entrance to Brenda's drive, looking at the ground. In a minute the patrolman went to his car, which was parked on the shoulder. He pulled what looked like a file folder out of the passenger's side of the front seat, and he and Sam knelt. The patrolman pulled a sheet of paper from the folder and compared it with something on the ground.

"What are they up to?" I murmured.

Buck brought his mug of coffee and stood beside me. He gave a guttural "Huh," which is Okie talk for "What do

you think about that?'' He and I watched as Sam and the
trooper walked slowly down the drive, stopping several
times to examine the ground. Athena's truck didn't move.
She was watching them, too. They progressed slowly past
the house and on toward the barn.

"They're following tracks," I said.

"Yep." Buck's voice was noncommittal, his face expres-
sionless.

Sam and the trooper continued toward the barn, still
pointing at the ground. Finally the trail seemed to become
plain, at least to the highway patrolman, and he walked directly ahead and kicked the back tire of a truck.

Sam stood fifteen feet away. He didn't move. His back
was toward me, but when he stands real stiff and solid that
way—well, I knew he was upset.

I snatched up my jacket and ran out the back door. Buck
came after me.

"What's wrong?" I yelled.

Sam didn't seem to hear. As I got near, he spoke to the
trooper in a dead monotone. "It can't be."

"Sheriff, you see the evidence yourself," the trooper said.
He knelt and pointed to the left rear tire. "You were with me
while I followed the trail. Look at that scarred tread. I'd be
willing to bet these are the tires that left the tracks at the
Pilkington place today. They're the tires that left tracks at
the pasture gate last Friday. This has got to be the truck that
killed Joe Pilkington."

"Oh, no!" I said. "That can't be right!"

The barn door swung open then, and Johnny and Billy
came out. Billy ran over the snow toward the house.
"Com'on, Johnny! Mama's got cookies!" He ran past Sam
and the trooper without stopping. "Com'on! They're
snicker-doodles!"

Johnny followed him, but he stopped beside Sam, who
was still standing like a stone. Johnny looked at the highway patrolman, and he frowned.

"What's going on?" Johnny asked. "What y'all doin' with my truck?"

I felt as if the broad prairie sky was crashing down all around us. It was absolutely impossible. Unbelievable. I refused to accept it. I didn't care what the evidence showed. The tires that had driven over Joe Pilkington were not on Johnny Garcia's truck. It was not true.

Johnny Garcia was not mixed up in cattle stealing. He was not having an affair with Athena. And he was not the person who had run over Joe Pilkington.

I watched the scene as if it were a dream.

"This is your truck?" the trooper asked.

"Sure," Johnny said. He turned to Sam. "What's going on?"

The trooper stood up. "We need to examine your truck. Any problem with us taking it for a few days?"

Johnny looked amazed. "Yes, I have a problem. I drive that truck every day. I need it to get to class. I can't let you just walk off with it for a few days!"

Sam spoke quietly. "You'd better let us take it, Johnny. It may be evidence."

"Evidence? Of what?"

"The tires look a lot like the ones on the vehicle involved in Joe Pilkington's death."

Johnny gasped. "Well, they're not," he said.

"Then we need to eliminate them."

Johnny made a dismissive gesture. "Sure! Take 'em then. But you'll have to lend me a truck for a couple of days."

The trooper answered. "We'd appreciate your answering a few questions, too. If you'll come with me—"

Sam swiveled to face the trooper then, and his voice was almost a shout. "I'll do it!"

"Do what?" Johnny's voice was incredulous.

Sam kicked the tread of Johnny's right rear tire. "See that gouge? Your tires look real close to the ones that ran over

Joe Pilkington, Johnny. We'd better get a more extensive statement from you. Down at the office."

Johnny looked as stunned as I felt.

Sam and the highway patrolman began to mutter to each other then. They seemed to be arguing. Finally the trooper walked away, and Sam turned to Johnny. "Get in my truck," he said.

"Sam! I've got to feed cattle!" Johnny said. "I can't be going down to your office now."

Sam's voice was like ice. "Get in the truck."

Johnny stared at him a long time, but he obeyed.

"Sam, I can feed for you tonight," Buck said softly.

"No, thanks," Sam said. "I'll be back in half an hour, and I'll get Nicky to drive. We'll manage. You've got your own work to do."

He drove off, leaving the Highway Patrol cruiser parked at the end of Brenda's drive. The trooper was talking into his radio, and I speculated that he was calling for a wrecker to haul Johnny's truck away.

As I turned to look after Sam and Johnny, I saw Brenda and Billy standing on the back porch. They both looked worried. Billy's soprano piped up. "What happened, Mama? Where did Johnny and Uncle Sam go?"

Then I heard a sobbing breath behind me. Athena Pilkington was standing in the snow with Brenda's jacket clutched around her shoulders. She was shivering, and once more tears were frozen on her cheeks.

"That devil," she said. "That devil."

She staggered as she went toward her truck. I didn't try to stop her, but I yelled after her. "Johnny didn't do it!" She didn't look around.

Buck and I followed Brenda and Billy into the house. Brenda, Buck, and I had a whispered consultation by the back window, where I could keep an eye on the truck, while Billy stood by, looking concerned.

"Mama, where did Johnny and Uncle Sam go?" His voice sounded whiny as he repeated the question, and I didn't blame him. I felt a bit whiny myself, and I knew where they'd gone. Billy couldn't get any one to answer his question, so naturally he was unhappy.

He tugged at Brenda's shirt, and she snapped at him. "Billy, will you let me alone! Take off your overalls and go watch cartoons! I've got to check on Lee Anna." She slammed out. Brenda was usually very patient and polite with her children, so I knew she was extremely upset.

"Come on, Billy," Buck said. "I'll help you with those boots."

But Billy's feelings were hurt. He glared at Buck. "I can do it myself," he said. He sat on the floor of the mudroom and tugged the rubber boots off, pouting and glaring at each of us in turn.

After he was de-booted and had skinned out of the padded overalls that covered his blue jeans, I tried a peace gesture. "How about some hot cocoa, Billy? And a cookie?"

Billy continued to glare, but he came to the table, skating across Brenda's clean and shiny kitchen floor in his socks.

"I'm not a little kid like Lee Anna," he said angrily. "I want to know where Uncle Sam and Johnny went to."

"We're not quite sure, Billy," I answered. "None of us really understands what's going on."

"What was Uncle Sam mad about?"

"Did you think he was mad?"

"He yelled at Johnny. I never heard Uncle Sam yell before."

"Well, I think he was more upset than mad," I said. "It's sort of complicated, Billy, and I'm sure it'll all come out all right. I know neither Uncle Sam nor Johnny would want you to worry. Okay?"

"When will they be back?"

"Well, Uncle Sam said he'd be back right away."

"When will Johnny be back?"

"I don't know, but I'm sure it won't be long." I hoped it wouldn't be long, I thought fervently.

"Well, he'd better be back tomorrow, 'cause that's the last day we can practice before the show."

Oh, God! The livestock show and Billy's debut with Dogie. And if those tires on Johnny's truck really were the right ones, Johnny might not ever be back.

Buck, who'd been leaning against the cabinet listening, gestured with his coffee cup. "Don't worry, Billy. If Johnny doesn't get back, I'll help you show Dogie."

"No!" Billy gave Buck a look that would have set a herd of Herefords right back on their hind hooves. "Johnny will help me! Not you!"

Then he ran out of the room. I took two steps after him. "Billy!" Then I heard his door slam.

I felt embarrassed as I turned back to Buck. "Kids!" I said.

Buck laughed. "I'm not equally popular in all circles," he said. "Listen, tell Brenda I'll call her later. She's going to have to settle Billy down, and I'd better feed my own cattle."

He left, and I rinsed cups and meditated on the recent events.

None of it made sense. I guess that Johnny Garcia did have the technical expertise to steal cattle, but why would he do it? He had a comfortable home, he had been awarded a scholarship that paid his tuition, he had a job he seemed to enjoy, and while his salary wasn't munificent, it was a living wage. I knew he'd bought his mother a new washing machine for Christmas, and he drove a good truck. He'd never seemed to be in need of money, and we all knew that he'd be in line for a good-paying job in some agriculture-related field after he got his degree in May.

Besides, cattle theft just doesn't pay a lot, when you consider how hard the work is. It's generally known as a hard-times crime, Sam had told me, one practiced by people who can't find work when the price of cattle is down. Of course, this current ring of cattle thieves had been working at it quite efficiently. They'd been making good money.

But Sam and the other law enforcement types on the case were convinced that the cattle weren't being sold anywhere in Oklahoma or north Texas. They were being taken far away before they were marketed, or law officers would have located some of them. That would require that the cattle be driven four or five hundred miles away, and Johnny hadn't been taking any trips. No, he'd been out there feeding cattle with Sam twice a day for the whole winter, not hauling stolen cattle to New Mexico or Nebraska.

And when Johnny had laid down his long, cowboy-style raincoat—the one Sam found draped over Joe Pilkington's body—he had inadvertently helped save the evidence that now threatened him—the tracks of the truck that killed Joe. Why would he have done that if he had killed Joe himself?

The situation didn't make sense. I could hardly wait for Sam to get back and explain it.

But an hour went by, and the wrecker had hauled Johnny's truck away to be impounded before Sam's truck turned into Brenda's drive again. By then it was growing dark, and the temperature was dropping. When the Titus Ranch truck stopped outside Brenda's barn, its interior lights showed me that Sam wasn't alone.

Had he brought Johnny back?

I wasn't sure, so I didn't say anything to Brenda or Billy as I pulled my jacket on and ran for the barn.

Inside, a dark head was bent beside Sam's blond one. Both of them were digging through a footlocker.

"Oh, good!" I said. "You brought Johnny back! I was afraid—"

The heads were raised, and my voice died. The black hair didn't belong to Johnny. The person with Sam was Tom Blacksaddle, the young brother of Sam's deputy, Sonny

Blacksaddle. Tom was a student at the University of Oklahoma.

"Hi, Mrs. Titus," Tom said.

"Tom's home for a long weekend," Sam said. "He said he'd help me feed. Do you mind driving us?"

I stuttered out a greeting to Tom and assured Sam I'd be glad to drive. Sam found some worn insulated overalls in the footlocker.

"These aren't much, Tom," he said, "but I think you're going to need them."

Tom grinned and sat down on the lid of the footlocker to pull the overalls on over his shoes.

"Sam," I said. "What's happening with Johnny? Have you arrested him?"

Sam looked miserable. "No, we have to get the lab report back. But that scarred place on his tire sure looks like it matches."

"If you didn't arrest him, why didn't he come back with you?"

Sam grinned slightly. "Oh, his mother took him into custody."

"His mother?"

"Oh, yes. The Garcia family may seem to be completely acclimated to Holton, America, but they've still got that Mexican-American family feeling. We barely got to the office when Mrs. Garcia showed up with another son and a daughter. She decreed that Johnny wasn't going to work for a gringo jerk like me any longer."

"Didn't you tell her you didn't think he had done anything?"

"I tried. But Johnny was none too happy either. We finally all decided to go our separate ways and talk again tomorrow. I'm just darn glad I didn't have to arrest Johnny. I believe his family would have torn the jail down."

I pictured the angry Garcia family with a certain sympathy. "I might grab a crowbar and help them," I said. "Sam, there's got to be some mistake. Something's wrong with those tire impressions.''

"Maybe so. It'll take a couple of days for the lab to sort it out. But that's— Well, that's not the worst of the evidence.''

"Not the worst! What's happened?"

Sam walked over to a stall and pounded it with his fist. Then he kicked it with his heavy boot. When he turned, he looked utterly desolate.

"They've found Joe Pilkington's shotgun. It was pawned over near the SOSU campus.''

"Oh, that could help! Who pawned it?"

"The pawnshop owner's description sounds just like Johnny. Right down to the red hat with earflaps.''

FOURTEEN

THE NEXT DAY WAS THURSDAY, and when I am eighty years old and compile a list of the worst days of my life, that particular day is going to be in the top ten.

The bitter weather returned, and I longed to pull the draperies closed to hide the view of the frozen plains, wrap up in the afghan Nora Rich had given us as a wedding gift, sit beside a fire, drink hot chocolate, and reread some Aaron Elkins book, which was my idea of a really good puzzle in the days before I married a lawman and found out how truly mysterious real life can be.

But no, my husband was not only a lawman, but was also a working rancher, which made me a ranch wife. So I tried to do my part. In bed Wednesday night I had offered to help feed cattle at dawn Thursday.

Sam scowled. "Tom's coming back to go with me."

"Yeah, but Tom doesn't really know what he's doing, and it seems to help you if I drive the truck."

"Yes, it does help. But I feel guilty when I make you do that."

"I'm offering, Sam. Of my own free will. I can take it."

"I know you can take it, but it wasn't part of the deal when we got married. You didn't sign on to herd cattle."

When Sam and I first met, he was a captain in the military police, and we both expected him to spend another fifteen or twenty years in the U.S. Army. Since I'm an army brat—my father just got promoted to lieutenant general, and he's got his own parking space at the Pentagon—I was complacent about juggling the responsibilities of an officer's wife with my own career as a photographer. But almost immediately after our honeymoon, Sam was called back to Oklahoma because an emergency left no one to run the family ranch.

We were still here two and a half years later—with Sam working at two jobs, and with our lives growing more separate each day. At least when we're feeding cattle we're doing something together, I thought.

I snuggled over to Sam's side of the king-sized bed and rested my chin on his shoulder. "Do I look downtrodden?"

"No, but you've got a mighty sharp chin for an assertive woman."

I dug the chin in deeper. "Yeah. And don't you forget it."

Sam put his arms around me then, readjusted my chin, and laughed. "Don't you ever get tired of being a good sport?"

"What do you mean?"

"Well, rural life wasn't exactly what you expected when you married a guy you thought was a former farm boy."

"It wasn't what you planned on either—then. I do fine. I have plenty of time to take pictures, and I have a beautiful home with a well-equipped darkroom. I'm actually selling my stuff! All I have to worry about is you."

"Me?"

"Right. I just wonder how long it's going to be before you stress out, and the guys in white jackets show up with a net. You're holding down two full-time jobs. You're wonderful, but can you compete with Superman?"

Sam held me tightly, resting his cheek against my hair. I could feel his throat work as he gave several big gulps.

"Nicky, I'm so grateful you're not like Athena!"

I pulled away and looked at him. "Thanks a lot! I really appreciate being compared to her!"

"You've got a lot in common."

"How?"

"You both were raised in another sort of life, but got plunked down in Catlin County."

"Well, judging from Athena's accent, the place she was raised wasn't too different from around here."

"She's originally from south Texas."

I considered the situation before I spoke. "Nora says the neighbors tried to be friendly to Athena, and I know the Maids and Matrons invited her to join. But all she would talk about was how much better she liked Houston. Joe must have hated living in a city that size."

"I'm sure he did. But he dragged Athena up here without asking her permission—just about the way I dragged you."

"Sam, I never felt that way about it—"

"And after he got her here, he worked at two jobs, ignored her, and neglected her—pretty much the way I've treated you."

"Sam! Don't be so hard on yourself!" I put my chin back on his shoulder and tried to grin. "You do almost make me feel sorry for Athena. But we're better off than she and Joe were. At least you and I usually go to bed at the same time."

He pulled me close. "I know I don't appreciate you enough, Nicky, but I do realize you could have reacted just the way Athena did—hated Holton, hated the ranch, hated me. Instead, you take pictures that make southwest Oklahoma look beautiful."

"It is beautiful! And so are you, buster!"

"No, I'm not beautiful, I'm just mixed up. I never thought I could be pulled so hard in different directions. After Johnny leaves, the ranch is really going to be time-consuming. But I sure don't want to quit law enforcement."

We were both silent a few minutes. Then I moved enough to look up at him. "I really do understand," I said. "The things you can give up are the things you don't want to give up."

"If we can just get through this emergency, prove Johnny didn't..."

His voice trailed off, and I kissed him. He kissed me back. It was quite a bit later before we said good night.

"Maybe I could get you some blue pajamas with a big golden S on the front," I said. "Sleep tight, Mr. Kent. I set the alarm for six."

So I began that miserable Thursday guiding the pickup through herds of expectant mothers and of never-to-be fathers while Sam and Tom served up cow chow from the truck's bed. I was wearing my double-knitted wool cap, my ski jacket, and my heavy boots, but I still shivered as I watched Sam swinging the big ax, chopping a rectangle in the ice near the edge of the frozen pond. He showed Tom how to tuck the edge of the rectangle under the remaining ice and slide it under, leaving open water for thirsty cattle. Tom wound up with one foot in the water, but at least it didn't go over the top of his rubber boot.

When Sam and Tom got back into the cab, they brought along a wind from the Arctic tundra, and I shivered again. It had grown light enough to see the rocks in the pasture, so I supposed that the sun was somewhere behind the blizzard-gray clouds, but it was not a nice day.

Tom slammed the door. "God! I'm sure glad I'm not an ag major! How do you stand doing this as a career?"

"I didn't start out to," Sam said, "But law enforcement's not much better, if you're looking for inside work. Nicky, I believe that does it. Let's head for the barn."

I turned the truck, and we bounced across the pasture. Tom got out to open the gate, then shut it after us, and we were back on the gravel road. The last herd, fifty mother cows, had been on what the Tituses called "the Wolf Creek ranch." It doesn't abut the main ranch property, so we had to drive several miles to get home.

"Tom, you're going to have breakfast with us, aren't you?" I said.

"Well, I've already eaten," Tom said, "but that was three hours ago. I could stand a snack. Thanks." He tapped on the window. "Sam, isn't there some way to automate this cattle-feeding chore? Standing in the truck bed tossing feed off the back doesn't seem very efficient."

"A cow's not like a cat, Tom. You can't just leave a bunch of feed out. You have to kind of ration it, or they'll eat too much. Or the birds and wild animals will carry it off. But at least the hay part of feeding is easier to handle these days."

"With the big bales?"

"Yeah. Those round bales weigh about eight hundred to a thousand pounds, some of them even more. A couple of them make a pretty good haystack. And since they have to be handled by truck, it's a lot less wearing on your back than slinging the small rectangular bales used to be."

"I guess this is a stupid question, coming from a guy who grew up around here, but how do you move those round bales? I've seen 'em going down the road in a pickup, but I've never known how they got them on the truck in the first place."

"Oh, it's not hard." Sam gestured ahead. "Nicky, stop up here at the Pilkington pasture. I noticed yesterday that somebody had been moving bales."

I slowed to a crawl, and Sam pointed at Athena's pasture. Half of Joe Pilkington's steers were huddled back beside the hay shed at the rear of the area, sheltering from the wind. Two of the giant round bales had been pulled from behind the wire that surrounded the hay shed. The cattle were clustered around them. But the long string of bales laid end to end, an arrangement I call a caterpillar, had disappeared.

The other half of the steers were up by the gate, chewing solemnly as they nuzzled feed from a trough near the spot where Joe had died.

"That's funny," I said. "Somebody's shifted all that hay. And that trough wasn't here by the gate the other day. I wonder why they moved it."

Sam sat silently. In a minute Tom spoke. "I see the bales, Sam, but how do they move them?"

Sam's voice was vague when he answered. "Oh, they have a sort of fork that sticks into the hay. It's attached to a hydraulic lift system."

He leaned forward and looked out the window intently. "Tom, let me out, okay?"

Tom stared at him, and I sort of yipped. "Out! You're getting out in this when you don't have to? What for?"

"Maybe I'll change my mind about buying Joe's cattle," Sam said. "I ought to look them over. Let me out."

Tom, looking amazed, opened the door and got out. Sam slid down from the truck cab and motioned for Tom to get back in. Once the door was closed, Tom and I stared at Sam as he climbed the fence and went out into the herd.

He appeared to actually be looking the cattle over, checking their condition. He looked at the bunch near the gate, then he ducked his head against the wind and walked clear across the pasture—the equivalent of half a city block—to look at the cattle huddled beside the hay shed. Once there he waved his arms and yelled. He got the cattle all stirred up, so that they milled around. Then he disappeared behind the shed. In a few minutes he reappeared at the other end.

Then he began to run across the pasture toward us.

Tom looked at me. "Did you ever think about sending your husband to a psychiatrist?"

"Usually there's some system to his insanity," I said. But I shook my head as Sam vaulted the gate and trotted over to the truck door. He swung it open and jumped in.

"Scoot over, Tom, and let me in. Damn, it's cold! Let's hit for home."

SAM WAS OUT of the truck as soon as I pulled to a stop in our machine shed, and he was on the phone by the time I got into the kitchen.

"Nadine," he said. "You get the paperwork ready, and I'll be along in an hour to take it to the judge. The Pilkington place. A search warrant for the whole property."

Tom came in then, and Sam didn't say anything more. When I started to quiz him, he muttered, "Later. I want to keep this strictly quiet."

But his mood had improved, even if mine hadn't. Over bacon, eggs, and English muffins, he entertained Tom with a couple of cop stories.

I figured out that he had spotted some sort of a clue in the Pilkington pasture, but I couldn't imagine what it was. Maybe it had been Santa Claus, carrying a bagful of evidence clearing Johnny, or the Easter Bunny, with the first sign of spring in his basket.

But Sam still hadn't let me in on the secret when he left for the office. I was dying of curiosity, and when Sam called about ten A.M. my heart jumped at the sound of his voice.

"Nicky, do you reckon you could take pictures while we search at the Pilkington place?"

"I'd be crushed if you didn't ask me! What are you looking for over there?"

"We'll know it when we see it. I'll pick you up in half an hour."

Sam was his matter-of-fact, straightforward self as he served the warrant on Athena. "We just want to look around, make sure everything's legal if we find any evidence," he said.

Athena looked at the paper, and she seemed to sag. "Whatever," she said dully. She sat down on a multicolored cut-velvet couch in a fake Spanish style and stared at her hands in her lap.

A deputy, Jake Whitaker, and Nadine, who does triple duty as a matron and a deputy as well as office manager, were left to search the house. Sam, Sonny, and I drove off in the sheriff's car, and I thought we were headed for the pasture. But instead Sam drove to his parents' place, passing their house and pulling up beside the machine shed.

Without a word Sam got out of the car and climbed into his dad's pickup. Sonny moved into the driver's seat of the sheriff's car, and we drove off. Sam followed us.

Big Sam came out on the porch and shook his fist as we went by. He looked furious. I rolled my window down in time to hear him yell, "—get Johnny back here, by Godfrey!"

"We're trying!" I yelled back.

I did the gate-opening honors when we did arrive at Joe's pasture, and both the truck and the patrol car rolled across the field, stopping short of the hay shed.

So that was what we'd come to look at. I realized then that the Titus Ranch's hydraulic lift for hay was mounted in the back of Big Sam's truck.

Sam had grown grim and purposeful. He asked for pictures of the overall scene, then he led me behind the shed. He seemed to be looking for a particular spot.

"Sonny, dig that old blanket out of the truck," he said.

Sonny complied. "Where do you want it?"

Sam pointed to a spot in the snow. "About here."

Sonny, his Kiowa braids dangling out from under a knitted cap that had a Dallas Cowboys logo on the front, laid the blanket over the snow. He looked as if he knew what was going on. I sure didn't.

"How's that?" Sonny asked.

Sam flopped on his stomach on the blanket. "About as good as it's gonna get," he said. "Nicky, lie down here."

I lay beside him on my stomach. "What is it?"

Sam gestured. "The light's not right," he said. "But can you see the tracks?"

Faintly, in the snow, I could see the tracks of two tires, side by side. They weren't tires from a pickup, the vehicle I would have expected to see used for work with that hay.

"The light was coming at a lower angle this morning," Sam said. "I could see it then. Think you can get a photo?"

"I'll use flash. Is it important?"

"I had to swear it was there to convince the judge to issue the warrant. So I'd better be able to prove I saw something."

Twenty minutes later I'd taken a roll at all sorts of angles and with all sorts of flash, and I stood up. "I think that's the best I can do."

Sam nodded. Sonny mixed up a batch of Denstone—it's the same stuff dentists use to make impressions of teeth and gums, and it does just as well on tire tracks as it does in patients' mouths. He carefully made a cast of the tracks.

"Now, to move the hay," Sam said. And he strode toward his dad's pickup.

For the next half hour Sonny and I sat in the car and watched Sam move giant cylinders of hay. Hay is worth money, and he treated it carefully, impaling the bales with the giant hydraulic fork mounted in the back of Big Sam's truck, then moving them into a row that snaked across the pasture, the row that had been there earlier.

The bales in the shed were stacked on their ends, three high, so he had to move six of them before a good-sized opening was cleared into the center of the hay shed.

By now, of course, I knew what he had deduced from the track of the cattle thieves' truck and trailer behind the hay shed. Sam believed the rig was hidden in the interior of the shed, behind walls of hay.

He turned off the pickup's motor after he had moved the sixth bale. All three of us got back out in the cold, walking toward the shed. Sam had already gotten a look at whatever was inside, and he didn't look happy.

I peered around the bales, looking into the dimness of the space inside the hay.

"There really is a room in there!" I said. "Wow!"

Sonny produced a giant flashlight, and the three of us walked inside. The space inside the shed was maybe ten bales long by three bales wide—fifteen by forty-five feet, I estimated. It could easily hold a pickup and twenty-five-foot trailer like the ones Sam believes the cattle thieves were using.

But it didn't.

The interior space was empty. Its floor was clear, except for a few hunks of trash and handfuls of hay. I knew Sam felt as let down as I did. I looked at the debris in the floor.

"Shit," Sam said.

I gasped. "You're right! Sonny, shine that flashlight over in that corner. There's something there. Maybe it's evidence."

The three of us approached the suspect object and knelt. "You were right, Sam," I said. "It is shit. Cow shit."

Sam didn't laugh. He nodded very seriously. "Just like the cow manure in the sheep barn," he said. "Looks like we need some more pictures, Nicky."

When we finished up at the hay shed, we headed back to Athena's house. Athena still sat on her cut-velvet couch, her apricot hair vivid against the red, green, and black of the pseudo-Spanish pattern. She didn't move, but her eyes cut nervously from side to side as Nadine and Jake Whitaker walked back and forth.

Sam went into the bedroom to check with them. He came out looking as impassive as ever.

"Well, Athena, I hate to put you to this trouble," he said, "but we've got to cover every possibility." He pulled a kitchen chair over and sat down facing her.

Athena took a deep breath. I could see her gather herself, getting ready to stand off an attack.

"Now tell me about that hay shed in the north pasture."

Sam's question seemed to catch Athena completely off balance. She seemed to deflate. "Hay shed? What about it?"

"Have you been out there in the past few days?"

"No! Why would I go there?"

"To get hay. To feed cattle."

Athena shook her head. "No, Dr. Mullins sent Daniel over to take care of that this week. I'll have to sell the cattle quick. I don't know how to take care of them, and I can't afford to hire anybody."

"So Daniel's the only one who's been working out there?"

Athena flashed a panicky look around the room. "Well, who knows? But I don't go out there and check. I guess Buck might have been over there. Or even Dr. Mullins. Or anybody who happened to drive by. I don't know. I don't even know of any reason that Daniel would have been around that hay shed. Joe had a pile of hay out in the pasture. I'd have expected Daniel to use that, since it was easier to get to."

Sam quizzed her a bit longer, but she'd found an answer. "I don't know" became her reply to any question Sam asked. After she had said it a dozen times, I wandered off to see if Nadine and Jake needed any photos.

The house was a single-wide, a form of manufactured housing. They can be nice, but the Pilkington place was cramped and ordinary.

It was really a sort of mobile home that had been plunked down on a cement block foundation I was willing to bet Joe had built himself. It had only four rooms—a living room, a kitchen with room for a table, a bedroom, and a small bath. There were few modern conveniences—no garbage disposal, dishwasher, or washing machine.

Nadine was in the bathroom, looking into an empty clothes hamper. She said she didn't need any photos, and she didn't think Jake did either.

She held up a bag of something icky. "The most exciting thing we got was the contents of the sink trap."

Soon we all left. Athena stared after us as we drove off.

Sam reached over and touched my hand. "Your car's ready. You want to ride into town with us and pick it up?"

"Sure. Then I'll go home and get these photos printed. Were you disappointed in what you found at Athena's?"

"Well, we had to check the shower drains and such, just in case we need the evidence later. But the main point was the hay shed."

"Okay, Sam. Confess! Now that it's just the two of us, what made you think that truck and trailer might be in Joe's hay shed?"

"The tracks."

"No, I mean really. You went out there in that pasture early this morning, and you were looking for those tracks."

Sam grinned at me and shook his head. "Nope. You saw me. I was looking at the condition of the cattle, deciding if they'd be a good buy or not. Which Athena had asked me to do. Or that's what I told the judge."

"Sam!"

He grinned again. "Actually, it was your remark about the trough being moved, Nicky. Moving the trough had made the cattle come over by the gate, and they messed up any evidence that had been left out in the pasture—including the traces of tracks we believed were made by the thieves' truck and trailer."

"But that didn't matter. You already had all the evidence—tracks and glass—that you needed out of the pasture."

"Right. But thinking about those tracks made me realize that you and I had looked all over the southern part of the county for tracks made by that outfit. But we had skipped Joe's pasture."

"Because we already knew the truck and trailer had been there. There was a reason for any tracks we would find. Oh!"

"Yeah. We knew the tracks were already there. So we wouldn't notice any new ones. And when I saw that hay shed, sitting back there like a potential garage—"

I patted Sam's shoulder. "Smart."

"And when you found that cow manure—"

"But Sam, does that prove anything? That shed's in the middle of a cow pasture, after all. Couldn't the dung have gotten there some other way?"

"It's not too likely, Nicky. It was inside that shed, and it was fresh enough. I feel sure it hadn't been there since before the hay was stored. It looked like somebody kicked it out of the back of a trailer."

"Is that cow dung good enough evidence to prove that the cattle thieves' truck and trailer had been there?"

"Probably not. But maybe some oil will show up in the dirt we sampled from the floor. We'll just have to wait and see."

"Do you think Athena was telling the truth when she said she didn't know anything about the hay shed?"

"Could be."

"Is any of this going to get Johnny off the hook?"

"No. None of this evidence directly affects Johnny. We've got a lineup this afternoon. I'm hoping that the guy from the pawnshop won't be able to pick Johnny out. That will take a lot of the pressure off."

I stared out the window at the cold, gray mountains looming ahead of us. What if the pawnshop owner did pick Johnny out? What then?

I didn't speak aloud, but Sam answered my question anyway.

"Whatever happens," he said, "Big Sam got Johnny a lawyer, and Johnny and I managed to calm his mother

down. He'll be back at the ranch by the end of the afternoon."

He leaned over and patted my hand. "I went by the
school and got Billy out of class to tell him that," he said.

But I was still nervous as I drove Big Boy home. I developed and printed the photos from the hay shed, but they
showed nothing surprising that I could see. The afternoon
dragged on, cold and dreary as my mood.

At the sound of the telephone, my nerves clanged louder
than its ring, and I almost gasped when I heard Sam's voice.

"I'll be late," he said, "but Tom and Jack Rich are going to take care of feeding the cattle."

"Do they need me to drive?"

"Brenda's going to drive; Mom said she'd keep Billy and
Lee Anna. Tom will help Jack with his herd, then do ours."

"Okay."

"I'll be home as soon as we get Johnny bonded out."

"Oh, no! Then the lineup didn't eliminate him?"

"'Fraid not." He sighed. "The pawnshop owner picked
him out."

I stood looking out the kitchen window, staring at the
bare branches of the pecan grove and, through them, at the
dry creek bed with its few patches of ice. A killdeer ran back
and forth in the sand alongside the creek. Closer to the
window, a cardinal landed in our bird feeder. He had fluffed
his feathers to conserve warmth, making himself into a ball
of red with a black mask and orange beak. That splotch of
red was the only bit of color in the gray, arctic landscape.

My internal landscape was just as gray and cold. A world
where a person I knew and liked and trusted as much as
Johnny Garcia could wind up in serious trouble—well, it
was a world of avalanches and thin ice.

I couldn't stand to look outside. I yanked the kitchen
shade down so fast it nearly flew off the window.

FIFTEEN

IT WAS DARK when I heard a car coming in our gate. I looked out the front window and saw the roof lights of Sam's patrol car, and behind them the headlights of a second vehicle. I went to the back door, hugging my sweatshirt around myself as I stepped out onto the porch. The wind had dropped, but it was going to be another bitter night. I waited, standing under the bright light Sam had mounted on the back of the house, as he came from the machine shed.

"Who'd you bring with you?"

"I don't know. But when I met them down the road, they turned around to follow me, so I guess they've got something to say."

The second vehicle pulled into the light then, and I saw that it was a Land Rover. "Dr. Mullins," I said.

Mullins got out and came around the Land Rover, leaving the motor running. His little head poked out of an enormous suede jacket with fleece collar and lapels, and his extra-wide hat seemed to be resting on the jacket, rather than his gray hair.

"Sheriff, just what are you up to?" he demanded. "Buck said you pulled Daniel off the job, kept him away from his work all afternoon."

"I needed some help figuring out what's been going on down at Joe Pilkington's hay shed," Sam said. "Daniel should be home by now."

"Surely you've got better things to do than harass innocent bystanders, Sheriff."

Sam's mild tone told me that Mullins had gotten to him. "Well, you know what they say. All that's needed to make evil triumph is for the good men to do nothing. We want all the help we can get from the good men. But what makes you so sure Daniel is innocent?''

Mullins bounced on his high-heeled boots. ''You made an arrest!''

''True, but the investigation is far from complete.''

''But I heard that you had the goods on this Garcia fellow! That he had the missing shotgun. This is way beyond a traffic accident. He was screwing around with Pilkington's wife, for God's sake!''

''Where'd you hear that?''

''It's common knowledge.''

''Common knowledge is often uncommonly ignorant and uninformed,'' Sam said. ''I suggest you keep your mouth shut.''

Mullins stared a moment, then he obeyed. He snapped his jaw closed so fast that his teeth clicked loudly.

But he couldn't keep quiet long, of course. He had to bluster.

''Well, Sheriff Titus, I know that this Garcia boy is a special pet of yours and your family, and the voters of this county know it, too. If you continue this favoritism, you'll find your political career dying.''

Sam took a step toward Mullins, and I knew he was strongly tempted to punch the doctor right in his pugnacious little jaw. I considered flinging myself between them, but my real impulse was to yell ''Sic 'em!'' If Sam knocked the doctor down, I planned to step over and kick him someplace real painful.

But before I could do anything, and before Sam could shake Mullins like a dust rag, the door to the Land Rover flew open, and Mike Mullins came tumbling out.

''Nobody is dying!'' he yelled. ''Nobody is dying! Oh, please stop!''

Mike's outburst made us all ashamed of ourselves, I guess. Anyway, it made me remember that something important was at issue here—two people had died violently within the past week. Instead of tearing at each other, the way Mullins and Sam had been, we should be keeping things cool and logical while we figured out what happened. Kids like Mike needed reassurance, and calmly seeing that justice was done would help all of us.

Or at least that's how I felt. Dr. Mullins calmed down, too, though he still sounded short-tempered as he spoke to Mike. "It's okay, son."

But Mike seemed to become aware that tears were now running down his cheeks, and he climbed back in the Land Rover, wiping his nose on his sleeve.

"Let's go home, Dad," he said.

Mullins ducked his head in Sam's direction. "Sorry if I spoke out of turn," he muttered. Then he left.

Sam came in then, but the ghastly day wasn't over. The phone rang.

"Aunt Nicky?" Billy's high-pitched little voice was weepy. "Where's Johnny?"

"He's just fine, Billy."

"But where is he? There's no light at his house. Uncle Sam didn't really put him in jail, did he?"

I looked at Sam and covered the receiver. "It's Billy. He's crying."

Sam reached over and took the phone from me. "Billy, are you worried about Johnny?"

I could hear the squeaking of Billy's voice, then Sam spoke again. "No, Billy, he's not in jail. But his mother was worried about him, too, so he went over to her house to tell her he was all right. I tell you what, I'll get him to call you, okay?"

Brenda got on the phone then, and Sam uh-huhed into the receiver. "No, he's just charged with possession of stolen goods, Brenda. The judge released him on his own recognizance."

He uh-huhed some more, then spoke again. "Alibi? Sure, that would help." More uh-huhs. "Okay. We'll come by in about an hour."

He hung up. "Brenda says she may be able to alibi Johnny for the time when he's accused of pawning the shotgun. I told her we'd come by and talk about it after dinner."

"Okay," I said, "but you've got to tell me what Daniel knew about the hay."

"He swore he didn't know a thing. Said he just got a couple of bales off the end and that he didn't know there was a hidey-hole inside it."

"Could Joe Pilkington have made that hole himself, Sam? Could he have been mixed up in the cattle thefts?"

Sam shook his head. "I don't see how, Nicky. First, he had a reputation for solid honesty; he didn't even cheat on B.J. Slater's oddball time-card system. Second, he was in financial hot water; there's no sign that he had any extra money. Third, Bubba says he hadn't taken off work any night this winter."

"And he would have had to if he'd been out stealing cattle."

"Right. Something sure smells good. Can we eat and get to Brenda's in an hour?"

I started steaming the broccoli.

When we got to Brenda's, two pickups were sitting in the drive. For a moment they looked identical. Then I saw the magnetic sign on the door of one, and the back porch light showed me the different colors of the trucks.

"Your dad's truck is here."

"Johnny's driving it. I see Buck's here, too. I hope we can run him off fast."

"How come?"

"Because I want to talk to Brenda without him around."

Buck was sitting in the living room nursing a cup of coffee when we came in. Lee Anna, wearing footed pajamas and looking like a four-year-old blond angel, was on the floor, playing with a set of Legos.

I sat down beside her. "What are you building, Lee Anna?"

"Barn." Lee Anna wasn't into lengthy answers.

Brenda came out from the bedroom. She shook her head. "Johnny's trying to calm Billy down," she said. "Honestly, that kid is in a real sweat about Dogie."

Sam frowned. "I guess we've put too much pressure on him over this show. We wanted it to be fun, but he's taking it real seriously. He doesn't have to go to the show at all."

"That's what Johnny's telling him," Brenda smiled ruefully. "But Billy says Dogie will be disappointed if she doesn't get to compete."

Buck, Sam, and I all laughed at that.

"Well, we can't let Dogie down," Sam said.

Buck stood up. "Listen, Brenda, I can see you're in a crisis situation here tonight. I'll come over some other time."

"It would probably be best, Buck," Brenda answered. "Give me a ring, okay?"

She walked to the back door with Buck, while Sam and I stayed in the living room so they could say good-bye in privacy.

It was an hour before we were able to start grown-up talk, because it took that long to get Billy and Lee Anna settled down. They both knew that their favorite friend Johnny was in some sort of danger, and they hung all over him. He finally wound up sitting in Brenda's platform rocker with kids draped around him until Lee Anna fell asleep and Billy could be persuaded to go to bed with a book. Billy's show stick had somehow made it into the house, and Brenda had to tuck it into his bed.

When we'd all pulled our chairs up close, so we could speak low enough to keep Billy Big Ears from listening in, Brenda began.

"Sam, I just found out this evening that Johnny's supposed to have pawned that shotgun between eleven A.M. and noon on Tuesday. I can swear he was in the SOSU library then."

"That's great, Brenda. But Johnny, why didn't you tell the OHP Brenda could vouch for you?"

Brenda took a deep breath, but Johnny waved a hand casually. "I wasn't sure she'd seen me."

Sam frowned. "But just knowing she was there would have given you a witness."

Again Brenda seemed to be ready to speak, and again Johnny shrugged as an answer.

"The crazy thing is that pawnshop guy," he said. "I don't see how he could pick me out of a lineup, when I don't even know where that shop is."

"Eyewitnesses are notoriously apt to make mistakes," Sam said. "But I think we can assume that whoever really was in there looked a lot like you."

"Maybe so," Johnny said. "I guess I'm a common type. Straight black hair, brown skin, brown eyes. Ordinary Latin."

I exchanged a glance with Brenda. She and I both knew there was nothing ordinary about Johnny's looks, unless you compared him to Hollywood's standard.

"Yeah, but he wasn't sure you were the one until he saw you in the hat and sunglasses," Sam said.

"Which I wear most of the time."

"Right. Brenda's alibi should help you, but it might not do any harm to say a prayer to St. Jude."

"St. Who?"

"St. Jude. The patron saint of lost causes."

Johnny shrugged. "I don't know anything about that stuff. But why did those guys keep questioning me about Mrs. Pilkington? I swear, I hardly know the woman."

"Your pickup tracks were found in her yard."

"Sam, I swear I've only been inside their gate twice. Once when I went to try to tell Mrs. Pilkington about finding Joe. Then yesterday, when your mom asked me to drop off a loaf of homemade bread for her."

Sam frowned. "And Athena had never been in your truck?"

"No way!"

Sam shook his head. "And you don't know anything about saints?"

"Saints? Huh-uh! That's Catholic. You know my mom's strong in the Iglesia de Dios. I never heard about any of that stuff."

Sam was still frowning, but the conversation seemed to die after that. Johnny announced he was going home, and we left as well.

But I was very curious about some of Sam's questions. As soon as we were back in the truck, I started on him. "What was all this stuff about saints, anyway?"

"Well, the guy who pawned the shotgun—whoever it was—also bought something at the pawnshop. He picked out a religious medal. St. Christopher."

I thought about that. "Sam, I can't imagine Johnny wanting such a thing. He never wears any kind of jewelry. No rings, no ID bracelet. No chains."

"I can't understand it either. Unfortunately, the medal was found in Johnny's truck."

"What!"

"Yeah. It was in a gift box, behind the seat. Right next to a couple of strands of hair. Kind of orangish hair."

A picture of Athena Pilkington's apricot tresses popped into my mind.

"Ouch!" I said.

"Yeah. Ouch. Either Johnny's been jazzing us about knowing Athena, or somebody's gone to a lot of trouble to make it look as if he has."

Sam drove on, but my mind was racing faster than the truck. Could Johnny be lying about seeing Athena? I simply couldn't believe it.

"Of course, anybody could have hair the color of Athena's," I said. "It comes out of a bottle. She must spend hours a month dyeing."

Sam hit the brakes, and the car hit a patch of ice, and we nearly hit the ditch.

My shoulder belt grabbed me, and I hung on to the armrest until we came to a stop sideways across the road.

I sat there panting, but Sam spoke with his usual calmness. "Sorry about that ice."

"My God! You scared me to death."

"You gave me quite a start, too." Sam gently turned the car and got us headed back in the right direction. "At least you gave me something new to work on."

"I did? What?"

Sam stared out the windshield. "It's unbelievable."

"What is?" I touched his arm. "What are you talking about."

He looked at me, his eyes blank in the light from the dashboard. "Surely I'm wrong, Nicky."

"Wrong about what?"

He shook his head. "I'd better not say anything more. I'm probably way off base."

HE WAS STILL REFUSING to talk the next morning as he headed for the office.

"Hey, wait a minute!" I said. I grabbed him and gave him a passionate kiss. Then I looked up and batted my eyes like an imitation Scarlett O'Hara. This particular act usually makes him laugh. I batted the eyes again. "Are you positive you're not going to tell me what you're up to?"

Sam grinned and shook his head. "Nope. But you can beg me some more." He kissed me again, then caressed the hip pocket of my jeans. "See you down at the fairgrounds in an hour or so."

I waved as he went by the house, then I started packing up my photographic gear. This was the first day of the Sooner State Cattle Growers' Association Junior-Senior Steer and Heifer Show, and every Titus in Catlin County was involved.

Big Sam, of course, was chairman, working with Buck Houston as Sooner State Association staff member in charge. Marty, who doesn't usually participate, had volunteered to do clerical chores for the judges. Brenda was chairman of the concessions, which were being run by the Holton Maids and Matrons. Billy, of course, was showing Dogie, and even Lee Anna had been issued a trash bag and assigned an area near the concessions stand to keep clear of litter.

My part was taking pictures. I wanted some for my own photo essay on livestock shows, of course, but I particularly wanted to get some good ones of Billy and Dogie. Big Sam would love them, and someday Billy would cherish them, too.

So I loaded my camera bag with plenty of T-Max for the Leicaflex, and I put in lots of 1600 ASA Ektachrome for the Minolta I planned to use for color shots. Both films should be good for available light. Extra batteries for the strobe unit and a couple of special lenses made the bag heavy, but I hoisted it into Big Boy and was headed for the fairgrounds by nine A.M.

The sun was out, though it was another bitterly cold day, after an overnight low of only twelve degrees.

"Hooray for the Sun Belt," I told Big Boy. "Let's hit the road."

The Catlin County Fairgrounds was already lined with rows of pickups, stock trucks, and trailers. A couple of king-sized recreational vehicles were parked at the back of the gravel lot. They were the kind retired couples use to tour the nation, but I knew these were owned by big-time stock show operations. They were both running, and their exhaust fumes fogged out into the cold air.

I turned into a parking space near Brenda's little Ford and pulled my red knitted cap down over my ears. As I lifted the camera bag out of the back seat, a car stopped behind Big Boy. It was Sam.

"Tell Big Sam I won't be here for a while," he said. "Something's come up."

"Oh? What's happened?"

Sam frowned. "I guess there's no secret about it. Athena Pilkington's gone."

"Gone?"

"Yeah. As in not home."

"Well, maybe she went to work."

"Nope. We called down there. They haven't seen her and didn't expect her back at work until next week."

"Well, maybe she went to the store or something. Not being home when the sheriff wants to talk isn't exactly a crime, Sam."

He was still frowning. "But it looks funny, when her car and Joe's truck are there and she's not."

"All that means is that somebody came by to see her, and she went someplace with them." Remembering Athena's house, I said, "She might have gone with a friend to do her laundry."

Sam squinted. "Laundry? Why'd you say that?"

"Because Athena doesn't have a washing machine. And her laundry hamper was empty, as if she'd gathered everything up. I noticed it when Nadine was searching the bathroom."

"Good God!" Sam yelled. "Why don't you women share this information with us dumb guys!"

The car jumped forward six feet, but then Sam hit the brakes and lurched to a stop. "Get in! I may need you!"

I ran around the car and jumped into the passenger's seat. The car shot forward before I could even reach for my seat belt.

"What's wrong?" I gasped.

"We're probably too late," Sam said grimly. "They're probably doing Athena's washing right now."

SIXTEEN

"WHERE ARE WE GOING?" I yelled.

"To the Laundromat. Where else would Athena send her laundry?"

"Then you think there may be important evidence in it?"

Sam nodded and wheeled the patrol car out onto the blacktop road. The Laundromat was way over on the other side of Holton—at least eight blocks away—and he didn't speak again until we pulled up outside.

He jumped out and hurried in. As soon as I disentangled myself from my lapful of camera bag, I went after him.

He was standing at the counter, in front of the big sign that said "Drop Off Bundles—3 Pounds for $1," talking to the owner of the Laundromat. I didn't know her name, but she was a short, square woman with a short, square haircut and a pronounced Okie accent.

"Yep, her warshings dun, but she had'en picked it up yit," the square woman said. I wondered again how "hasn't" can be turned into "had'en" by a genuine southwest Oklahoman. And "had'en" does not stand for "hadn't." That's pronounced "haddent."

Sam pursed his lips and turned to me. "We're too late," he said. "It's already been washed."

"But what were you looking for?" I said.

Sam shook his head. "Maybe the junk in the drain will prove it," he said.

"Prove what?" My voice was getting sharp.

"I'll tell you in a minute." Sam turned back to the square woman, who was gaping like the biggest fish in an Oklahoma bass contest.

"I appreciate the information," he said. "Sorry to hear I'm too late."

"Oh?" The square woman ran a hand through her short, square haircut. "Weel, I'm sorry, but it was warshed yesterday afternoon."

Sam nodded and turned away, but the Laundromat operator wasn't through speaking. "Not that Athena's going to be happy about it," she said.

"Why not?" I touched Sam's arm to stop him. "Was there some problem with Athena's laundry?"

"Well, those towels."

Now Sam turned back. "What towels?"

"Some plain white towels." The woman leaned across the counter. "Or at least they used to be white."

"What was wrong with them?" I asked.

"They had these big black stains, and she didn't mention it when she dropped her bundles off."

"Stains?" Sam's voice was soft.

The woman nodded. "We just cain't be responsible if people don't tell us about these things. They should have been pretreated, soaked in somethin'. But not only did she not mention it, she left them wrapped up in a bright plaid shirt, so they accident'ly got warshed on cold."

I'd become impatient. "Are you saying that these stains didn't come out of the towels?"

"That's right. And I hope she doesn't have the nerve to ask us to replace them—'specially since I'd be willing to bet she snitches those towels from that beauty shop where she works in the first place."

Sam took a deep breath. "Could I see the towels, please?"

"Well, I was puttin' them through another warsh," the short, square woman said. "But I'll pull 'em outa the dryer, if you're sure it's okay for you to look 'em over."

Sam followed her across the room, assuring her his search warrant gave him the proper authority. I didn't quite see why

Sam was so concerned about Athena's laundry being whiter than white.

I looked at the stack of laundry the woman had identified as Athena's. There was a certain sadness about it; mixed in with the sheets, towels, and wash-and-wear slacks was a week's worth of men's white cotton briefs, T-shirts, and socks. The T-shirts were stacked crookedly. I adjusted the stack. It stayed crooked. I saw that one shirt had been folded oddly and was throwing the whole stack off.

I pulled the offending shirt out and shook it, ready to re-fold it. It was a V-necked shirt smaller than the ones Sam wore. But Sam was unusually broad through the shoulders; he wore undershirts only under wool shirts, and he liked them loose, so he bought a size 42-44. This shirt was labeled size 38.

A picture of Joe Pilkington lying in his casket loomed before my eyes. Joe hadn't been tall, but he'd been broad. He could never have worn an undershirt size 38. That was the size someone slim would wear.

Someone built like Johnny Garcia. Damn! I dropped the shirt in disgust.

I still refused to accept Johnny as Athena's lover. It was all wrong. Just not possible. I picked the shirt up again and began to fold it, shoulder seam to shoulder seam.

That's when I saw the stain. Something black had stained the knitted neckband, and it was still dark, deep in the ridges.

I was staring at it as Sam came back. He held out a couple of white towels. "It's not going to be much use," he said in a disgusted tone. "They almost got the stains out."

I held the T-shirt out to him. "It's a size 38," I said. "It was in the middle of the stack. All the rest are size 46."

Sam took the shirt, frowning.

"Sam, I can't believe that Johnny is carrying on with Athena Pilkington—"

"I agree. And this shirt may help prove he's not."

"But it's about Johnny's size."

Sam leaned close and whispered in my ear. "I'll tell you a guy secret. Johnny wears bikini underwear in sexy colors, and the only undershirt I've ever seen him wear was long-sleeved."

"Oh." I felt relieved. "What were you looking for in the laundry?"

"Something stained."

I pointed to the collar of the T-shirt. Sam gave a low whistle. "That might do it," he said. "Add that to the towels." He handed me the towels. They were slightly damp. "I'll get some evidence bags."

Sam whizzed out the door, and I looked at the towels. They were small white towels of the type used by most beauty shops, and the stains on them were faint. I was no scientist, but when I find beauty shop towels and a man's T-shirt, all with similar stains and all in the same load of laundry, I'd suspect some hair dyeing had been going on. In this case, black hair dyeing.

But nobody would dye Johnny's hair black. It was already as black and shiny as the stout and murky coffee that Big Sam makes when Marty lets him get out his old enam-eled coffeepot. So black dye would point away from Johnny.

Sam was back with the evidence bags, and my mind moved on to another piece of evidence against Johnny.

"But what about the tires on Johnny's truck?"

"That's the easiest thing in the world, Nicky, if you start with the premise that somebody decided to frame Johnny. They simply switched the guilty tires to his truck."

"But how could they do that?"

"I'm not sure, but if I were going to do it, I'd follow Johnny over to the college, then steal his truck from the parking lot. It wouldn't even be hard to get Johnny's extra keys. He never locks his doors. He has classes all day on

Tuesday, and his schedule isn't that hard to find out—for someone who lives around close."

"They switched the tires and put the truck back? But wouldn't Johnny notice that the tires were different?"

"With all this mud and slush? All they'd have to do would be hit a few mud roads and puddles on the way back to the parking lot. And be sure they brought it back during classes, while the lot is pretty well deserted."

"It would be a big gamble."

He nodded. "I think we're already sure we've got a guy on our hands who's willing to gamble."

His mood was cheerful as we climbed back in the patrol car, and he picked up the radio mike.

"Holton, this is Catlin One. Nadine, any word from the lab?"

Nadine's voice crackled. "Yep. They just called in and said you were right 'bout the hair in the drain. It had no Asian characteristics."

Asian? I knew that lab technicians can identify race from hair. But as far as I knew, no Asians were mixed up in this case. Then I realized that persons of Mexican ancestry, such as Johnny, were partially from Native American racial stock. And that comes out as Asian as far as the lab is concerned.

We knew that the person who had hocked the shotgun—a person I was ready to believe was the killer of Joe Pilkington—must look quite a lot like Johnny. But if his hair had no Asian characteristics, he probably did not come from the same Mexican-Latino racial stock. Johnny himself had described his own looks as "standard Latin."

Sam was still talking to Nadine, but I kept on with my own thoughts.

The guilty party was not a Native American or from a related gene pool, according to the evidence of the hair in the drain, but he probably had a dark enough complexion to pass for a Latino. He was around Johnny's size, according to the evidence of the T-shirt. But he did not have black hair, according to the evidence of the hair dye. In fact, if he had left the hair that Joe Pilkington had found in the shower drain, he had gray hair.

And if Sam's speculation about the tires was correct, he was someone who knew at least a few things about Johnny's schedule—maybe a neighbor?

And he was attractive enough to appeal to Athena Pilkington.

I could think of one person who fit the bill right off. As Sam hung up the mike, I took a deep breath and spoke.

"Daniel Bibb."

"You're right." Sam turned the ignition key over. "We already knew he had the best opportunity to hide the truck in Joe Pilkington's hay shed. The hair in Athena's drain and the dye in the shirt should clinch it. Sonny's going to meet me at the fairgrounds for the arrest."

"Do you expect him to give you trouble?"

"It's smart to be ready for anything."

I considered the events of the past week. Daniel was apparently responsible for two deaths and an attempt to frame Johnny Garcia for a serious crime.

"He ought to be feeling pretty desperate," I said. "Two people are dead."

"Maybe three." Sam's voice was grim.

"Three?"

"I've had Sonny and Jake out looking, but nobody's found Athena Pilkington yet."

"She may just be shopping in Wichita Falls or Lawton. Something like that," I said.

Sam shook his head. "Somehow I don't think Athena would be in the mood for a shopping trip."

"Do you think she's fled the county?"

"Not without a vehicle."

He slowed to turn into the fairgrounds. "Nicky, I'm going to ask you to do something for me."

"Sure."

"Just walk through the fair barn, real casual, and see where Daniel is and what he's doing."

I nodded.

"Now, don't speak to him. Okay?"

I traced a big X on my ski jacket. "I promise. I won't scare him off."

Sam gave me a kiss. "I'll be here, waiting for Sonny."

As I got out of the car, I saw Buck Houston standing in the doorway to the barn. Sam gave him a wave, then ducked his head and began to make notes on his clipboard. He was acting extremely casual. Now I had to do the same thing.

I slung the camera bag on my shoulder and walked into the blue metal barn. "Hi, Buck. How's it going?"

"Shapin' up pretty good, Nicky."

I passed him and started a circuit of the huge building. It wasn't too noisy yet, since it was still before ten-thirty and the first competition wouldn't be held until four o'clock in the afternoon. But a dozen or so heifers and steers were tied to the metal fencing that divided the barn into lanes. At least two dryers were blowing noisily, and eight or ten people were busy with grooming chores.

The cattle stood hoof deep in shavings or straw that had been spread out as bedding. Billy and Johnny were halfway down the row. Billy was dragging along a clear plastic bag of cedar shavings, a bag that was as tall as he was and twice as bulky. Of course, the shavings weighed practically nothing.

As I stopped opposite them, Billy looked up at Johnny solemnly. "Can I use your knife?" he asked. Then he saw me, and he grinned. "Hi, Aunt Nicky! We're making a good bed for Dogie."

Johnny produced a pocketknife and carefully opened a blade, which Billy used to slit the end of the sack. He handed the knife back, then began to strew the cedar shavings over the cement floor in front of a computer-produced banner that read "Titus Ranch Herefords." He was very serious.

Johnny and I grinned at each other, and I went on.

Down the row was a larger space, marked off by blue pennants and by wooden plaques with "Circle M" burned into them. The directors' chairs and walnut show box once again were arranged to form a sitting room at the end of the area.

It contrasted strongly with the simple Titus Ranch lay-out. It just showed which ranch was seriously into raising cattle and which was a Rexall rancher's hobby, I thought.

Mike Mullins was leading his heifer to her place.

"Hi, Mike," I said. "Looks like you're all ready."

Mike peeked at me over the heifer's back and nodded. Then he ducked his head. His eyes were puffy, and his mouth sullen. I wondered if he'd had another run-in with his dad.

I walked on. At the rear of the fair barn a big double door stood open, letting in an excessive amount of fresh air. A man came in carrying a bag of shavings on each shoulder. He was silhouetted against the light, making it hard for me to see his face. He had nearly passed me before I realized it was Daniel.

I tried to be natural. "Hi!"

Daniel smiled and gave me his heavy-lidded look. Once again I marveled at the contrast between his deep tan and his blond hair.

"Hello there, Miz Titus," he said. "Glad to see you got Johnny out of that jail."

"I had nothing to do with it," I said, "but I'm glad he's out." And I want to see you in, I added silently.

I went on past Daniel and turned back at the next lane, heading toward the door I'd entered. I could see Daniel and Mike through the metal fence. Daniel began spreading the cedar shavings, making additional bedding space for the Circle M cattle. They usually showed three or four.

I tried to keep my pace slow and casual as I went back through the barn. I spoke to Buck again as I went out, and I conquered the desire to run from the barn door to Sam's patrol car.

Beyond his car, at the entrance to the fairgrounds, I saw Sonny's car turn in. I glanced back at the barn. Buck was disappearing inside. Good. There'd be no witnesses to my report to Sam.

It took me only a moment to tell Sam that Daniel was on the right-hand side of the fair barn, just beginning to spread two big bags of cedar shavings in the Circle M space.

"Mike's there with him," I said. "And Billy and Johnny are right down the row. Should I call them away?"

"Maybe it would be best," Sam answered. "Tell Mike that Jack Rich is looking for him outside. Jack's his 4-H adviser; he ought to buy that. And then tell Johnny I want him to take Billy over to the concessions for a little while."

I admit that my nerves were jumping when I went back inside the barn. I felt like a spy inside enemy territory. But Mike didn't give me any argument when I sent him outside to look for Jack Rich. I didn't speak to Daniel. He gave me one of his bedroom looks, then he went back to his cedar shavings.

I took Johnny aside and quietly told him Sam wanted Billy out of the fair barn for a few minutes. He frowned, but he didn't argue. "Come on, Billy. I need something hot to drink," he said. "Let's get us a snack before we bring Dogie in here."

Billy followed him docilely. I headed back to the door, using all my willpower to keep from turning my head to check on Daniel's whereabouts. I managed to avoid the temptation to look back until I got out the door. Then I couldn't resist. I turned around and looked back into the fair barn.

Daniel had disappeared.

I assured myself that everything was fine. He was probably only getting more shavings. Sam and Sonny would find him.

But thirty minutes later Daniel still hadn't returned to his spot beside Mike's heifer. Sam and Sonny had walked the whole barn and the whole arena. They had looked behind and around the two dozen trucks and dozen trailers parked in the gravel parking lot. They had checked the concession areas and the men's rooms.

I pretended I didn't notice what they were doing. I got out my cameras and began shooting. But when I saw Buck come in the back door leading one of the Circle M steers and whistling cheerfully, I moved over and took some pictures of Mike. So I was there when Sam asked Buck where he could find Daniel.

Buck seemed exhilarated. He grinned as he answered. "Darned if I know, Sam. That guy's been givin' me trouble all mornin'. If this keeps up, I'm gonna run him off."

"What's his problem?"

"I don't know, but he keeps disappearin'. If you find him, tell him to get back here and start workin'."

But it was another hour before Sam located Daniel, and when the hired hand turned up, he was in no shape to get back to work. He was hidden under a pile of hay in a corner of the sheep barn, stuffed inside a giant plastic bag that had once held cedar shavings.

The bag had originally been clear, but now a pool of blood seemed to have stained it a rich red.

SEVENTEEN

DANIEL HAD BEEN BEATEN to death.

I offered to take pictures, since I was on the spot and I happened to be holding my camera in my hand, but Sam hesitated.

"It's pretty gruesome," he said. "As bad as I've seen in a long time."

I gulped and offered again, and he finally nodded. I had to do some more gulping while I snapped, but I managed. Daniel was a bloody mess.

The strange thing was that almost all the blood was inside the plastic sack. There were a few spots over by the back door, spots Sonny found hidden under some loose hay, but nearly all the blood was inside the sack. Only a little had trickled out of a ragged tear in the plastic.

"This is weird, Sam," I said. "It looks as if someone made Daniel put the sack over his head, then beat him to death while he was in it."

Sam nodded. "It's neater that way. Keeps the blood off the assailant."

"But how could anybody talk Daniel into that?"

"He could have used a gun as a persuader, but that would have required two people—one to hold the gun and the other to manipulate the sack. I think there's a simpler explanation. We found a work glove over there by the door. It'd been filled with sand—it would have made a handy cosh. More likely the killer stunned Daniel, then stuffed him into the sack and beat him to a pulp."

"A pulp" was definitely a good description of what was left of Daniel. His whole head was soaked in gore, but with a strange irony, one side of his thick blond hair remained untouched by blood.

I shuddered. "It looks as if somebody used a sledgehammer on him."

"No, not a sledge. Anything with hard edges would have ripped the sack open. It was something softer, something with padding around it." Sam raised his eyebrows and held up a dirty padded jacket, the kind most farm workers would pick for outdoor wintertime work.

"What's that?"

"Buck identified it as Daniel's jacket. The killer apparently wrapped it around something, used it to pad the club."

"What kind of a club?"

"I don't know yet. Lots of things would do the job—a chunk of wood, a piece of pipe."

Sam looked back at the body, frowning. "But I do know one thing," he said. "Whoever did this hated Daniel's guts."

I knew Sam was right. Daniel had been beaten viciously, with far more violence than was necessary to cause his death. A lot of hate had gone into his killing.

When I got angry at the world as a child, my mother would tell me to beat the throw rugs. She had an old-fashioned rug beater, and she'd loop the rugs over a clothesline and make me beat them until my frustrations were gone.

I shuddered again. Whoever killed Daniel should have been feeling mighty loose emotionally after Daniel was dead. His frustrations should have completely disappeared after the exertion he'd put into the killing.

"Hey, Sam!" Sonny called from the outside doorway. "The OSBI guys are here. And your dad wants to talk to you."

Sam and I started over toward Big Sam, but his dad began to talk before we could reach normal conversational distance to him.

"You're not gonna close this show down, are you? It'd sure be an unpopular move for an elected official! We've got folks here from clear up in the Panhandle. Drove hundreds of miles on icy roads to compete. Spent plenty on gas and motels and food. Hired people to handle things while they were gone. Kids'll be disappointed, and so would their folks."

Sam's chin twitched. He almost grinned. "And you'd have to give everybody's registration fee back."

Big Sam glowered. "I'm ready to do that—by God-freys!—if you think this bunch will impede your goldarned investigation."

Sam shook his head. "Nope. If it gets right down to it, I don't have the authority to close y'all down in the first place. But since you're not using the sheep barn, and that's where the crime occurred, all I ask is that you keep everybody away from this area. I think Sonny and Jake have already put up crime scene tape. Just tell everybody to stay clear."

I left the scene as the OSBI's mobile lab came in.

When the news of the body had hit, I'd been in the fair barn taking a picture of Mike Mullins brushing his heifer, Proud Mary. Everybody had rushed out. Suddenly Mike and I and a bunch of cattle were the only living creatures in the barn.

Now, as I returned an hour later, the barn was jumping with excited conversation. Not only was everyone discussing the murder, but Sam had also announced that Athena Pilkington seemed to be missing. Her bed hadn't been slept in, so apparently she had been gone since the night before.

Between the killing and the missing woman, the fairgrounds had gone wild. Mothers were yelling for kids, cattle were bawling, 4-H members were running back and forth, teen-age FFA boys were assuring teen-age FFA girls that they'd protect them from the bad guys, and normally stolid ranchers were looking excited and whacking baseball caps against their thighs. Dr. Mullins ran past me, calling, "Mike! Mike!" impatiently.

When I went into the arena, I discovered that the county employees had abandoned the small tractor they'd been using to smooth a thick layer of dirt over the concrete floor and had stopped bolting together the metal framework of the platform that was to elevate the officials and their table of ribbons and trophies. They were walking back and forth, talking to the officials. Organization had been replaced by turmoil.

Then Big Sam took charge. He was chairman of the show, after all.

He entered the show ring from the side nearest the sheep barn, and he limped to the center of the arena, dragging his bad leg through the dirt that had been heaped on the floor as footing for cattle. He stopped near the semi-assembled officials' platform, knocked soil off his boot with his cane, then imperiously beckoned to one of the workers. Almost immediately a microphone was produced.

"Attention!" Big Sam roared into the mike. Loud whistles of electronic feedback issued from the loudspeaker. After a few false tries, the sound level was adjusted to accommodate his basso, and he continued. With that sound system, I knew his voice was echoing through the cattle, sheep, and hog barns, as well as the arena.

"Yes, a body has been found in the sheep barn. The sheriff has cordoned off that building and an area around it, and he's asking that everyone stay away from there," he rumbled.

"But he says the Sooner State Steer and Heifer Show can continue. As far as he can tell, there is no particular reason to think that anybody who's exhibiting or attending the show should be in danger. He thinks it would be smarter for us all to keep goin' at our usual activities. Just stay away from that sheep barn! And keep your kids away from it!"

Almost immediately, of course, a group of men and a few women clustered around Big Sam, asking for the inside stuff. I didn't fight the crowd, but I could hear his voice boom out some answers.

"Yep, it was a guy Sam had been trying to find because he wanted to arrest him," he said once. "He was mixed up in somethin' crooked."

That seemed to reassure most people. It's very soothing to the ordinary citizen to think that crimes are only committed against people who are getting what they deserve. The crime rate in Washington, D.C., is high only because of the drug dealers killing each other, or so my dad assured me when he was reassigned to the Pentagon. He changed his tune slightly after somebody stole his hubcaps in a nice neighborhood, but I recognized an attitude like his among the members of the Sooner State Cattle Growers' Association standing around that arena. Being assured that the victim was only a criminal eased their minds. They might have felt differently if they'd been aware that Sam believed this was the third murder in this case.

I locked my crime-scene film in Sam's patrol car, then I tried to continue my own activities in a normal fashion. I took some pictures of Johnny and Billy working on Dogie. The cattle barn was full of talk, too, with grown-ups standing around in clumps. The kids were more excited than usual and kept running back and forth. It was only a little different from the usual scene.

The only adult who seemed to be stewing was Dr. Mullins, who continued to yell for Mike. Buck worked on the Circle M cattle, glaring at his employer and operating a noisy blow-dryer at the same time. Dr. Mullins was acting so stupid that I didn't much blame Mike for hiding out or Buck for glaring.

I tried to stay away from the doctor and from Buck. I knew they'd both given Sam preliminary statements just after Daniel's body was found. He'd told them to stick around the fairgrounds.

It was two hours later when I saw Sam again. He left the OSBI's mobile lab in the sheep barn and headed for his car. On impulse I picked up a cup of coffee from the concessions stand and took it out to him, along with a Milky Way.

He almost grinned when I rapped on his window. I hadn't expected to talk to him at this stage of the case, but he motioned for me to come around the car and get in.

"You're a lifesaver," he said. "I don't mind telling you this has left me badly in need of stimulation"—he lifted the coffee cup—"and quick energy"—he lifted the candy bar.

He blew on the coffee, then took a sip and set the cup on the dashboard. He laughed humorlessly as he ripped into the Milky Way. "Just think. At ten-thirty this morning we had this case solved."

"I guess Daniel can't be victim and bad guy both."

"Oh, yes he can! Just like Otis Schnelling was."

"Then you're still convinced they were both mixed up in Joe's death?"

Sam nodded. "I thought I had it making sense until this happened. I figured Daniel was seeing Athena Pilkington on the one hand and stealing cattle with Otis Schnelling on the other. A busy guy. But when Athena decided the theft of Joe's cattle would help matters—"

"But why would she steal her own husband's cattle?"

"For the insurance. Joe had borrowed money to buy the cattle, and he'd insured that herd. But the price of cattle has been dropping all winter. Joe was very close to the point that the sale of the cattle wouldn't bring in enough money to pay for the feed it took to raise them and the bank loan he'd taken out to pay for them. But if anything happened to the cattle—they were drowned in a flood or killed by a bolt of lightning—"

"Or stolen."

"Or stolen—he'd have gotten the insurance. He would have come out better than if he'd sold them."

"If that herd had been a building, you mean, it would have been smart to burn it down."

"Sure. If you don't mind a little dishonesty."

"But Joe doesn't sound like the kind of guy who would do that."

"Right. He was even too honest to cheat on his time card. So Athena must have talked her boyfriend into taking care of the situation."

I shook my head. "If Daniel was already stealing cattle, then he probably talked her into it."

Sam sipped his coffee. "He sure could have suggested the deal. But Joe figured out that something was wrong and took off from work early. Either he wanted to catch Athena in bed with somebody with gray hair—"

I broke in. "He'd assigned that role to Dr. Mullins, but it was really Daniel. His hair is actually blond, but it could be mistaken for gray."

"Right. Anyway, Joe came home early, and he didn't find anybody in his bed. Instead he caught one of the cattle thieves, either Daniel or Otis, in the pasture. He fired the shotgun at the truck and trailer, and he probably damaged the truck. But the other thief, either Daniel or Otis, was down the road in a pickup, and he ran Joe down."

"Is that why I saw the OHP towing the Circle M pickup away?"

Sam nodded. "There's a bump in the hood. Daniel had covered it up with that tire he wired onto the radiator grill, as if he was going to push somebody."

He sipped his coffee and chewed a Milky Way. "Joe's death must have been a severe shock to Daniel and Otis."

"Why?"

"Because they'd been stealing cattle over a period of months, and they'd been very careful to keep anybody from seeing them. They worked only in the dark, and they picked

cattle in pastures that were isolated. They never went anywhere near anybody's house. Of course, they mainly did this
to keep from getting caught. But I think this also shows they
didn't want to hurt anybody. I doubt either of them was
even armed."

"If they'd had guns, they might have shot Joe, instead of
using a truck as a weapon."

Sam nodded. "That would follow."

I pictured the scene Sam had painted. The cattle thieves
were stuck in somebody else's pasture with a dead body and
a truck that would be easily identified by the damage from
Joe's shotgun blast. They must have been scared stiff.

"It's easy to see why they lost interest in stealing Joe's
cattle," I said. "But they must have known the truck had
left traces in the pasture."

"Yep, but they may have figured we wouldn't find those
traces until spring."

"Why not?"

"Because of the snow. It started snowing around three
A.M. the morning Joe was killed. We know from Bubba that
Joe left work around four-fifteen, so he should have gotten
there and been killed right around the time the snow was
coming down good. Daniel and Otis must have figured that
the snow would cover their tracks. If they left the cattle, no
one would know they'd been there."

"Which would have happened if some weird sort of irony
hadn't intervened."

"Yep. Joe landed on a track from the pickup that hit him,
and the snow didn't continue."

"Then Johnny came along and put his raincoat over the
body."

"Right. He just meant it as respect for Joe, but he helped
save the tracks of the pickup. And even though we couldn't
identify the tracks made by the truck and trailer, we were
able to see that some vehicle had been out in the pasture.
That led Sonny and me to look around out there carefully.

And close beside one of those tracks were some shards of safety glass.''

"So you figured from the first that the cattle thieves were involved.''

Sam nodded. "But right away Athena's sex life got dragged in.''

"Well, if she was mixed up with Daniel—''

"So what? That didn't have any direct significance, if the thieves were involved. Joe tried to keep them from stealing his cattle, and he got killed. Bing. His wife's morals didn't really have anything to do with it.''

"Then why bring Athena in at all?''

"That's bothered me all along. I've finally concluded that it was all an effort to make Johnny a scapegoat from the first.''

"Somebody had it in for Johnny?''

"Maybe. Or maybe they just wanted to provide a handy person to look guilty. In any case, the rumor that Johnny was seeing Athena could have originated with Daniel. Though Buck told me he had seen Johnny's truck over there.''

I thought about that for a minute. "But how does Otis's death fit into all this?''

"Well, Otis began to panic. So he had to go.''

"Otis panicked? How do you know that?''

Sam lifted a finger. "First, he followed me to Lawton when we went to the machine shop to talk about Joe with B.J. Slater and Bubba. Remember how peculiar he acted when we caught him on the road later?''

"Oh! When he hid by lying down in the seat.''

"Right. He wasn't drunk, but something sure was bothering him. Second, he showed up at the funeral and Athena yelled at him.''

"I remember.''

"Third, he wrecked you and Big Boy.''

"You're sure that was Otis?''

"It must have been. Split Creek Road is a back way between the fairgrounds, where I believe the truck and trailer had been hidden in the sheep barn, and Joe Pilkington's hay shed. Otis had the bad luck to run into the sheriff's wife while he was moving it."

"Oh." I thought about that a minute, then I decided to object. "Sam, that can't be right. The reason I followed that truck was the Mozart."

"Right. Since the window had been shattered by the shotgun blast, the music on the tape deck sounded real loud."

"But why would Otis have been playing Mozart? He was a country music fan, judging by the tapes and posters and books and junk we found in his house."

"Well, I can't explain that, but Sonny went out to search Daniel's trailer, and he found a travel case of tapes. Three quarters of them were Mozart. Maybe Daniel was with him."

"That's crazy, too. Daniel was a country musician."

"He was!" Sam turned to look at me. "I'd forgotten that! I just thought of him as a hired hand."

"No, that one time I talked to him, when he rescued me after Big Boy was wrecked, he said he was trying to get the money together to start a new group and make some tapes."

Sam nodded. "That would explain why he didn't throw his money around on television sets and dishwashers."

"The way Otis did."

"Right."

We sat silently a minute. It was sad, I realized. Daniel had been working all day as a cowhand, then doing much the same work at night, trying to get money for his musical career. When had he found time to write the songs he claimed were going to make him famous? When had he had time to use the theories on creativity he had paraded when he gave me a ride after Big Boy was wrecked?

The recollection jogged my memory, and I gasped. "Oh! I think I understand about the Mozart. Daniel told me he used all sorts of music to inspire him. He said he'd listened to nothing but John Philip Sousa for a month, then he wrote some patriotic song he was real proud of. Maybe he was doing the same thing with Mozart."

"That's as good an explanation as any."

"But why would Otis have been playing the Mozart tapes? And why so loud?"

"Because he couldn't hear them!" Sam turned to me and gestured with his Milky Way. "Remember! We found literature on hearing aids in Otis's house. And Queen Anne Tudor said he was hard of hearing. I'll bet Daniel had left a tape in the truck, and Otis just let it play. It wouldn't have been as loud as you might think, since the window had been shot out of the truck. You were hearing the sound straight—unmuffled."

"Exactly!" I took a deep breath. "Okay. You've explained the Mozart and why Otis had to be killed by Daniel, his accomplice. Next Daniel had Athena dye his hair black so he'd look like Johnny. She could use that spray stuff we bought for the Halloween Haunted House. It washes right out, but it sure does mess up a lot of towels. With this disguise, Daniel stole Johnny's truck and wore the crazy red hat he found in it while he pawned Joe's shotgun. He could switch tires from the Mullins Ranch pickup and Johnny's truck at the same time. Then he went back to Athena's house and she washed the spray out, staining her towels and his undershirt in the process. It all makes sense."

"Yeah, I had a real good case against Daniel—if he hadn't gotten himself killed and ruined the whole thing." Sam sipped coffee, we both stared out the windshield.

"So there's some third person mixed up in this," I said.

"Yeah, I figured that out myself."

"Cut that out!" I punched Sam's arm. "The other person has got to be Athena."

"Her disappearance makes that look likely." Sam stared out the window. "But—"

I waited until he turned back toward me and spoke.

"Think of Daniel's injuries. Could a woman have done that much damage?"

"She would have been angry enough to do it, Sam."

"I could see that, Nicky. I just wonder if she has the physical strength."

"Well, with the right weapon—but you're probably right. I don't think Athena ever lifted anything heavier than a bottle of hair dye. Besides, she's not the right kind of an accomplice for a cattle thief."

Sam grinned. "Well, what kind of an accomplice would you want, if you decided to take up stock theft?"

"I wouldn't want somebody who was always worried about chipping a fingernail."

"Okay, I can agree with that. Athena wouldn't have been any help on the cattle-theft angle. I can't see her tromping around in a pasture luring cattle into a trailer. She never even helped Joe around the place."

I nodded. "I suppose she might have made the contact with the person who bought the stolen cattle. She's always down in Wichita Falls. It could be somebody down that way."

"We've checked all the sale barns in north Texas, and there's no evidence any of them were involved. She would have had to go farther away."

"I don't think she's taken any long trips, Sam. Joe would have known if she was gone for very long."

I thought about the cattle-stealing operation. A lot of cattle had been stolen over the past few months.

"You're overlooking one thing," I said. "You've said from the first that these guys were running a very efficient reconnoitering operation. How did Daniel and Otis do that?"

"Scouted the country, I guess."

"But when? Daniel worked right under Buck's supervision. He couldn't be running around looking for likely herds of cattle to steal without Buck noticing he wasn't doing his work. And Otis had to be here at the fairgrounds. The county commissioners would have noticed if he was gone."

"And if they hadn't, Big Sam would have."

I nodded. "Exactly. Sam, somebody had to be scouting for them, telling them what cattle to steal. It may not have been the electrical co-op man, but I'll bet it was someone with a job like that."

Sam nodded. "Makes sense. Maybe only two of them worked—"

His voice broke off and he focused his eyes behind me, toward the cattle barn. He frowned. "What's Sonny up to?"

I turned to see Sonny walking rapidly across the icy parking lot. Dr. Mullins was with him, frisking around like a Pomeranian in a big hat.

When they got within ten feet of the sheriff's car, I rolled my window down.

"What's up?" Sam said.

"Mike's missing!" Dr. Mullins yelled.

The two men leaned down and looked in the car window. Sam ignored Mullins and looked at Sonny. "That right?"

Sonny nodded solemnly, his braids bouncing. "Sure is, Sam. We've looked everywhere, and we tried paging him on the public address system. No foolin', Sam. I think he's really missing."

EIGHTEEN

IT TOOK ABOUT twenty minutes to figure out who had seen Mike last, and the answer turned out to be embarrassing.

It was me.

Mike and I had been the last ones to leave the cattle barn when news of the murder spread. Nobody—not any of the 4-H kids, not Buck, nor Dr. Mullins—would admit they had seen Mike Mullins after I had.

"Oh, Lord!" I said when Sam finally got this narrowed down. "I just stuffed things in my camera bag and ran out as quickly as I could, Sam. Mike was tying up his heifer. He was saying, 'Wait for me, you all!'—yelling at the other boys. I'm sure he came out right behind me. But, no, I didn't see him after I left the barn."

Somehow I felt guilty. But that was silly. Mike hadn't been my responsibility. His dad and Buck always seemed to be looking after him. Besides, as Sam reminded me, there was no particular reason to think that anything bad had happened to Mike.

"He probably went down to The Hangout for a Coke or something," Sam said. "Just to make sure, we'll get the Holton patrolman and the deputies to look for him." Then he bent his head close to mine. "Stick around and talk to Dr. Mullins, okay? He's babbling, and I haven't got time to listen to it. He may tell you something useful. At least you can help keep him calm."

Sam had described Mullins accurately. The man was almost falling apart. He seemed grateful when I led him to one of the director's chairs beside the handsome walnut show box in the Circle M show area. I sat down on the edge of the show box, and Dr. Mullins gripped the wooden arms of his chair and talked.

All I had to do was nod now and then, because little of what he was saying made sense. But I suppose his babbling reflected what was going on around us. Because a lot was happening.

We might have had a murder, and a twelve-year-old boy might have been misplaced, but the Sooner Cattle Growers' Regional Junior-Senior Steer and Heifer Show was going on as scheduled. The members of the Sooner State Association had braved icy roads and frigid temperatures to compete, and they were hard at it. Ranchers in rubberized suits were leading freshly shampooed steers from the cattle shower room. Every kid had a currycomb tucked into a back pocket and held a show stick in one hand. Some of the children were smaller than Billy, since this was one of the few shows that had a junior division. Most shows limit competition to FFA and 4-H members, and children must be eight before they can join 4-H. No adults competed in this show.

Brenda had come in, and she was helping Johnny finish Dogie's beauty treatment. As I listened to Dr. Mullins I watched her. She sat on an overturned bucket, teased the clump of white hair at the tip of the heifer's tail, molded it into a ball of angel hair, then sprayed it with tail goo as Johnny and Billy looked on anxiously. I realized that the first event, which was Billy's junior heifer competition, was about to begin.

I may have groaned aloud. I wanted to watch Billy compete, not sit around listening to a worried father. I couldn't convince myself to worry about Mike. Most of the people around us didn't seem to think he was in danger.

Jack Rich, Mike's 4-H adviser, stopped and patted Dr. Mullins on the shoulder. "Hey, the boy'll turn up!" he said. "He's a good'un. He's just upset about Daniel, and he's gone off someplace to take it in."

Mullins smiled weakly. "I hope you're right."

Jack Rich walked on, leaving Mullins staring at the toes of his fancy boots.

Brenda came by next. "Don't worry, Dr. Mullins," she said. "I've seen how Mike loves that heifer of his. He wouldn't miss showing her. I know this is scary for you, but he'll be back."

Then she looked at me with troubled eyes. "Won't he be back, Nicky?" I knew she was remembering the days when Bill, her husband, was missing. Brenda had been frantic then. Even finding Bill dead had been easier for her to bear than those days of not knowing.

I tried to sound reassuring as I answered her question. "Sam and his deputies are looking everywhere for Mike. I know they'll find him."

Brenda gave Buck a quick smile—was I imagining the message it sent?—and went back to Billy. She made him stand still while she tucked in the tail of his red western shirt and combed his wavy, tow-colored hair. He took his show stick in his left hand, carefully holding it down beside his leg, and reached for the leather strap that was hooked to Dogie's halter in his right. Johnny and Brenda both smiled at him proudly, and I called out, "Good luck, Billy!"

He squared his six-year-old shoulders, gulped solemnly, and said, "Come on, Dogie." I saw Big Sam in the door that led over to the arena. He was beaming. The fifth generation of Tituses was entering the cattle business.

I resigned myself to missing Billy's performance in the effort to comfort Dr. Mullins. And so far Mullins hadn't been comforted.

"God!" he was saying. "I never thought I'd want to hear that Mike has run away. But if I heard that somebody had seen him out at the edge of town, hitchhiking for his mother's house, I'd be so relieved—"

"Dr. Mullins, Jack Rich knows Mike very well, and I'm sure he's right," I said. "Mike's just gone off by himself to think about things. Daniel's death must have been a shock to him."

But Mullins shook his head. "No. He didn't like Daniel very well. I'd been after Buck to fire that guy, but he wouldn't do it for some reason. Mike wouldn't be upset about Daniel."

"Sometimes when we don't really like someone, it makes it harder—"

"No!" Mullins's voice was firm. "No, Mike would never leave his cattle over Daniel. He didn't give a damn about Daniel, but he sure does love those cattle." He gulped. "He's always loved animals. That's why I wanted him to have the ranch experience. The wholesome life. Not like Oklahoma City, where the public schools are full of drugs. And some of the private schools are good scholastically, but they're designed to keep the kids insulated from real life.

"I wanted Mike to learn about life first hand, to have freedom, to be able to run as far as he wanted across a field, to have a creek to wade in, to have a horse, to do all the things—" His voice almost broke.

I kept my voice soft. "I know you've done your best for Mike."

"It's been hard knowing what to do. After his mother—" Mullins ran his hands over his face. "If anything's happened to Mike—God! If I have to tell her that—"

He stopped, and we both sat silently. I sure didn't know what to tell him. His outburst had killed the optimism sparked by Jack Rich and common sense, and a lump of fear was beginning to fill my stomach.

There was a murderer loose. Sam felt sure the killer was a cattle thief, along with Otis Schnelling and Daniel Bibb— a partner who had turned on his accomplices and had brutally killed them. And Mike Mullins had been in daily contact with Daniel, one of the victims. Mike could know something, could have some clue that would make him a danger to the killer. I didn't know anything hopeful to tell Dr. Mullins.

Our silence lasted until Buck came up and sat down in the second director's chair.

"Any word?" he asked.

Mullins silently shook his head. "Can you think of anything, Buck? Anyplace to look?"

"No!" Buck's voice was curt and he glared at his employer.

"Mike looks up to you." Mullins was pleading. "Sometimes I even get jealous—"

"Damn it!" Buck said. "I was hired to raise cattle, not Mike! I don't know where the hell the kid could have gotten to."

Mullins dropped his eyes, and Buck turned to me.

"Where's Sam?" he demanded. "If Mike's taken off, we can't show today. I want to get my equipment out of here."

I guess I blinked blankly, because Buck went on, speaking as if he were explaining things to a three-year-old. "Sam told us to stick around. But I'd like to get these cattle and this gear out of here. I'll load up and take it out to the ranch, then come right back. Would you mind"—he put a sarcastic spin on the word—"helping me find Sam to tell him what I'm doing?"

Buck's attitude was infuriating, and I stared at him a moment. Then I told myself that he was entitled to be nervous and upset. His hired hand had just been murdered, and Sam might have just told Buck that that same hired hand was implicated in a scheme to steal cattle. His employer's son had disappeared, and his employer had tried crying on Buck's shoulder and had been rebuked. I certainly wasn't the only person Buck was yelling at. If Brenda showed up in the next few moments, their romance might be over.

I decided that I could act like an adult even if Buck couldn't. "Certainly, Buck," I said in my sweetest voice. "Sam asked me to stay here with Dr. Mullins, but if you need me to find him, I'll certainly be glad to help you out. I feel sure he hasn't left the fairgrounds."

I rose and walked toward the opposite end of the barn, toward the door to the parking lot, where I hoped I would find Sam.

As I walked I was once again struck by the surreal quality of the events. Dr. Mullins was incoherent with worry, frantic about his son. Yet all around us people were completely concentrated on a task they seemed to find of earth-shattering importance—the task of making cattle beautiful.

It seemed utterly stupid. Suddenly I wanted to jump on one of the show boxes, stamp my feet on its lid, beat a galvanized water bucket with a currycomb, and yell at the astonished faces that would turn in my direction.

"Pay attention!" I wanted to yell. "A man was killed here today! A boy disappeared! He may be dead! Those things are more important than hairdos for a bunch of stupid cows! Pay attention!"

I paused in the door of the barn to zip up my ski jacket and looked back at the scene. Dr. Mullins still sat with his head bowed. Buck was winding up a heavy electrical cord, making a figure eight between his palm and his elbow.

Sam could have stopped all this routine activity, as Big Sam had pointed out. He could have requested that the show be halted and that everyone go home. He thought it was better for the show to continue. I could see why. It kept everyone on the scene, for one thing, and it kept them occupied and out of his way.

Outside, I stopped and looked up at the sky. "Damn!" I said. "Sleet!" The last thing we needed was sleet. In fact, the whole world would be a better place if sleet didn't even exist. I lowered my head and slogged on, toward the roof lights I could see across the parking lot. At least the gravel hadn't become too slick yet.

As I expected, Sam was in the front seat of the car, talking on the radio.

"Anything?" I asked, climbing in beside him.

Sam shook his head and hung the mike under the dashboard. "Nobody's seen him. I had a patrol car on each gate to the fairgrounds—Jake Whitaker on the highway side and a city patrolman on the Holton side. They were there to take names and license numbers of everybody who tried to leave in a car or truck, but I believe they'd have seen Mike if he walked away."

"You mean Mike may still be here? At the fairgrounds?"

Sam stared at his clipboard. "I don't know what I think. I suppose Mike could have left the fairgrounds after you saw him but before we got patrol cars at the gates. It's a damn scary situation."

"Rule Number One doesn't seem to apply here."

"Rule Number One?"

"You know. You're always telling me that killers are usually close to the victim—husbands, wives, parents, business partners. Who else cares enough to kill somebody?"

Sam's gaze focused somewhere over behind the cattle barn, but I kept talking.

"The most obvious person that Rule Number One would apply to would be Athena. She was married to Joe, she slept with Daniel, and she knew Otis well enough to share a beer."

Sam spoke, but his manner was absentminded. "She knew Otis well enough to yell at him."

"Well, that might not mean much. She yelled at Buck, too. But I can't picture Athena getting mixed up in cattle theft. So I guess that leaves you with the MOM rule."

"The MOM rule?" That got Sam's attention. "I don't think I remember that one either."

"You talk about it now and then—means, motive, and opportunity. M,M, and O. But MOM is easier to remember than MMO."

"Well, I already know who was closest to all the victims—and the possible victims—and who had the means and the opportunity. But the guy is completely without a motive."

"Who's that?"

Sam shook his head. "I'm not sayin', even to you. It's too unlikely. And I'm prejudiced against the fella. I may not be giving him a fair shake."

He put his brain back in Cruise Control then, and I sat and tried to figure out who he was talking about. It was a man, a man Sam didn't like for some reason.

Dr. Mullins. For a minute I was sure that was right. Dr. Mullins had known all the victims—his neighbor, his employee, and Otis. Well, Mullins hadn't known Otis. But if Mike suspected his father was involved in a crime, he might well have run away. And Sam didn't like Dr. Mullins much.

But that wouldn't work. Nobody liked Dr. Mullins, and we all had pretty good reasons. Dr. Mullins was a small-minded, obnoxious jackass. Sam hadn't been talking about somebody who was simply unlikable. Sam had been talking about some man he didn't like for a specific reason. Some reason Sam wasn't sure was fair.

The name that tumbled into my mind was Buck Houston.

Yet I had never been consciously aware that Sam didn't like Buck Houston. Now I was sure of it. I didn't like him either. The nervousness Buck made me feel was not because he threatened the status quo of the Titus Ranch, not because he might know more about running it than Sam did. It was because I felt, down deep, that Buck was more interested in the ranch than he was in Brenda.

And, like Sam, I was afraid I was being unfair.

But Buck did fit the situation of both my rules for detection, Rule Number One and the MOM rule. He knew all the victims well; Joe had been a neighbor, Daniel an employee, and Otis had worked with him on the stock show. He knew at least one of the missing people, Mike, very well. I remember Athena chasing him down the road in a pickup, and I suddenly felt sure that Buck knew her better than he'd admitted, too.

But how about the MOM rule? Buck certainly had the means to kill both Joe and Daniel—a pickup truck and a bludgeon. He even had brought the dryer that killed Otis to the fairgrounds, and we had only Buck's own word that he had warned Otis about the electrical short that caused the man's death. He could easily have rigged the accident. And he had the opportunity for all three killings—he'd been on the scene for Otis's and Daniel's deaths, and he'd been only thirty miles away when Joe was run down. Nobody would have noticed if he'd left the motel to drive over to kill Joe.

I began to get quite excited about the prospect of Buck as a killer. Besides having the means and opportunity to kill people, Buck was in the ideal position to be the scout for the ring of cattle thieves.

Then my excitement died. Sam was right. Buck had no motive. Zilch. *Nada*. No way. Buck's primary personality trait was personal ambition. He would never get involved in a scheme that could endanger his professional aims for a paltry financial return.

Sam was still staring into space. I realized that I hadn't passed Buck's message on to Sam, but Sam seemed so disheartened I didn't speak. I looked at the cattle barn. A little boy, bundled to the ears, was lugging in yet another vacuum cleaner-sized blow dryer. The giant tin barn was nothing but a big beauty shop.

I remembered Dr. Mullins, sitting in the cattle barn agonizing over Mike, and the whole situation suddenly seemed ridiculous. I had to fight the impulse to giggle. The contrast between Dr. Mullins's worry and the frantic grooming of cows was simply ludicrous. I gulped and made such a peculiar sound that Sam came back to earth and looked at me.

"Sorry," I said. "The irony of the situation just got to me. Here you're so worried, and Dr. Mullins is frantic, and Buck is so upset he's snarling at everyone, including me, and it's all happening in a beauty shop."

"A beauty shop?"

I gestured toward the barn. "A beauty shop for cows! They're trimming and blow-drying their hair. They're painting their nails. They're teasing their topknots and tails and spraying them as stiff as—as stiff as Otis Schnelling! The only things not going on in there are permanent waves and dye jobs! And that's only because nobody wants a curly cow and dyeing is illegal!"

My outburst seemed to leave Sam stunned. He stared at me, and his mouth slowly opened, as if he were going to speak. Then he grabbed my arm.

"Nicky! Where's Dad?"

"In the arena watching Billy compete, I think."

"Maybe he can tell me if I'm right." Sam picked up his mike. "This is Catlin One to Base. Nadine, tell Sonny to get over here to the cattle barn right away. Catlin One, out."

He jumped out of the car, heading for the arena on the run, skidding on the sleet that was beginning to coat the gravel.

"Hey, wait!" I was just behind him. "Sam! I didn't give you the message."

He didn't slow down. "What?"

"It's Buck. He wants to know if he can leave."

Sam abruptly swung to face me, his face an iceberg. It was colder than the wind whistling down my coat collar. I shivered. "He says he'll come right back, but Buck wants to take the Circle M cattle and gear out to the ranch."

"I'll bet he does," Sam said, and his voice was as quiet and slick as the sleet falling on his hat. He stamped his feet a couple of times and looked up at the sky.

"You can't play it safe all your life," he said. "I'll see Buck before I talk to Big Sam. It might make a difference."

Then he swiveled again and took off for the show barn.

His purposefulness—so different from his mood of only a minute before—left me amazed. He was definitely ready to take action. And that action required a backup, I gathered, since he had called for Sonny to join him. I ran after him.

I caught up as he reached the door to the show barn, and I grabbed his arm. "What are you up to?"

Sam stopped with his hand on the door. "Is it that obvious?"

"You definitely look like a man who's decided what action to take."

"I guess I'd better calm down, then," he said.

We stood there a moment. There was no sound except the grating of sleet hitting the metal wall of the cattle barn. Then Sam did something that chilled me clear to the bone. He took his revolver out of its holster and made sure it was loaded.

Then he whispered under his breath. "There's no reason to think he's armed. I can't wait another minute. Mike could still be alive."

Even though no one was in sight, I whispered back. "Who is it?"

"The person I should have suspected from the first time he poked his nose in," Sam answered.

He turned abruptly and went into the barn. I tagged along, more mystified than ever.

I wanted to ask Sam more, of course, but he was walking slowly along the right-hand aisle of the show barn. At first I thought he was making an effort to appear casual. Then he pulled off his glasses, and I realized they had fogged up.

He was walking slowly because he couldn't see where he was going.

Sam pulled his blue bandanna out of his pocket and began to clean the lenses. When I reached his side he was squinting down the barn. I knew he couldn't identify anybody more than twenty feet away.

"Is Buck still down there by the Circle M gear?" he asked.

I looked. "Dr. Mullins is sitting there alone—No, here comes Buck. He's coming in the back door. Guess he took some of his gear out to his truck."

Sam nodded and put his glasses on. He sauntered down the barn, passing the cattle, kids, fans, dryers, show boxes, and general stuff and scuffing his feet through the straw and shavings that covered the floor. When we reached the Circle M area, he touched Dr. Mullins on the shoulder. Mullins looked up and jumped to his feet.

"Sheriff! Is there any word?"

"Not yet, Dr. Mullins, but I had officers on duty at both the gates of the fairgrounds, and neither of them saw Mike leave. That makes me think we could be missing some obvious answer in all this."

"What's that, Sheriff?"

As he spoke, Mullins stepped closer to Sam, leaning toward him eagerly, but Buck—who had been so eager to talk to Sam—ignored the scene. The big guy began to push the Circle M show box, the one I'd been sitting on, out of its spot. Its wheels rolled smoothly, moving toward the door where contestants had been taking cattle over to the arena. I realized that Buck must have pulled his truck up there, in a spot sheltered from the wind, ready to load up as soon as he got the okay from Sam.

He must really be ready to get his equipment home, I thought. Apparently he didn't think Mike was coming back in time to show the cattle.

"I think Mike might have left a clue to what was on his mind around here someplace," Sam was saying to Dr. Mullins. "I'd like to look through his stuff."

Mullins gestured hopelessly. "Anywhere you want to look, Sheriff. Buck's been loading up."

Buck was still loading up, I realized. He and the show box were almost to the back door. He must feel really confident that Sam would let him leave.

Sam spoke so suddenly that I jumped. "Buck!"

Buck stiffened, but he didn't turn until Dr. Mullins also called to him. "Buck, the sheriff wants to talk to you. Come here."

Buck turned, but he didn't move. Sam took three long strides and reached the side of the show box. "Buck, you can't take this out of here," he said.

"Yes, Buck," Dr. Mullins said weakly. "The sheriff wants to see if Mike left a clue."

"Sam, this is stupid!" Buck's voice rumbled angrily. "The kid's fought with his dad for a year. So he's finally decided to run away. It's too bad, but it's no skin off my nose. I've got my gear all packed up, and I want to get it out of here so I can come back and concentrate on the show. I don't have time to fool with this."

"I have to insist, Buck."

"Dammit! You can't paw through my stuff!"

Sam reached over and touched the Circle M logo on the side of the show box. "This isn't your stuff, Buck. According to this brand, all this equipment belongs to the Circle M."

Sam's voice was sleet-cold again, and he sounded perfectly calm as he went on. "Do you have a key to this box, Dr. Mullins?"

Mullins, his mouth gaping, shook his head.

Sam looked at Buck and spoke softly. "Where's the key?"

Buck scowled. "I left it in the truck. This is stupid!"

Sam made one of the quick motions that surprise people who don't know him well. He grabbed up a shovel that was propped against the grooming frame, thrust the blade under the hasp of the show box, made one quick motion, and the padlock popped off.

He immediately threw the lid up.

The box's contents were covered with a tarp, a gray tarp that was tucked neatly into the corners. Sam grasped one end and pulled it back. Underneath was a yellow waterproof jacket, the outfit Mike had worn while washing his heifer earlier that afternoon.

As I watched, the yellow jacket moved slightly. Sam snatched it up.

There was Mike Mullins.

NINETEEN

"HE'S STILL BREATHING," Sam said.

Dr. Mullins shoved Sam aside and grabbed for his son. "Mike! Mike!" he said. Tears were running down his face. I yanked a tarp, a blanket, and another waterproof suit out of the box, giving us a full-length view of the boy.

Then Dr. Mullins slipped into his professional persona. He felt his son's head. "Contusion," he said calmly. "And he's nearly smothered."

Even I could see that Mike's color was improving quickly. His eyelids fluttered, and his eyes opened.

"Dad?"

"It's okay, son. Don't try to talk."

Mike seemed to be struggling to speak. "I didn't want him to hurt Skunky," he said. "I'd never tell."

Skunky? Had he said Skunky? I couldn't believe my ears. Why was Mike talking about Skunky? Skunky was the line-backed calf who'd been killed by a pack of wild dogs. The calf had been dead for months, and Mike hadn't had anything to do with her anyway. She'd been a Titus Ranch heifer.

"I wouldn't tell," Mike muttered.

I couldn't keep quiet. "Tell what, Mike?"

But Mike's eyes rolled back, and he seemed to drop off to sleep again.

Dr. Mullins looked up, glaring. "Call an ambulance!"

Jack Rich was in the front of the crowd that was beginning to gather. "I'll get it!" he yelled. He ran for the front of the barn, where there was a wall-mounted telephone.

Mike stirred again. "I wouldn't tell on him. I was afraid for Proud Mary. After she won..." His voice sank to a murmur, and I only caught the last word. "...dying."

Dying?

I was dying to know what the heck he was talking about. Especially because I felt sure Sam already did know.

Where was Sam? I moved back to get out of Dr. Mullins's way, scanning the crowd for Sam.

He was nowhere to be seen.

Whom had Mike meant when he said he "wouldn't tell on him?"

At that moment I stepped back, tripped, and abruptly sat down. Luckily, I had fallen over one of the director's chairs from the Circle M "parlor," so I wasn't hurt. I simply found myself sitting in the chair that Dr. Mullins had been occupying a few moments before.

I was staring at a similar chair. That chair had a name stenciled on the back. "Buck."

And I realized that—whether Buck had a motive or not—Sam and I had both been right. Buck was guilty. He had killed Joe, Otis, and Daniel. He had tried to kill Mike. And he might have killed Athena, too.

But Sam had cited him as the least likely person to be involved. Why would a person who had two good jobs—and whose whole career depended on his professional reputation and expertise—be a party to something as shoddy as cattle theft?

I was completely confused. Buck might have been the only person with the opportunity to stuff Mike in the show box. And he'd been trying to move the show box out of the barn when Sam stopped him, pried the box open, and found Mike.

Buck had to be guilty, even if his guilt made no more sense than Mike did when he talked about Skunky and Proud Mary.

I looked frantically around the barn. Buck had disappeared. Sam was not there, and Sonny hadn't arrived in answer to the call for a backup. No law officer of any kind was in sight. I felt certain Buck had his truck right outside the door to the arena passageway. He was about to escape. He might already be gone. Somebody had to do something.

I ran for the arena door.

I don't know what I thought I could do. I was unarmed. I was not a professional law officer. I had no radio, no car, no nightstick, no handcuffs, no siren. I was a foot shorter than Buck Houston, and he had a lot more muscles than I did.

But I ran for the door anyway. I kept remembering Sam's whisper, "There's no reason to think he's armed." I didn't think I could stop Buck, but I couldn't simply let him drive away.

I burst out the door of the cattle barn and into a deep freeze. The lights on the outside of the barn had been turned on to fight the early darkness and the gloomy day. The sleet was falling more heavily than ever, forming icy curtains that clattered against the gravel surface of the parking lot and piled up on the hood of Buck's sapphire-blue truck, parked on my left.

I swung toward the pickup and took a deep breath. Sam was already there.

He had pulled his pistol, and Buck was spread-eagled against the side of the trailer. Sam stood behind Buck, talking into his radio. "Yeah, Jake, I need you to help take in a prisoner."

As usual, Sam was on top of the situation. He had anticipated Buck's try at a getaway. As I exhaled in relief, the door to the arena opened, and Billy ran out.

"Aunt Nicky!" he yelled. "I got a blue ribbon."

Johnny and Dogie appeared in the doorway behind him.

And all hell broke loose.

Buck, I realized later, saw that Billy, Johnny and Dogie would be in Sam's line of fire. Their unexpected appearance had nullified Sam's pistol as a weapon.

Moving as quickly as a lasso snakes toward a cow's neck, Buck kicked at Sam's gun.

Sam dodged the kick, but he jumped back, and the sleet—the hateful, horrible, nasty, rotten, god-awful sleet—nearly got him. He slipped and landed on his back.

Buck kicked his pistol flying, then aimed another kick for Sam's head. Sam parried with his right arm—taking a blow that might have cracked the bone—but managed to catch Buck's boot with his left hand. Buck went down, but he wound up on top of Sam. Sam's in good shape, but Buck was several inches taller and maybe thirty pounds heavier. We needed help.

I ran toward the arena, grabbing Billy as I went by him. "Johnny! Get Billy out of here. And get help!"

I opened the door to the arena and began to shoo Billy and Dogie inside.

"You get help!" Johnny yelled. "I'll get the gun!"

He turned, but his hand got caught in Dogie's lead, and suddenly we were a Keystone Kops mixup of calf, boy, cowhand, woman, leather straps, and show stick, each of us shouting and jumping and bawling and getting more tangled by the minute.

Then I pulled the show stick out of the middle and Johnny popped his hand out of Dogie's halter, and—in one of life's minor miracles—we were all sorted out. I started shoving Billy into the arena again, but it was too late.

"Hold it right there!" Buck was doing the shouting, and he had the gun.

I looked over my shoulder, and the scene was as frozen as the sleet that was falling on all of us. Sam was on his knees, his hand still stretched out toward the spot where the pistol had been a moment earlier. Johnny had stopped in mid-step and stood stiffly, his fists at shoulder level. Billy and I clutched each other, immobile. Dogie was the only one moving. She was tossing her little Hereford head nervously, maybe because nobody was holding the lead attached to her halter.

"Nobody move!" Buck yelled.

We all obeyed for a long moment.

Then Sam spoke very quietly. "Somebody's going to be coming out one of those doors any minute, Buck. You'd better put the gun down."

"Shut up!"

"You can't kill us all." Sam still sounded calm. "You'd better give it up."

Buck took a step backward and gestured toward Sam with the pistol. "Get down! Down on your belly!" Sam slowly dropped onto the sleet-covered gravel.

"Stay there!" Buck snarled. "If you think I'm going to death row because I killed a filthy blackmailer, you've got another thing coming! I know how to get a ticket out of here." He pointed the pistol at Sam's head. Then he beckoned.

"Billy! Come over here. Your Uncle Sam needs your help!"

"No!" I was the one who yelled. I held Billy tightly.

"Let him go, or your husband gets it!" He shoved the pistol close beside Sam's head.

"No!" I yelled it out again, but this time I did let go of Billy, and I raised my hands in fury.

My right hand held Billy's show stick.

Dogie bawled in fear. She gave a mighty leap, then ran straight toward Buck.

I dropped the stick, grabbed Billy, and tossed him in the door of the arena, waiting for the shot, the shot that might kill Sam.

But no shot came.

When I whirled around, Buck was flat on his back, Sam and Johnny were both on top of him, and Dogie was disappearing around the corner of the cattle barn.

I heard a cry of mingled fear and anger, a scuffle of hooves, and another loud bawl. Sonny Blacksaddle came around the corner of the barn, leading Dogie.

"I nearly got trampled by a calf," Sonny said. "And what the heck's goin' on here?"

"I couldn't even begin to explain it," Sam said. "But get out your handcuffs."

Johnny knelt on Buck until Sam and Sonny got him handcuffed.

The three of them had just hauled him to his feet when Billy burst out of the arena door again.

"See, Mama! See! Uncle Sam pulled his gun!"

Brenda! Oh, God! She was coming out of the arena just in time to see her boyfriend taken away to jail. She'd be crushed. I turned toward the door, dreading the look on her face as she came out and saw Buck in handcuffs.

Her look of dismay was just what I expected, but she didn't wring her hands, or wait for me to comfort her.

She rushed across the passageway.

"Are you all right?"

She ignored Sam, Sonny—and Buck. She threw her arms around Johnny Garcia and held him in a mighty hug, looking up into his face. "Johnny! You could have been hurt!"

For a moment, Johnny stared at her in what seemed to be complete incredulity. Then he took his cue.

As Big Sam would have said, Johnny kissed the Ol' Harry out of her.

TWENTY

AT TEN O'CLOCK that night I was still kicking myself for an idiot.

Why hadn't I understood that Brenda was never interested in Buck? She and Johnny had been getting closer for months, and the signs had been plain—if I'd been looking for them. They'd shared classes, met for coffee in the SOSU student union, worked with Billy and Dogie, studied together in the library. Brenda had custody of the Titus Ranch computer, which Johnny used to type his papers. Just the night before, I had noticed how Lee Anna had ignored Buck, then had climbed into Johnny's lap. Obviously, Johnny had been around the house enough to get well acquainted with the four-year-old.

I had taken Johnny for granted. He was simply part of the ranch equipment. Maybe Big Sam and Sam had taken him for granted, too. Maybe we'd all have to reassess our relationship with Johnny.

The thought was sure easier to take than the idea of Buck joining the clan had been.

The phone rang, and I picked it up.

"Catlin County Sheriff's Office."

"Listen," Big Sam roared in my ear. "You tell that boy of mine that he'd better get by here to 'splain all this! And I mean tonight!"

"Big Sam, it's getting awfully late," I said.

"Well, if you think either Marty or I is goin' to get a wink before we understand what's goin' on, then you're crazier than a snake-bit steer! You tell Sam to come by here! Or I'll whup him!"

"Yes, sir!"

Marty and Big Sam had taken Billy and Lee Anna home from the stock show, giving Brenda and Johnny a chance to talk. Both kids had fallen asleep before we got there. Lee Anna was on her grandparents' bed and Billy, still clutching his show stick and blue ribbon, was on the day bed in the office.

Sam had asked all Catlin County ranchers and farmers to look for the cattle thieves' truck on their own places, and the missing truck with the broken window—with Athena inside the attached trailer—had been found in an unused barn on Jack Rich's place. Buck had locked her inside the night before, she said, after she had been foolish enough to let him know she'd had enough and was going to tell Sam all she knew and all she'd found out from Daniel.

Athena had burrowed in some old straw and saved her fingers, but she was in the Holton Hospital being treated for frostbite of the toes.

Mike Mullins was doing okay, his dad said. He was being kept in the hospital overnight, too, in Lawton, where there was a neurologist, but the prognosis for his head injury was good. The prognosis for the injury to his heart—the organ Buck had injured even more severely—was unknown, but Sam said he thought Dr. Mullins was doing his best to tend that injury, too.

Brenda and Johnny arrived just after we got settled in Big Sam and Marty's comfortable kitchen. Johnny hesitated in the doorway, looking from Sam to Big Sam with an expression that combined caution and defiance, as if he were waiting to see if they accepted his new relationship with Brenda.

"Come in this house, Johnny!" Big Sam said. "Sam's about to tell us what's behind all the excitement. Sit down here!" So Johnny sat next to Brenda at the kitchen table. They kept their hands in view, but I had the feeling their knees were bumping.

There was still one thing that had me completely confused. "Sam, you cited Buck as the type of person who wouldn't be mixed up in cattle theft any more than your dad would," I said. "Now it seems he was."

"Daniel was blackmailing him into it."

"He called Daniel a blackmailer. But what did Daniel have on him?"

"Just what Mike said. Skunky and Proud Mary."

"But Skunky died. And she had nothing to do with Proud Mary."

"She sorta did," Big Sam rumbled. "If they were humans, you'd say they were cousins."

"Right." Sam nodded. "They came from the same bloodline, and they were born the same week. Actually, they looked a lot alike—except that Skunky was line-backed."

"A pretty obvious difference."

"Yeah. I didn't link them up until you made that remark about a 'cattle beauty shop' and the only reason the people in the show barn weren't doing dye jobs was because they were illegal. And by some quirk, I suddenly remembered a couple of things Mike Mullins did."

"What?"

"Well, he was real antsy about shampooing Proud Mary along her backbone, and he got mad when his dad told him to scrub harder. Then over at our house Thursday night, he overheard his father yelling about 'dying.' He jumped out of the Land Rover and yelled, 'Nobody's dyeing!' At the time, we all thought he was upset about Joe's and Otis's deaths. But this afternoon I finally realized the word 'dying' could also mean 'dyeing,' as in changing colors."

Sam turned to his father. "Then I remembered Skunky."

Big Sam nodded. "The calf the wild dogs got."

"She was a pretty little heifer," Johnny said, "'cept for that stripe down her back."

"Right," Sam said. "She couldn't be registered."

"After the dogs got her, I figured there would have been some other genetic fault," Johnny said. "Maybe she was weaker, easier prey."

"Huh! I figured that stripe was just a kind of birthmark," Big Sam growled.

I remembered Skunky very well. Sam had explained to me that the variation in her markings was an unacceptable trait in Herefords. They have white heads, legs, and bellies, but their backs are supposed to be a solid, mahogany red. A white stripe along the backbone is a no-no for the breed.

Sam, Big Sam, and Johnny had had a big discussion about it, I remembered, wondering if the white streak on Skunky's back showed a genetic weakness in the Gillespie Ranch line. They'd called Buck over to look at her, asking if they should inform the other Hereford breeders. But the next week Skunky had been killed—apparently by a pack of feral dogs.

"I wanted you to take a look at Proud Mary," Sam told his dad. "I figured you could recognize Skunky if anybody could. But Buck forced my hand."

"You mean Buck stole Skunky and substituted her for Proud Mary?" I said.

"I think so. I'm hoping Mike can confirm that."

"Why would Buck do that? What happened to the original Proud Mary?"

Big Sam rumbled an answer. "She musta died, and it was Buck's fault."

Sam nodded. "Right. This evening Mike told his dad that the original calf had diarrhea. He mentioned it to Buck the day Dr. Mullins and Mike left for that trip they took last spring."

"Scours." Big Sam's voice was grim. "The calf musta had scours."

"Right. If the calf had scours, and Buck didn't treat it—" Sam shrugged.

"Especially after Mike had called it to his attention," I said.

"Right. Buck would have been in big trouble. And that same week we found a dead calf we thought was Skunky, remember? But the hide was real torn up. Buck must have done something stupid and actually caused Proud Mary's death. He didn't dare let Dr. Mullins find out what had happened. It could have meant his job."

"And it would have made him look like a fool," Big Sam said. "Buck's too proud to stand for that. And making such a grade-school mistake mighta cost him his job with the Sooner State Association, too."

"Right. So he put Proud Mary's body in our pasture and stole Skunky."

"Oh!" I said. "That was the real reason Proud Mary's mother rejected her.

"Right. Because he had to put the real Proud Mary's body in our pasture, he couldn't use the skin to fool her mother, the way it's normally done with an orphan calf. So Buck and Mike had to raise the calf on a bottle."

"That should have told us something was wrong right there," Big Sam said. "All those Gillespie cows are good mothers."

Sam nodded. "Anyway, Daniel found out what Buck had done."

"How?" I asked. "Surely Buck didn't allow any witnesses to his dye job."

"On the contrary, Nicky. I'll bet he needed help."

"Oh! Athena!"

"Right. Athena's trying not to say much, but she's admitted she and Buck had a little thing going at one time—"

"Sure, they did," I said. "He's her closest neighbor, and when Athena decided to make her husband jealous, he would have been the handiest guy for her to turn to. And Buck doesn't seem like the type to say no. Turning down free sex wouldn't fit his asinine idea of the macho image."

Johnny hastily took a drink from his Coke.

"—and I'll bet he turned to Athena for help in dyeing Skunky," Sam said.

"But Buck and Athena broke up, and she starting fooling around with Daniel," I said.

"And she blabbed about the dye job to Daniel, who was desperate for money—"

"—to jump-start his country music career!" I said.

"Right. He had a contact—somebody we're still looking for—who would take the stolen cattle. And he'd found an accomplice in Otis, a country music fan he'd met at Crawdad Corner or some other beer joint. But neither Otis nor Daniel had an excuse to cruise the gravel roads of southwestern Oklahoma looking for cattle to steal."

"Buck's job with the Sooner State Cattle Growers' Association put him in jes' exactly the perfect spot to scout for cattle," Big Sam said. "And Daniel was able to force him to do it by threatening to tell about the dyed calf."

Brenda spoke then. "I wonder if Buck even made any money out of the stealing."

"There's no evidence that he did," Sam answered.

"Was Athena in on it?" I asked.

"Not directly," Sam said. "She admits that she conspired with Daniel to steal Joe's cattle, but that was just to cheat the insurance company. And by the way, she had no idea Joe had term life insurance to cover the mortgages the bank held. Brock was waiting until we made Joe's cause of death official to tell her—just in case the law decided she was involved. Then the insurance wouldn't have had to pay off."

"Will she get the money?" I asked.

"She may not get it until after things are sorted out a little better, but I really don't believe she conspired to cause Joe's death. In fact, she says she didn't figure out that Daniel and Buck were part of the cattle-theft ring until after Joe and Otis were killed."

"If Otis, Daniel, and Buck were mixed up in the cattle thefts, which one killed Joe?" Marty asked.

"Athena says Buck did, Mom, and there's some evidence to back that up. He registered at the Lawton Holiday Inn the night before—driving the ranch truck, according to the license number he put on the registration card. But Nicky and I can swear his own truck, the sapphire-blue number, was at the stock show the next morning."

"Circumstantial, but damning," I said. "Theoretically, he hadn't been back to the ranch in the meantime."

"Right," Sam said. "Buck was upset at the idea of Daniel and Otis stealing cattle right next door to the Circle M, and he didn't like Athena knowing about it. So he went down there, maybe to try to talk them out of the plan. When Joe showed up, or so Daniel told Athena, Buck was parked in the Circle M truck down the road. When he saw Joe get out of his truck with his shotgun, he panicked and ran him down. They all figured the snow would cover the tracks, so they didn't worry about them. They didn't realize Joe had landed on a set of tracks Buck made when he turned around to head back to the north, before Joe came along and caught them."

"Why did they take the shotgun?" Brenda asked.

"Because they couldn't clean it," Sam said. "If they'd left it there, we might have guessed Joe had fired it at something. So Daniel took it away. He went to his trailer, where Athena was waiting, and told her what had happened."

"So that's where she was when I tried to tell her about Joe," Johnny said.

"Right. But you'd already messed up their plan. You put a raincoat over Joe—and that was one factor that saved the tracks of the Circle M pickup. When Sonny and I started investigating the scene, Daniel was hanging around, pretending to be a concerned citizen. He realized that we'd been able to get a cast of those tracks, and that we'd found tracks in the pasture."

"So Daniel warned Buck," I said. "And they came up with a plan to switch tires with Johnny's truck. And to frame him by dyeing Daniel's hair and having him pawn the shotgun."

Big Sam rapped on the table. "I'd never of believed that anybody could mistake Daniel for Johnny. They don't look a thing alike."

"I don't think Athena and Daniel really tried to make them look alike," I said. "I think they just tried to turn Daniel into the same type of person."

"But he's blond and got real blue eyes!" Big Sam said.

"True. But he has a deep tan. And with his hair dyed black, and his eyes covered with a pair of those sunglasses like Johnny's—"

"And wearing the hat he took from my pickup—" Johnny said.

"Right. It would be perfect for him to use to tuck that ponytail up inside," Sam said. "Plus, he used a Spanish accent."

Big Sam glared. "But Johnny doesn't have a Spanish accent!"

"I know. But a few words of Spanish made the pawnshop owner think in terms of a Latino customer. And Johnny does look Latin. Daniel used the pawnshop owner's preconceptions against Johnny. But he goofed when he bought the religious medal. Johnny wouldn't have done that."

Marty spoke for the first time. "But after Daniel and Buck had gone to so much trouble to frame Johnny, why did Buck suddenly kill Daniel? And why did he do it at the stock show, where it was so crowded? Wouldn't it have been safer to do it out at the ranch?"

Sam frowned and stared at the table before he answered. "Mom, I believe I caused Buck to take fast action against

Daniel—though I do think the guy wouldn't have been around much longer in any case. As I came back to the fairground to arrest Daniel, I sent Nicky inside to locate him."

I gasped. "And Buck was standing in the door of the cattle barn!"

"Yes," Sam said. "Nicky walked inside, located Daniel, and walked directly back to the patrol car."

"That didn't prove a thing," Marty said.

"Guilty conscience," I said. "Buck must have been in such a state that he saw the whole episode as suspicious. He would have immediately told Daniel to meet him in the sheep barn. And that was the end of Daniel. It's a miracle he didn't try to use Johnny's boot as a weapon. He'd done everything else he could to try to frame him."

Sam sipped his coffee. "Buck had already laid the groundwork for making Johnny a suspect by telling me that yarn about seeing Johnny's truck over at Athena's house."

Johnny shook his head. "Why'd he pick on me? I barely knew the guy."

Sam sipped his coffee slowly. "Well, you'd been the first one on the scene and . . ." His eyes flickered toward Johnny and Brenda. "And maybe Buck figured out that you were his main competition with Brenda. But that claim to have seen your truck at Athena's house was the first thing that made me suspect him. I couldn't figure out how Athena's sex life would fit in with stealing cattle. It called my attention to Buck from the first. But I couldn't believe he was guilty. I couldn't see why a person like Buck would get involved in such a scheme."

Johnny hid behind his Coke again, but Brenda smiled. "I've been trying to figure Buck out," she said. "I'm going to talk to my psychology professor about him."

Sam laughed. "I wouldn't think a guy was nuts just because he wanted to date you, Brenda. That seems to have been one of the more sensible things he did."

"Thanks," Brenda said. "But he was real odd. I'd about made my mind up I wasn't going out with him again—even if I couldn't get Johnny to ask me for a real date. Or even admit we got together in the SOSU library nearly every day."

Johnny ducked his head and looked sideways at her. "I didn't want people to think—"

Brenda touched his arm, then leaned forward earnestly and spoke directly to Sam. "See, everybody always told me that men expected a widow to be hot stuff—you know, real sexy. I hadn't been feeling real sexy, which was one reason I was cautious about starting to date. But Buck treated me so...well, distantly. I began to wonder if he was really interested in women at all."

"According to Athena, that's not Buck's problem."

Brenda shook her head. "No, I think he has a Madonna-whore complex. We talked about it in psych."

Big Sam narrowed his eyes. "What the Sam Hill is that?"

"According to Dr. Barnes, men with that complex classify all women as either pure or impure. Mothers usually fall into the pure complex. Madonnas. But women who sleep around—the way Athena did—well, they're impure. Whores."

"That's not too far from the way we all thought when I was growing up," Big Sam growled.

"Maybe not," Sam said, "but when it becomes a complex, it takes odd forms. As I understand it, for example, these guys may lose interest in their wives sexually after they give birth to a child."

Big Sam looked contemptuous, but Brenda nodded.

"Right," she said. "Buck treated Athena like dirt because she stepped out on her husband. But he treated me with almost exaggerated respect because I was a mother. To be honest, I don't think he was as interested in me as he was in the Titus Ranch."

We all sat silently. None of us had wanted to say it out loud, but it was good that Brenda had figured it out for herself.

Big Sam sighed. "You know, I knew ol' Buck's father years ago, when I was in my first term on the Sooner State Association board. He 'droughted' out a while back, nearly went bust. Had to sell everything, right down to the land. Even the house. Buck wasn't gonna inherit anything there. I guess that Buck saw a long haul ahead before he could buy himself a ranch."

He clenched a fist. "Godfrey Daniels! I sure hate to see times like these, times when a feller's got to inherit or be a millionaire to get hold of some land. The Rexall ranchers are goin' to take over the cattle business!"

ONE THING DID IMPROVE for the cattle business after that night. The bitter winter weather abruptly went away. We got up the next morning to sunny skies, and the snow and ice were gone by noon. Three weeks later the wheat fields were lush with thick, brilliantly green growth, and we hadn't had an overnight temperature below twenty-five for two weeks.

Daffodils began sending up green spikes all around the steps of our house. I was eyeing them for signs of blossoms when Johnny arrived for a business conference with Sam and Big Sam on the first Sunday afternoon in March.

"How 'bout this weather?" Johnny said.

"I'll keep it," I said. "Come on in. The Sams are in the living room."

"Should I be scared?" Johnny didn't look as if anything would scare him.

"Come and see," I told him.

"Basically," Sam explained to Johnny, after the three of them had discussed the weather, "we're suggesting that you and I switch jobs, and we'll double your salary. You'd be the ranch manager, and I'd be the helper. And we'd hire another hand, part time."

Johnny smiled, but he shook his head. "I can't tell you how much that offer means to me. But I have to turn it down."

Big Sam sighed. "Well, I guess some feed company's offered you a high-powered job as a salesman. Well, what salary would it take to get you to stay? You know you're just like one of my own boys!"

"Yes, I know!" Johnny blinked a couple of times. "That's why I have to leave, Big Sam. I'm not one of your boys. I can't just move in here—take over a spot at the Titus Ranch." He sat back on the couch. "Listen," he said, "I know y'all have figured out Brenda and I are going to get married."

"Well, that's just fine." Big Sam said. "But that makes no nevermind to this offer."

"I can't just move in on Brenda and the kids—and the ranch, too!"

"Godfrey Daniels! None of us looks at it that way!"

"I understand that. But I can't just spend my life here, having everything handed to me. I have to learn to stand on my own feet, Big Sam." Johnny leaned forward. "I have to fly off on my own, get out of your shadow. The way Young Sam did!"

Big Sam dropped his jaw. I had the feeling he wanted to answer, but for once he couldn't think of a thing to say.

Had he never realized that he was the main reason Sam had felt compelled to rebel against the sanctity of the Titus Ranch? Was this a new idea to him? It seemed to be.

Johnny laughed. "You have a very powerful personality, you know. I guess I'll handle cattle the way you do for the rest of my life."

Then Johnny turned to Sam. "But there's plenty of guys in the SOSU ag department who'd love to have a crack at a job over here. Let me know when you decide if you want full time or part time, and I'll round you up a bunch of applicants."

Sam grinned. "Okay!" I was amazed to realize he was a bit relieved at Johnny's refusal.

Maybe Big Sam wasn't the only one learning something today. It could be that Sam had never before analyzed the real reason he decided to leave the ranch and go into law enforcement.

"But you'll stay through May, won't you?" Sam asked.

"Sure."

"Good. Because I want to take off the last two weeks in April."

It was my turn to stare then. "What's this?" I asked.

"April is when you're in that fancy photo show in Houston, isn't it?"

I nodded.

"Well, I thought we could go to that, stay at a good hotel, and take in the sights of Houston. Then the next week we could head for New Orleans for a few days. Or down to Padre Island. Unless you've got a better idea?"

I got up from my chair and sat down in Sam's lap. "It sounds great," I told him. He gave me a kiss right there in front of Big Sam, God, and everybody.

Big Sam grinned. "You reckon the Catlin County crime scene will be quiet enough for you to be gone?"

"According to the law of averages, we've had enough killings to last us five years," Sam said. "And we haven't had time for a new gang of cattle thieves to get organized."

"Well, I hope they don't." Big Sam turned to Johnny. "Spread the word that we're lookin' for a full-time ranch manager. I wouldn't want to see Sam become a Rexall sheriff!"

LIFE ON THE TITUS RANCH is going to change. Johnny's been accepted for a graduate program at Oklahoma State University, and Brenda's going to finish her degree there. They've set a wedding date for late May, rented a house, and both found jobs. OSU's close enough that Billy and Lee

Anna can come back to the ranch often, but far enough for Johnny to spread his wings outside the shadow of Big Sam Titus.

Billy's only worry was about Dogie. With some guidance from Brenda and Johnny, he finally decided she should stay with her mother, No. 78, but he plans to check on her every time he comes back.

Buck's father has hired him a defense attorney who's prominent in Oklahoma, and the legal process has barely started. But Sam and the district attorney feel confident about their case.

Dr. Mullins has sold the Circle M and bought a spread on the north side of Oklahoma City. Mike and Skunky—Proud Mary will move up there as soon as school is out. Mike tried to give the heifer back to the Titus Ranch, but Big Sam suggested a swap instead. Mike got the line-backed heifer, and the Titus Ranch got the walnut show box. Dr. Mullins said he doesn't mind having one unregistered animal in his herd. He and Mike seem to be getting along a lot better, now that they see more of each other.

Sam took a lot of kidding from his fellow lawmen about being rescued by a cow. The Oklahoma Law Officers' Association even gave Dogie a medal designating her a "heifer heroine." Billy hung the medal up with Dogie's blue ribbon, and Big Sam said he thought it was a very suitable honor for Dogie.

He punched the air in front of Sam's chest with a forefinger. "I tell you one thing, boy! That ranch raisin' of Buck's and all those years of working with cattle, that may have saved your life!"

Sam grinned. "I thought I had Dogie to thank."

"Exactly! When Ol' Buck saw that calf runnin' at him, he just naturally jumped sky high. He might wella killed any one of you all, but the idea of shooting a heifer calf was completely foreign to his nature."

Big Sam cleared his throat portentously. "You can take the boy off the ranch, but you'll never get the ranch out of the boy."

He made it sound like a warning.

About the Author

EVE K. SANDSTROM is a columnist and former reporter and editor for the Lawton, Oklahoma, *Constitution*. She received her B.A. in journalism from the University of Oklahoma. A fourth-generation Oklahoman whose Choctaw ancestor arrived in the state before the Civil War, she lives in Lawton. Her first mystery, *Death Down Home* (Scribners, 1990), won the best-novel award from the Oklahoma Federation of Writers. She is also the author of *The Devil Down Home* (Scribners, 1991), which was an Alternate Selection of the Mystery Guild.

Take 3 books and a surprise gift FREE

SPECIAL LIMITED-TIME OFFER

Mail to: The Mystery Library™
3010 Walden Ave.
P.O. Box 1867
Buffalo, N.Y. 14269-1867

YES! Please send me 3 free books from the Mystery Library™ and my free surprise gift. Then send me 3 mystery books, first time in paperback, every month. Bill me only $3.69 per book plus 25¢ delivery and applicable sales tax, if any*. There is no minimum number of books I must purchase. I can always return a shipment at your expense and cancel my subscription. Even if I never buy another book from the Mystery Library™, the 3 free books and surprise gift are mine to keep forever.   415 BPY ANQ2

Name	(PLEASE PRINT)	
Address		Apt. No.
City	State	Zip

* Terms and prices subject to change without notice. N.Y. residents add applicable sales tax. This offer is limited to one order per household and not valid to present subscribers.

© 1990 Wolrdwide Library.

MYS-94

JUDAS PRIEST
RALPH McINERNY
A Father Dowling Mystery

First Time in Paperback

HIGH PRIEST OF SIN

Chris Bourke has abandoned his vocation, married a former nun and made a career out of attacking the church. His Enlightened Hedonism movement called for untrammeled pursuit of sensual pleasures—and his following was, not surprisingly, enormous.

But what does a professional apostate do when his only child announces she is going to enter a convent? He asks Father Roger Dowling for help.

Not in the business of turning away those with the call, Father Dowling agrees to speak to Sonya. But her brutal murder involves the venerable priest in a sordid tale of duplicity and deadly intent...and a clever killer with a calling of his own.

"Characterizations are excellent...."
—Chicago Tribune

Available in November at your favorite retail stores.

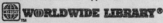